Praise for the novels of Donna Fletcher

Whispers on the Wind

A HAUNTING HEARTS ROMANCE

"Donna Fletcher's ghostly romance is a treat for those with a taste for the spectral world. The main characters are 'lively,' passionate, and engaged in a fine adventure."

—*Affaire de Coeur*

"*Whispers on the Wind* is an exquisite mixture of suspense, fantasy, and blazing passion. The plot is fresh and the characters are remarkable. This is a magnificent book that is worth another read."

—*Rendezvous*

The Buccaneer

"Donna Fletcher has written a joyous adventure on the high seas that will delight all her readers. The witty characterizations, unique situations, and swashbuckling action combine to make a terrific fast-paced romance that is thrilling to the very last word. This sensuous romance is a delight—right down to the very last sigh!"

—*Affaire de Coeur*

"*The Buccaneer* is a ... np on the high seas. Fas ... "

... *um*

Titles by Donna Fletcher

WEDDING SPELL
WHISPERS ON THE WIND
THE BUCCANEER

Wedding Spell

DONNA FLETCHER

JOVE BOOKS, NEW YORK

WEDDING SPELL

A Jove Book / published by arrangement with
the author

PRINTING HISTORY
Jove edition / April 1999

For information address: The Berkley Publishing Group,
a member of Penguin Putnam Inc.,
375 Hudson Street, New York, New York 10014.

The Penguin Putnam Inc. World Wide Web site address is
http://www.penguinputnam.com

ISBN: 0-515-12482-6

A JOVE BOOK®
Jove Books are published by The Berkley Publishing Group,
a member of Penguin Putnam Inc.,
375 Hudson Street, New York, New York 10014.
JOVE and the "J" design
are trademarks belonging to Jove Publications, Inc.

PRINTED IN THE UNITED STATES OF AMERICA

10 9 8 7 6 5 4 3 2 1

To Alisande,

the extraordinary woman who bewitched
my son and taught him the true
meaning of magical love.

Welcome to our family.

One

"You need a lover."

Alisande Wyrrd smiled and swung her long slim legs over the side of the chaise lounge. The white gauze cotton dress she wore brushed her ankles as she walked barefoot across the white marble tiles to join her aunt on the natural wicker settee.

Her aunt reached out to give Alisande's hand a comforting pat. "I would be remiss in my duties as your aunt, but even more remiss in my duties as a witch, if I failed to remind you of the necessity of finding a lover."

"At my age, Aunt Sydney, I don't think a lecture is necessary."

Her aunt waved a finger in her niece's face. "Then do tell me, my dear Ali, why have you waited three hundred years?"

Before Alisande could offer an explanation, her aunt continued.

"All these years on this earthly plane without one lover has dwindled your magical powers considerably, and now only a magnificent love affair with a powerful man will restore your abilities. And powerful men can be difficult to deal with."

Alisande understood her aunt's concern, especially given

the fact that her aunt assumed that she would choose a male witch, and male witches, particularly potent male witches, could prove much too difficult to handle. But Alisande had a different idea. She had long studied mortal males and found them quite appealing. They could be charming and loving, and a few exceptional ones could be extremely powerful in presence and attitude. She planned on finding such a male.

"I knew it," her aunt said with a concerned grin. "You want a mortal male, don't you?"

Alisande ran a long pale pink fingernail down the front of her dress and toyed with the tiny pearl button that sat nestled between her full breasts. "I find them fascinating."

"Mortal males can be dangerous," her aunt warned. "They come with mortal flaws."

"I think I'm up to the challenge of dealing with simple mortal traits."

"You must remember that your powers aren't up to snuff."

Alisande laughed, throwing her head back, her long honey-blond hair rushing in wildly riotous waves down her back to rest at her slim waist. "Which means the man I choose may just have a fighting chance."

"Not even in his dreams, my dear, will he have a fighting chance," her aunt said with a catlike smile.

Alisande giggled. "You're right. After all, he's only mortal."

"Which leads me to ask, where do you intend to find this exceptional male?"

Alisande bestowed on her aunt the courageous smile of a child about to ask for a forbidden sweet. "I thought perhaps you would help. You are a powerful seer, the most powerful seer I have ever had the privilege to meet, and—"

Aunt Sydney stopped her. "Flattery will not help you in this situation, and you know full well I am not the most powerful seer you have ever met, and you also know full well that a wise seer never interferes in matters of the heart. You will never learn life lessons if the answers are easily provided.''

Alisande cast her a petulant and playful pout. ''Then I have no choice but to read through the many magazines and newspapers I have collected over the last few weeks and comb the pages to see if anyone of interest stands out.''

Aunt Sydney offered her own advice. ''Being only a short distance outside of Washington, D.C., you shouldn't have any difficulty in finding a powerful man.''

Alisande smiled as she shook her head. ''I don't know about a politician, too many can be manipulated and bought. I want a man rich in character and strong in integrity.''

''Then stay out of D.C., darling,'' her aunt said with a laugh.

''With a little research and a spark of determination, I'm sure I can find the man of my dreams.''

Aunt Sydney stood and adjusted the jacket of her almond-colored silk suit. ''Be careful, my dear. Sparks ignite into uncontrollable fires, and sometimes we dream of more than we can handle.''

Alisande completely understood her aunt's implied warning, and promised herself that she would proceed with caution and care. After all, she had to remember that she would be dealing with a mortal male on the most intimate level. And intimacy had a way of ruling one's most basic emotions while easily disregarding intelligent thought. But then, there was no room for intelligence when lust and passion ruled.

''I'm off to the Wyrrd Foundation, dear. Last-minute details for the fundraiser we're hosting next week need my attention.'' Her aunt leaned over and lightly brushed Alisande's cheek with her own. ''No, I don't require help, and besides, you will be too busy looking for a lover to lend me a hand.''

Alisande shook her head and playfully chastised her favorite aunt. ''I thought the seer who taught you warned against intruding on people's thoughts without permission.''

''On occasion and when necessary,'' her aunt corrected and waved as she hurried out the door of the solarium with a quick good-bye from Alisande.

Alisande admired her aunt. She was a renaissance woman of extraordinary intelligence, having earned numerous degrees in various areas of interest as well as studying subjects thought to be objectionable during her six hundred years.

She often sought out her aunt for counsel and was glad she had come to stay with her while her mother and father were off on a lengthy adventure.

She, herself, was about to begin her own grand adventure. Many times through the years she had thought of taking a lover, and once or twice had come close, but always in the end she had decided against it. She wanted someone special, a magical lover, possessed of a strength not often found. Only *she* would find him and make him hers.

Alisande hurried out of the solarium, down the hall, through the foyer, and out through the front screened door. She took a deep breath of fresh air, catching the many rich scents of a warm summer's day, honeysuckle and mint in particular, and with a sigh of satisfaction she glanced out on the land she loved so much.

The two-hundred-acre estate had been purchased by the Wyrrd family several years before Alisande's birth. The rolling hills and pastures had changed little over the years. The twenty-room manor-type house had been modernized several times, the stables updated, a swimming pool and tennis courts added, and the gardens extended. Here was where family and friends came for shelter and comfort. Aunt Sydney mended many a broken heart here, Uncle Thaddeus hid from two wives, Aunt Vivien gave birth to Josh and Nicole, mother and father were married, and she herself was born here, and countless more milestones were celebrated right here on the Wyrrd estate. And right here was where Alisande would marry and give birth to her babies.

But first she needed a lover. She walked to the far end of the porch where it jetted out in an octagon shape and smiled at the stack of magazines and newspapers waiting for her on the pine table. Adele, not only a house servant for forty years but a close confidant of the Wyrrd family, had left a pitcher of mint iced tea and a plate of tea biscuits for Alisande to enjoy.

Eager to begin, she pulled one of the pine rockers up to the table and plopped down in it, tucking her feet beneath her. She reached for a magazine and a biscuit and began to read.

Alisande read the article five times. Could she be this lucky? This was only the third magazine she had picked up an hour ago, and here he was, the perfect man, staring her right in the face.

Sebastian Wainwright, CEO of Wainwright Security. His multimillion dollar business was based in D.C., though his client list was global. His security firm supplied protection to top government officials and foreign diplomats. His security personnel were the best in the field; only the most experienced and exceptionally talented people worked for Wainwright Security.

One whole floor of the Wainwright building was dedicated to research and development of security devices. What type of security devices, the article failed to mention. The article did, however, stress Sebastian Wainwright's impeccable reputation. It seemed that the man possessed the uncanny ability not only to successfully track an opponent, but to uncover every detail of that person's life. His talent for finding the unfindable was considered remarkable.

As one person interviewed stated, "Wainwright could find the proverbial needle in the haystack."

Sebastian Wainwright was also known to be practical in nature, serious-minded, and a no-nonsense businessman who always got the job done successfully, and he was the most eligible and sought after bachelor in D.C..

Alisande smiled as she traced her long pink fingernail over the photo of Wainwright. Dark hair, stylishly cut short and tight surrounded a tanned complexion. Dark eyes, brownish black like the color of the rich, potent soil during planting season, addressed the camera with a look of supreme confidence. A black tuxedo, obviously tailor made, accented his well-endowed athletic body and his height of at least three inches over six feet added to his masculine appeal.

Alisande brought the picture of him to eye level and stared at his handsome face. She ran her finger over his strong jaw line, high cheekbones, and the narrow bridge of his nose. His long dark lashes fascinated her, but it was his lips that tempted her the most. They were thin, barely noticeable, yet so utterly beguiling. How would they feel against her full ones? Strangely enough she felt they possessed the potency of his power. Latent and hidden, yet once unleashed . . .

She smiled and continued running her finger slowly over his picture. "Poor dear, you have no idea what you're in for."

Two

Alisande emerged from the cool interior of the silver Rolls-Royce out into the full summer heat of D.C. Though most of the capital's elite were vacationing worldwide, there were enough junior staff members around to stop and admire the beauty who emerged with eye-catching grace and confidence from the expensive vehicle.

Alisande had taken extra care with her appearance, and now, standing in front of the Wainwright building being eyed with obvious appreciation and interest, she was glad she had chosen simple elegance.

She wore a white silk suit that conformed to her shapely body and a skirt that rode high enough to enhance her long, slim legs. The white high-heel slings she wore added two inches to her five feet six height and her honey-blond hair fell freely in soft riotous waves down her back. Of course, she sprinkled a handful of gold dust to add sparkle to the silky strands and to catch the eye.

She marched right through the front door of Wainwright Security, and as she approached the first-floor security desk she smiled, dipped her hand in her pocket, brought it out, and with a gentle rush of breath across the palm of her hand, she sent the silver dust skimming through the air.

The tiny particles took instant flight and descended over

the security guards. With stupefied grins the men nodded politely as she continued past them to the elevators. A short, uninterrupted ride brought her to the top floor and the private offices of Sebastian Wainwright.

More security guards smiled foolishly as silver dust sprinkled down around them. In no time and without the slightest difficulty Alisande reached the office of Sebastian Wainwright's private secretary. She decided against dusting the woman and marched straight for the large double mahogany doors to Wainwright's office.

The tall, reed-thin woman frantically began shouting at her to stop and pressing buzzers on her desk. Alisande cast her a sympathetic smile before entering, unannounced, the hallowed office of Sebastian Wainwright.

"Ms. Smithers, I told you that—" Sebastian momentarily lost his voice when his dark eyes caught sight of the beautiful woman that stood just inside his office doors. She was simply stunning. Actually she was much more than stunning, but adequate words escaped him. He wasn't only speechless, he felt breathless from the sight of her.

She possessed the most extraordinary features he had ever seen on a woman, somewhere between exotic and common, which, combined, were exquisite. And her body was . . . damn he didn't want to think about it. Curves, dips, angles, fullness waited to be explored and charted and definitely claimed. His own body was already responding to her and at an alarming rate, and if he didn't reign in his raging schoolboy reaction, he might just find himself reacting foolishly.

It took him several minutes to compose himself, and when he did he threw down the report he had been holding and rushed around from behind his desk to approach her.

He was angry. This mysterious woman walked right into his office without invitation, and like an idiot he had simply stood there staring at her. Not only had she breached his building security, she had breached his own mental security, and that highly disturbed him.

"Who are you and how did you get past my security guards and into my office?"

Ali feasted her eyes on him for a few seconds before she answered. Her slow and audacious appraisal was meant to unnerve, and it did, but only for a mere moment. Within seconds he moved, walking right up to her, crossing his arms over his chest and raising an impertinent brow.

"I'm waiting," he said with a strength to his deep voice that sent a ripple of pleasure straight through Ali right down to the tips of her toes.

"Alisande Wyrrd," she said and held out her hand to him.

He made no move to take it, which brought a smile to Ali's face and a frown to his already stern composure.

"I wish to speak to you about an extremely important matter," she said softly, though with a firmness that was meant to remind that she would be heard regardless.

"I don't recall an appointment with a prospective client at this time." Though the Wyrrd name was known to him and almost everyone in Washington. He wondered if she was part of *The Wyrrds*, an influential and wealthy family whose roots dated back to the Founding Fathers. She certainly possessed the arrogance of the affluent.

"I don't have an appointment," she said and stepped around him, walking toward his desk. "Actually, I just realized this morning that I needed you."

Sebastian approached her slowly. "You need me?"

She turned a blatantly seductive smile on him that would melt the most celibate of men and answered in a mere whisper. "Yes, I need you."

How could a voice feel erotic? Sound yes, but feel? He felt as if she temptingly stroked his bare flesh with each short, emphasized word, and damned if he didn't hunger for more.

That was it. He took control of his confused emotions and reined in his insurgent hormones and marched to the office doors, flinging one open with such force that it would have smashed into the wall if he hadn't held it so tightly. "Ms. Smithers, where the hell is security?"

The flustered woman held a phone to each ear. "I'm trying to contact them, but there seems to be a problem."

"Get them here now!" he bellowed and slammed the door. His strides were purposeful and his muscles tense beneath his gray suit as he bared down on her like a mighty warrior charging into battle. "What do you want with me?"

Ali stood as she was, and he purposely came to a stop within only inches of her. His intimidation tactics were lost on her.

Confidently and with a clear voice she said, "I want you to be my lover."

He shook his head twice, positive he had misunderstood her.

"Let me explain," she said, reaching out to casually stroke his black and gray silk tie. Her fingers casually slipped beneath the cool material to faintly touch his white cotton shirt.

He made no move to stop her intimate gesture; he favored the subtle pressure of her slim fingers against his chest. "While you're explaining, don't forget to mention how you slipped past my security guards."

"That was the easy part," she said. "You see, I'm a witch, and a sprinkle of magic dust here and there goes a long way."

This time he shook his head three times. "Did you say witch?"

"Yes, I'm a witch, and that is part of the reason why I need you."

Sebastian took a step away from her. ''A bona fide card-carrying, broomstick type witch or the modern witches of today who play at Wicca without understanding a lick about the ancient religion?''

''Darling, we've never used broomsticks. Why should we when with the snap of my fingers I could pop right out of here.''

Sebastian nodded. ''Okay then, demonstrate your powers. Pop right out of here.''

''Now therein lies the problem,'' Ali said and took a step toward him, though he took another step away from her. ''You see that's why I need you to be my lover. I have neglected an important part of securing my powers and now I require a powerful man to sort of—''

''Stimulate your magical abilities?''

''Something like that.''

Sebastian rubbed the back of his neck as he once again shook his head. Was she a certifiable nut or a woman looking for sex? ''Look if you want to go to bed with me, why don't you just come right out and say so instead of making up some dumb story?''

Ali wasn't at all disturbed by his insensitive remarks; after all, he *was* only mortal. ''I can understand how strange this all must sound to you, but once you get to know me—''

''Know you?'' he nearly shouted. ''I know enough about you, and crazy women don't interest me.''

''What about witches?'' she said with a laugh.

Her laugh felt like a gentle caress across his face, and once again his body sparked to life. Her hair even glittered as if moonbeams danced off every silky strand and—

He caught his rebelling thoughts and shook his head as if shaking them away. He'd had enough, especially with his mutinous body responding so adamantly to her obtrusive advances. She was obviously nuts, and he wanted her out of his office, out of his building, and then he would immediately do a thorough background check on her to determine her exact identity and whether someone, mainly a competitor, could possibly have sent her.

Sebastian pressed the red button on his phone. "Ms. Smithers, where is security?"

"On their way, sir?"

"On their way?" he asked puzzled. "What about the guards on this floor?"

"They appear indisposed at the moment, sir."

He sent Ali a scathing look.

She was not at all repentant, though she did explain. "The magic dust is just beginning to wear off. They will all be fine soon. Which means I best hurry and finish here."

Sebastian stared at her skeptically. "Finish? Oh, you're finished all right. Now get out."

Ali shook her head slowly as she approached him with a sinfully erotic sway of her gently curved hips. "Oh, but I can't do that just yet."

Her suggestive sway caught his attention, and he could think of nothing but her completely naked beneath him moving in that languid rhythm that could drive a man wild. With a brief and sharp shake of his head forcing him back to the reality of this absurd situation he asked, "And why not?"

She stepped nearer, their bodies dangerously close to connecting. A fraction, just a mere fraction, and they would share the intimacy of first touch.

Sebastian stood his ground, never having backed down from anyone, not even a nutty woman. He could handle her if necessary. He really could, even if his body demanded otherwise.

She pressed her finger gently to his lips, those thin lips that so excited her. "You're my destiny," she murmured, "and I am yours, nothing can stop our intimate union. We shall have a glorious love affair."

"You're crazy," he said, moving away from her and feeling just as crazy for wanting her so badly.

Ali laughed. "No, not really and soon you will understand. I promise."

Her expression turned serious, and she raised her hands to the heavens and traced an imaginary circle in the air around them. Diamondlike dust sprinkled down over them, and in a soft, sensual rhythm she recited her spell.

"True love is often rare; forever love is always shared; mistaken love cannot be denied; make-believe love cannot hide; practical love makes two people whole; but *magical love* touches the soul."

Gently she tapped his chest, just above his heart with her long pink fingernail. Her spell was cast.

The office doors burst open, and ten security guards rushed in. Sebastian stared at her speechless and in astonishment as she waltzed past all of them as if she didn't exist, as if she was invisible, and left his office as mysteriously as she had entered it.

Three

Sebastian shook his head, stopped and shook his head again. If he didn't know any better he would swear that he shook something loose in his brain, he had shaken his head so often these last two hours.

Endless work on the computer and countless phone calls and still he was unable to uncover anything significant about Alisande Wyrrd.

He rubbed at his temples, the dull ache of an impending headache just beginning to form. He had barked orders at his men to go after the blond woman who had invaded his private sanctum and return her to him for questioning. They had stood gawking at him as if he had suddenly sprouted two heads. Ms. Smithers saved the day when she announced that the woman was making her escape on the elevators. The men scrambled out of his office, gratefully without tripping over one another. Several took the fire stairs and the others the elevators, and lobby security was alerted to the intruder's impending arrival.

All reported the same findings, the mysterious woman seemed to have vanished. She couldn't be found anywhere in the building or the surrounding area.

Sebastian had then resorted to the computer and noteworthy contacts, coming up with only basic information.

Alisande Wyrrd was actually part of *the Wyrrds*. She lived on a two-hundred acre estate in Virginia. Sydney Wyrrd, Alisande's father's sister, presently resided with her. Both women were known for their charitable natures and eccentricity which appeared to be a long-standing family trait. The Wyrrd Foundation, a nonprofit organization, hosted numerous fund-raisers throughout the year, helping to raise millions for worthy causes.

Alisande Wyrrd appeared to be legit—crazy—but as normal as one would expect from an eccentric.

Sebastian rubbed at the spot on his chest where her finger had gently poked him. The skin there was warm and highly sensitive almost as if she had branded him with her simple touch.

"Impossible," he muttered. He was letting his imagination and the nutty woman's suggestive words play on his mind. No doubt she had dabbled some in Wicca and now thought herself a bona fide witch. Though he had to admit that she didn't fit his image of a witch.

A cauldron-stirring crone like in *Macbeth* was more his idea of a witch. He laughed to himself; of course, there was always Kim Novak in *Bell, Book and Candle*.

"Damn," he mumbled and tapped angrily at a computer key. Here he was a practical and successful businessman debating with himself over good and bad witches. When all along Alisande Wyrrd was nothing more than a wealthy heiress with too much time on her hands, playing foolish games.

But then her family wealth could just about buy her anything. It certainly could help keep her privacy private. Further investigation was necessary, Sebastian didn't care for unanswered questions. A sensible explanation could be found for any situation, and he intended to find out what Ms. Wyrrd was up to.

Besides, his business reputation was at stake. If word got

out that a woman had breached security in his own building, his business would be in jeopardy.

Ms. Smithers buzzed him with a reminder about his three o'clock appointment and supper with two senators. His investigation into Ms. Wyrrd would have to wait.

"Tonight, when I get home," he promised himself and reached for the folder on his desk.

Sebastian stared at the digital clock on his nightstand. It was almost midnight, the witching hour. He was about to shake his head and stopped himself. He had hoped to be home earlier, but the senators had much to discuss with him regarding private security in their homes, leaving him to walk in the door only twenty minutes ago. A quick shower and he had dropped into bed.

The day had taken its toll, and being an early riser, never later than six and closer to five, he felt the drain of his long day catching up to him. He had intended to research the Wyrrd family at greater length and read some on the history of witches, but presently he found himself too exhausted to lift a finger.

He did manage to set his alarm and turn off his light, but as soon as his head touched his pillow his eyes closed and he instantly fell asleep.

"Really, Ali, do you think this is fair of you? After all, he is only mortal. And if it is a mortal male you wish, then you should play fair," Sydney said, watching her niece about to cast a spell to the heavens.

"All is fair in love, dear aunt. And besides, he spent a good portion of the afternoon investigating me; now I wish to do a little investigation myself."

"Investigation?" her aunt asked with a glint in her blue eyes. "I would say you are about to torment the dear man."

A slow smile spread across Ali's face. "I must determine if he fits my needs."

"Then take some advice," her aunt said. She poured herself another glass of wine and walked to the edge of the flagstone terrace, where her niece stood barefoot in the thick carpet of grass. "Make certain that he excels in kissing. So few men know how to kiss well. Only a handful possess the skill to kiss with passion and promise."

"Kisses it shall be," Ali said and with a ripple of laughter that sounded like the tinkle of wind chimes she raised her hands to the heavens and silently cast her spell.

He stood in a field naked. It was night and the stars twinkled brilliantly overhead. The rush of a warm summer's breeze swept around him, and the scent of fresh heather filled his senses. It was a dream—it had to be—since Sebastian Wainwright would never do anything so absurd as standing naked in a field of heather.

Sebastian cast a curious glance around him. The place didn't look familiar. He cocked his head to listen to the soft sound that suddenly caught his attention. Wind chimes. No, more like laughter, a gentle female laughter.

He caught sight of the shapely image that floated effortlessly across the field toward him. He had no doubt to the person's identity. She had invaded his personal thoughts all evening. No matter how many times he had pushed the image of Alisande Wyrrd from his mind, she would pop right back into it and always with a shake of her finger at him as if warning that she would not be so easily dismissed.

So it was only fitting that he dream of her, and since this was his dream, he could enjoy himself.

She settled only inches in front of him, wearing a white transparent gown that covered her from neck to toes yet displayed enough of her intimate beauty to tempt and tease.

He remained as he stood, waiting for her to make the first move.

She didn't disappoint him. Her hand reached out and her fingers faintly caressed his lips. ''I have wondered how you would taste.''

His tongue gently sampled her finger as it passed over his lips once again. ''You taste sweet and—''

He grasped her wrist, feeling the sudden urge to sample more. Slowly he drew her toward him, his dark eyes focused on her lovely face, his free hand circling around her narrow waist and his head tilting at just the right angle to capture her full lips as their bodies gently came together.

He lost all thought and reason after their first initial contact. A faint brush of the lips, a small electrical charge, and like magic they were locked in each other's arms, their bodies snug against each other and their lips sharing the heated passion only true lovers experience.

He tasted and enjoyed her as one would a rare vintage wine. He intended to drink his fill, make himself heady with her potent taste, and then vanquish her from his mind forever. But like a good, old wine, one can never get enough, never feel satisfied, always wanting more of the rare flavor and pleasure it leaves you with.

So he continued to enjoy her. His tongue mating with hers in appreciation, wanting to show her how very much he savored the intimate essence of her.

He wasn't sure when or how they wound up stretched out on a soft mound of grass or how the fresh heather lay sprinkled across them, and he didn't care. His only thought was of Alisande, the rare taste of her and the feel of her pressed so intimately against him.

He felt her move as only a woman does when she wants more from a man. She slipped her leg over his, urging it down between her own, urging him closer, urging him for more.

"Damn, why can't this be real," he murmured.

"It can be," she whispered. "Come to me, Sebastian. Come to me and love me."

She kissed him then. A kiss that threatened to rob him of his sanity, it was packed with such passion and promise.

"Come to me," she whispered again and floated out of his arms.

He reached out for her, a feeling of such utter loneliness invading him that it brought him to the edge of tears.

"Don't go," he said in a choked sob.

"You must come to me, Sebastian. Come, don't keep me waiting."

She drifted up into the starlit sky and vanished in the blink of an eye.

Sebastian lay with his arm draped over his head, watching where only seconds ago she had hovered above him. Rarely in his life had he felt lonely. He always had family and friends around, and even when he spent time alone it was with a sense of peaceful solitude. But now, lying here with the night sky so splendid above and the potent scent of nature surrounding him, he felt alone, dreadfully alone. Something was suddenly missing from his life, and he couldn't quite understand what it was.

"Wake up, you fool, it's only a dream," he warned himself.

But he remained in the field, the scent of her still upon him. It was a strange fragrance that suited her, sweet, tart, and womanly. He had never smelled it before and doubted it would suit any other woman.

He sniffed at his hand and smiled. He liked her scent on him, it was almost as if a small part of her lingered with him, teased him, tempted him.

"Come to me."

Her parting words sounded once again in his head and

continued in a steady rhythm, lulling him into a deeper sleep.

Alisande's smile was unusually bright when she joined her aunt for breakfast on the terrace.

"Do I need to ask how your night went?"

She deposited a peck on her aunt's cheek and took the seat opposite her at the glass-top table. A white umbrella trimmed in Belgian lace provided shade from the brilliant early-morning sun.

Ali reached for her glass of pineapple juice. "He's so much more than I imagined."

"That good?"

Ali put her glass down without taking a sip. "Aunt Sydney, you know I have kissed many a man during my many years, but never have I had a man kiss me with the power, passion, and prowess of Sebastian Wainwright. He's simply remarkable. I couldn't get enough of him, though I did see enough of him. He's simply a splendid male."

Aunt Sydney raised a questionable brow. "You didn't go beyond the acceptable, did you?"

Ali sighed. "I so wanted to, but I am not a foolish young girl who cannot control herself. And I fully understand the consequences of my actions. The decision must ultimately be his. And besides how was I to know he slept naked."

"Correct," her aunt said with obvious relief and a smile. "You may go only so far. He must come to you the rest of the way himself, dressed however he wishes."

Ali picked with her fork at the fresh slices of melon on her plate, her thoughts straying. "Do you think a kiss can taste rare, sort of like a fine wine that has waited ages to be tasted, savored and enjoyed by just the right appreciative person?"

"Definitely," her aunt said and laughed. "Uncorking a fine bottle of wine is like sampling your first kiss. You taste lightly at first, testing the texture, and then you sip, savoring the flavor, and finally you enjoy the rich, full body of it.''

Ali sighed, recalling her evening tryst. ''That's something how I felt last night. His initial taste was pleasant, then his flavor became more potent, and in the end, I must admit, I was mindless to anything but the taste of him.''

''And his response to you?''

''He wanted me, of that I was certain, but then, most mortal men respond to a woman who stands near naked in front of them.''

''Continue to take the necessary steps, and then you will discover for certain if he is what you desire and you are what he desires, or if it is only his mortal male hormones reacting,'' her aunt advised. ''And remember one other important fact.''

Ali looked to her aunt, cherishing any advice she offered.

''Half the fun of finding a lover is the chase.''

Both women laughed and raised their juice glasses in a salute.

Sebastian eyed the clock and groaned. He must have repeatedly hit the snooze button. He never slept past six, and here it was seven-thirty and he felt as if he hadn't slept a wink.

He rolled over and dragged himself out of bed. He headed straight for the shower, needing the pulsating spray to bring him to life. He shocked himself with a burst of cold water before adjusting it to lukewarm.

He worked a heavy lather of soap over his arms and chest before his thoughts wandered to his dreams. He had experienced vivid dreams before, they were nothing new. Many a time when he was on a mission for the agency and found himself in a tight situation, his dreams would turn vivid, almost lucid as if he were actually living them.

Last night was one such lucid dream. He could almost

still taste Alisande on his lips. And the feel of her supple body next to his was simply unforgettable. He wondered if she would feel so erotically appealing if he really held her in his arms, or if his dreams produced his euphoric state.

Perhaps it was a bit of her craziness that he found appealing. He was always practical and sensible about things. Alisande on the other hand seemed not at all disturbed or uncomfortable in announcing she was a witch.

Did he need a little magic in his life?

He was about to shake his head when he stopped himself. He would resort to no head shaking today, especially when he intended to further investigate Ms. Wyrrd. And heaven knew he shook his head enough when she was around or in his thoughts.

Though last night he didn't shake his head at all. He was too busy kissing her and enjoying it. When was the last time he had enjoyed sharing a kiss with a woman? And when last had he felt so completely desolate at the prospect of a woman leaving him?

Never.

Then why last night when Alisande slipped out of his grasp and floated away . . .

He shook his head.

Floated.

Just listening to himself gave him cause to wonder if being crazy in the head was contagious. Or had Alisande cast a spell?

Spell.

He almost shook his head but stopped himself. Now he had himself thinking that the nutty woman could actually cast a spell.

He shut the shower off with an angry twist of the knobs, grabbed a towel from the brass towel bar, and dried himself off while he mumbled.

"Sure, the witch cast a spell and zapped me out of my

bed, naked, which of course, being a witch, she knew I slept naked, and plopped me down in a field of heather, where she proceeded to seduce me.''

He draped the towel around his waist and reached for another towel, roughly drying his hair with it. When he finished, he draped the towel around his neck and peered at himself in the mirror.

''Then the crazy witch teases you near to seductive death with kisses and leaves, but not before practically begging you to come to her.''

He slowly shook his head. ''You idiot. Not another thought of her until you get to work.''

He gave himself a quick shave and brushed his teeth, feeling like a new man. With his thoughts more focused and in control he headed to his bedroom to dress.

''A mere dream, nothing more,'' he said as he dropped the towel in the hamper on the way out.

A small gurgle of water from the drain caused him to stop and check the sink. He found nothing and headed for his bedroom, but a second gurgle stopped him short. He walked over to the shower stall and opened the door.

His eyes rounded in shock as he stared down at the sprig of heather that blocked the drain.

Four

Three days of near sleepless nights would put any man on edge. But three nights of near erotic dreams about a woman who claimed to be a witch could drive the most sane man over the edge.

Sebastian was close to that edge.

He stared at the computer, at the same information he had stared at day after day, nothing new. Absolutely nothing new on Alisande Wyrrd. He had put his best men on the case with explicit orders to uncover anything and everything they could on Alisande and the Wyrrd family.

All returned with the same information, basic information that any amateur investigator could uncover. His own personal investigation proved just as fruitless, or was it that he discovered all he could about the strange woman?

He ran his hand over his face in frustration and glanced at the digital clock on his desk. Eleven in the morning. He had spent the last four hours going over redundant material and getting nowhere.

Sebastian hit the intercom button on the phone. "Ms. Smithers, fresh coffee, please."

Enough. His thoughts had lingered far too often on Ms. Wyrrd. She was an eccentric who dabbled in the absurd, and he had no intention of allowing her to interfere with his life.

A gentle knock on the office door announced Ms. Smithers. The thin woman quietly served him coffee and slipped a plate with a warm blueberry muffin, butter melting and dripping down the sides, in front of him.

Sebastian smiled. "Have I told you how much I appreciate you lately, Carol."

Wrinkles creased into a wide smile. "Every week in my paycheck, sir."

He laughed. "Good, I wouldn't want to lose a gem like you."

Ms. Smithers cleared her throat and Sebastian looked directly up at her. Carol Smithers had worked for him since he started his business, and when she had something important to say she always cleared her throat. Sebastian always listened, often hearing advice he didn't favor, yet proved necessary.

"What is it, Carol?"

The woman pulled no punches, she spoke directly. "I'm concerned with your health. You don't look as if you have been getting enough sleep."

"I've been getting plenty," he snapped.

"Plenty grouchy," she retorted.

He was about to snarl back at her but caught himself when he watched her cross her arms over her chest ready for battle.

"I'll leave early today," he said, attempting to appease her.

"Good, make it one since you have a one-thirty at the health club for a massage." She walked to the door.

"I don't remember scheduling a massage today."

"You didn't. I did."

Sebastian smiled with the close of the door. She was right. He needed to get away early and relax. And she was right about sleep. Too little of it caused tension, and at the moment he could feel every muscle in his neck and shoulders screaming in protest.

Those damn dreams.

They haunted him night after night. No. She haunted him night after night. He could not for the life of him get Alisande Wyrrd out of his mind. And what was even more crazy was that his thoughts of her were intimate, bordering on erotic.

Only this morning he had awoken with the taste of her on his lips, the fragrant smell of her surrounding him and his body aching for her. In his dream he had kissed her until he thought he would go mad with the want of her. Those full lips drove him insane and her silky soft skin seem to pulsate at his touch.

And yet as much as he tasted and touched he felt empty, denied, and he knew all too well that was because his dreams lacked reality.

But reality was that the very woman whom he fantasized about was a nut. Or was she?

Sebastian straightened in his seat and hit the computer key. He reached for his coffee, took a sip, and then broke off a piece of the muffin. Perhaps he wasn't seeing this clearly, his mind too focused on sex.

He laughed. How could one focus too much on sex when it was so damn pleasing to the soul? And maybe, just maybe that was Ms. Wyrrd's intentions all along. She was interested in nothing more than an affair. Plain and simple sex with a dash of intrigue to excite.

He studied the computer while finishing his coffee and muffin and smiled, pleased with his findings. Ms. Wyrrd had had no significant relationship as of late. She had been seen at several fund-raisers with various escorts but no repeat performance by any one in particular.

So was it simply that Ms. Wyrrd was horny?

He grinned. A sensible explanation could be found for anything if one looked hard enough and in the right places. And the right place was an unexpected visit to Alisande Wyrrd.

The Wyrrd estate took one's breath away. Sebastian eyed the beauty of the rolling hills and pastures dotted with spreads of wildflowers as he drove along the single-lane dirt driveway to the house. The place teemed with history. He could just imagine it a century or more ago before modernization took over, though the Wyrrd's did seem to retain its dated appearance as though time stood still around this patch of land and forever blossomed forth in historic grandeur.

He pulled his black Jaguar to a stop in the circular driveway in front of the house. With a quick admiring glance to the large three-story brick house he strode up the few steps and pressed the doorbell.

He suddenly felt nervous. A strange feeling and one he had rarely experienced since his teen years. He had learned to control his emotions, keep them at bay. It was a matter of survival. First, when he was twelve and his parents had been killed in a car accident. Their unexpected passing devastated him and almost destroyed his orderly life. But sensibility and determination took root and so did his father's sister, Mildred. She became his legal guardian, and though at first it was a difficult adjustment, he soon came to realize she was a lot like his father. Practical and sensible. Their similar characteristics helped him to settle in, and he and his aunt to this day enjoyed a close relationship. She had retired from teaching several years ago, moving to Arizona. He visited her whenever he could.

The second time his innate sensibilities and skill to judge a situation wisely and react just as wisely won him the attention of a top government agency. He was hired immediately out of college. He learned quickly that his missions required full concentration and strict attention to detail—that was why he was exceptional when it came to security. He knew how to track, hunt, and capture. And Ms. Wyrrd was about to be captured.

A spry woman in her sixties answered the door and surprised Sebastian when after introducing himself was told that Ms. Wyrrd was expecting him.

And as if by magic, the woman in question appeared like a gentle breeze sweeping into the room and taking his breath away.

She was simply stunning. A flowing dress of white curved and glided over her slim waist and ample breasts, and her hair was a riot of curls, some caught up in a gold clip while others fell freely and outrageously around her face.

She hurried to his side as if he were a long-lost friend and hooked her arm in his, startling him and sending his hormones into overdrive.

"How wonderful you've come to visit," she said excitedly, her naked feet peeking out from beneath the white gauze dress as she hurried him along beside her. "I was so looking forward to seeing you again."

He followed reluctantly but inquisitively. What was she up to now? And damn if those bare feet of hers didn't entice him, especially her right pinkie toe. She wore a gold toe ring, and a tiny bell dangled from it and tinkled ever so lightly as she walked. It was barely audible, and yet the gentle chime unnerved him.

The warmth of the solarium hit him as soon as he entered the bright room, Alisande still clinging to his arm. The room reminded him of an old Victorian solarium filled with a variety of foliage, wicker furniture, and eye-catching objects like the regal black ceramic cat statue that sat at least four feet high and looked to be guarding the place with its sharp, stunning green eyes.

"Mint iced tea?" she asked and slipped her arm from his, but not before running her fingers over his forearm and squeezing his hand firmly.

He nodded, his breath once again caught somewhere in his throat. This would not do at all. This loss of mental and physical control when around her. She just plain bewitched him.

Damn.

He couldn't even think of her in any other terms but witching. This had to stop. He had to take the upper hand here and keep firm hold of it.

He accepted the tall glass from her, avoiding the tips of her fingers as they attempted to graze his own.

"Ms. Wyrrd," he said, clearing his throat and thinking of his secretary's long-standing habit. "I felt it is important we talk."

"Good, good," she said with excitement and seated herself on the wicker settee, tucking her feet beneath her, leaving her one foot with the toe ring to peek out.

Tempting?

He shook his head and she smiled at him, patting the spot beside her. "Come join me."

Her voice was much too soft, her words much too coaxing. He remained where he was, standing.

He spoke firmly and with a sternness that bordered on sounding harsh. "I think you need to explain yourself."

The warm air rippled with her laughter, like wind chimes caught in a summer breeze, and his body froze. It was the familiar sound he heard so often in his dreams. *Dreams.* Just damn dreams.

"I would love nothing better than to explain everything. Absolutely everything."

Sebastian placed his glass down on the glass-covered wicker table and waited.

"Please," she said gently, again patting the seat beside her. "Join me."

Her suggestive words sent shivers down his spine and testosterone levels soaring. Damn, but if he didn't want to join her, but not to sit beside her, to be inside her. The intimate thought rocked the foundations of his emotional security.

"An explanation," he snapped sharply.

"Yes, Sebastian, I will offer you an explanation, but will you believe it?"

Casual, confident, competent, Sebastian thought. This woman certainly did not give the impression of being crazy, but then she had yet to offer her explanation. An explanation worth believing?

"Let's give it a try," he offered and sat in the wicker fan chair looking like a king about to pass judgment.

Alisande studied him carefully before speaking. He was interested, perhaps curious, definitely skeptical, which brought him here. He had to satisfy his doubts, have answers to unanswerable questions, and solve the perplexing mystery.

And through it all he appeared in control. His dark hair was perfectly groomed, his face clean shaven, a splash of casual cologne, nothing enticing, pure business cologne. His suit was light gray, smoky perhaps dusky in color with a starched white shirt beneath and a geometric tie that blended well. The diamonds in his Movada watch sparkled, and he rubbed at the gold ring on his right ring finger. A ring that carried an insignia of a top Ivy League school.

Yet beneath the controlled and polished exterior he presented, she knew raged unbridled lust. He wanted her and he fought his desire with the tenacity of a drowning man going under for the last time. He was much too practical to accept the impractical. But then, she was much too impractical ever to be content with the practical, and Sebastian Wainwright was about to take a step into the impractical.

She locked her green eyes with his dark ones. "As I said in your office, I am—"

"How did you get past my security guards?" he demanded, darting forward in his chair.

She smiled. *Impatient.* Mortals could be so easily manipulated through their faults.

"What do you really want to know, Sebastian?" Her question was a whisper, tempting him to ask the unaskable.

The fresh scent of mint drifted off her and around him. When had he moved so close to her that he could feel her warm sweet breath on his face?

Concentrate, he warned himself, and moved back in his seat. He had come for an answer. "What do you want from me?"

She stretched her leg out and casually rested her foot on his knee, the tiny toe bell ringing a faint chime. "I want you."

Sebastian glanced down at the bell and damned himself for the erotic thoughts that flooded his head.

Alisande continued. "I told you that I am a witch looking for a lover."

"Not a lover looking for someone to bewitch?"

She shook her head slowly. "Bewitching is the easy part."

"Finding the lover is the difficult?"

"I found him."

"But if old tales prove true, then he must submit to the witch's will," Sebastian said.

"Is that so difficult?"

"One would have to believe in witches, cauldrons, toads, and such. And of course that witches need sexual recharges. That's pushing the old tale a bit."

"Witches have grown in knowledge and strength since the dark ages. I rarely use a cauldron these days, and I never did care for touching a toad or turning someone into one. Sexual recharges have always been a part of our nature. Nature itself must replenish to survive. Witches follow nature and must replenish as well. Sound and sensible practices I am sure you can relate to."

"And you are asking a *sound and sensible* man to accept this explanation as to why you wish to make love with me?"

"A truthful explanation."

He raised a brow. "Come now, why not just tell me I excite you sexually and be done with it."

She smiled and licked her lips appreciatively. "Oh, but you do excite me. Why else would I have chosen you? You have the strength and stamina I require."

"This is ridiculous," he said and stood, brushing her foot off his knee. "I'm not on the auction block for you to choose at whim."

"Hmmm, an interesting concept."

The way her eyes blatantly roamed over him nearly brought him to his knees. She was simply outrageous in her pursuit of him. A seductress. A siren. A sorcerer!

"Are you going to admit the truth to me?" he demanded, not at all happy with his thoughts or his body's mutinous response every time he laid eyes on her.

She remained calm. "I already have."

"You're a witch looking for a lover."

"A special and consenting lover. He *must* consent."

"You're horny, but you want me to consent to have sex with you."

She laughed and threw her arms wide. "Heavens, no, not just sex, we shall make glorious, rapturous love. You will experience a passion unlike anything you ever imagined. You will become part of me and I part of you. We will unite in an age-old bond that defies time and meaning. We will love unconditionally for time and all eternity.''

While part of him ached to experience such unimaginable wonders with her, another part of him, the sensible part, warned of her sanity or lack of. She thought herself a witch whose powers required a boost. Was this rational thought?

''Why do humans fear witches?''

Her question startled him, but at least here was rational thought. ''Witches don't exist. Ignorance breeds fear, and manufactured tales spread by gossip helped to breed that fear of witches.''

Alisande smiled. ''I am pleased with your answer.''

''Good, then tell me what you want.''

She sighed. ''You. Simply you.''

He walked over to her and leaned down, his face a mere breath from hers. ''Then tell me the truth and dispense with the theatrics, and I might consider—*might*—making love to you.''

Her frown was genuine and it disturbed Sebastian as did his admission that he would consider making love to her. But then, hadn't that thought haunted him since he met her. He wanted her and damned but if he didn't have a hard time coming to terms with his overwhelming desire for this strange woman.

She hesitated for a moment. ''I want you. That is the truth, but so are my reasons. I am a witch and I have chosen you. I must be truthful. You must consent knowing full well what I ask of you.''

He shook his head. ''Crazy,'' he murmured and leaned down to capture her lips, wondering whether it was him or her he berated.

Five

''Breathless. His kiss left me breathless,'' Alisande said, sinking back against the salmon-colored swooning lounge in her Aunt Sydney's bedroom.

The older woman sat at her antique rosewood vanity table fussing with her long white hair that she had just secured in a perfectly executed French braid. ''An excellent kisser. This is definitely a point in his favor.''

Alisande melodramatically draped her arm over her forehead. ''*Excellent* is not a sufficient-enough word to describe his kiss.''

Her aunt cast a curious eye in the three-mirror vanity at her niece draped in dramatic pose across her lounge. ''And what words *would* sufficiently describe this kiss?''

Ali's eyes fluttered. ''Hot. Passionate. *Electrifying*.''

''Alisande.''

Her name spoken in parental scolding made Ali sit up and look contritely at her aunt.

''This affair is in the prenatal stage. It needs time to develop and mature. Do not rush your emotions.''

Ali sighed. ''But he is so much more than I expected. The dreams are one thing, Aunt Sydney. You know yourself they are of a spiritual nature and therefore can only hint at reality. But his kiss only hours ago was real. His lips were warm and gentle, at first, and then . . ." She sighed again.

"And then," her aunt urged.

Ali smiled with contented pleasure. "And then he took full possession as though he couldn't taste enough of me, couldn't satisfy his hunger, couldn't stop himself."

Ali closed her eyes and lapsed into silence, recalling how his kiss turned intimate, his tongue stealing its way inside her, teasing her own to consort with his until he demanded she respond, and she did without hesitation.

Her aunt interrupted her thoughts. "What prevented him from going further?"

Ali shrugged. "Reality, I suppose. He drew back surprised by his own desires, and I gather the strangeness of the situation. He rushed from the room without saying a word or without a backward glance."

Aunt Sydney nodded knowingly. "His emotions frighten him. He cannot understand them. He does not like losing control."

Ali grinned. "Oh, but I do so like when he loses control."

"Be careful, my dear, remember I warned you about wishing for something that may be more than you can handle?"

"I can handle Sebastian Wainwright."

Aunt Sydney shook her head. "He is much more of a mortal man than you think. His physical and mental strength go beyond the ordinary. He has tamed his emotions to respond accordingly."

"Then I will untame them."

"And unleash a fiery dragon."

"I like dragons."

"Not one you cannot tame."

"He will surrender."

Aunt Sydney laughed. "Dragons never surrender, dear,

they pretend to and then before you know it you are trapped and they consume you whole.''

Alisande stood. ''You forget who has the powers.''

''No, dear, you do.''

Ali frowned, her aunt's words leaving a strange sensation stirring in her. ''I have work to do.''

''Be careful,'' her aunt called after her as she hurried out of the room. ''His power is far greater than you think.''

Alisande did not hear her warning. She was too busy planning her next act of seduction.

Sebastian entered the health club an hour late for his appointment and in dire need of a massage. He was on edge, even more so than this morning in his office. He had thought a confrontation with Alisande would solve everything. It had only made matters worse.

How in all good sanity could he be attracted to a woman who professed to be a witch? And does not even dispute the ridiculous claim when given the opportunity. She had to be crazy. What other explanation was there?

The muscles in his neck constricted to the point of pain, and he rolled his head from side to side hoping to ease the tension his unplanned visit had caused. But was it the visit, or was it the kiss?

''Damn,'' he muttered, unfastening his belt. All he wanted was to slip out of his clothes and go stretch out on the massage table and let Gladys work her usual miracle on his taut muscles.

Instead he found himself focusing on that damn kiss. Lord, but she tasted *hot*. Full-blown passion, that's what he felt when his lips connected with hers. If he hadn't pulled away, if he hadn't reined in his sanity, he would have taken her right there and then on the wicker settee. He would have thrown that white gauzy dress of hers up, spread her legs ever so slowly, and entered her just as slowly so she could watch every possessive step he took. And then, then when he was buried deep inside her, he would have taken her with an unbridled passion that brought her to the edge. And when she finally toppled over he would have been there to join her in a climax that went beyond satisfying to mystifying.

"Damn," he muttered again and concentrated on getting undressed. He needed this massage. He needed to relax. He needed to forget Alisande Wyrrd, that kiss, and that damn toe ring.

Sebastian finished undressing, wrapped a towel around his waist, and hurried to the massage room ready to receive some much needed relaxation.

"Don't hold back, Gladys," Sebastian said as he stretched out face down on the leather massage table covered with a warm linen cloth.

"Yes, sir," the woman answered and set straight to work on his neck.

Sebastian almost sighed with pleasure. Gladys was a big woman at five feet ten and almost two hundred pounds, and her talented hands were well in demand. It took months to get an appointment with her. But she always made room for him, since it was he who first gave her a try when she started at the health club five years ago and he who had helped spread the word about her.

Her expert hands dug into him, kneading the tense and tight muscles until they gave in to her demands, and while Gladys worked her magic on him, Sebastian drifted into a hazy slumber.

He stood on an auction block, his hands tied in front of him with black silk scarfs. He knew he could break free of the puny bonds if he chose to. But he stood where he was, his body taut and glistening with a fine sweat of anticipation. He wore a white cloth draped low around his lean hips, the sparse material doing little good in hiding his potent arousal. He was ready. Waiting. Waiting for her.

Hundreds of candles filled the close quarters, and thin gauzy veils were draped from ceiling to walls. Large numerous pillows lay scattered about the tentlike room, and a compelling scent drifted in the air. A thick aroma that tempted the body and teased the senses.

A large man stood silently beside the heavy block of wood Sebastian stood on, his stare concentrated on the veils at the far wall while his thick hands tightly grasped the ends of the black silk bonds that enslaved Sebastian.

He heard it then, the faint tinkle of chimes. She drifted in on the enticing sound from behind the veils. Her hair was done up in a thousands curls that fell rebelliously around her face and along her slim neck. Her dress was pure white and veil thin, running down the full length of her, and beneath it he could see the shadows and curves that shaped her naked body.

She stepped forward and held out her hand. The large man handed her the end of the black silk scarf and disappeared. She said nothing, her intense green eyes focused on his face. Then slowly her glance drifted over him like a warm, possessive caress, and he could have sworn her hands had traveled the same route as her eyes.

He fought the unbearable urge to break free and take her fast and furious. But he forced himself to maintain control. He was man to no master, not even a beautiful and wickedly tempting witch. He was in command. He was his own master. And she would soon learn that.

She reached up and tugged at the corner of the cloth that covered him. It stayed tied at his hips, refusing to budge. She tugged again, and still the cloth refused to move. She then tugged at the black silk restraints at his wrists, and they, too, remained firmly in place.

She grew distressed as she attempted again to free him

of his shackles. To bend him to her will. To possess him. Her full lips pouted, her eyes grew misty, her hands began to tremble, and she looked to him with wide panicked eyes.

He snatched the black ties from her grasp and tore free of them, then he stripped free of the cloth and stepped naked off the block.

His fingers gripped her chin. ''I cannot be bought.''

A tear slipped from her eye, and he licked the clear bead from her cheek with the tip of his tongue.

She sighed.

He lifted her in one swift motion into his arms and carried her to the mounds of scattered pillows, dropping her gently down and lowering himself over her.

''Come to me,'' she whispered. ''Please, Sebastian, come to me.''

''I'm here,'' he said and lowered his lips to hers.

He woke with his lips plastered to the leather table, the linen cloth having slipped off to the side.

''Hell and damnation,'' he muttered and grabbed the loose towel as he sat up on the massage table. He was alone as he had expected. He often drifted off during a massage, and Gladys never disturbed him. She would shut the door and leave him to rest.

He ran his hand through his dark, damp hair and shook his head. What was he to do? He was acting like a teenager in the throes of his first sexual experience. This had to stop.

He had to regain control over his outrageously rebelling hormones. He was an adult male, not an adolescent teenager. Of course, he could always surrender and make love with the crazy woman; perhaps that would satisfy this unbridled lust.

He shook his head. *No.* He wouldn't be drawn into her little game. Hadn't his dream proved he was in control and not her?

He had to be logical and practical. He hopped off the table. He hadn't had a practical thought since he met the loony woman. What made him think he could start now?

"Because you have no choice, you idiot?" he said and walked to the door. "Now see what you've done. You're talking to yourself."

He swung open the door and stormed out of the room to the showers.

Alisande breathed a heavy sigh and allowed a single tear to streak down her cheek. She tucked her feet more firmly beneath her in the big wooden porch rocker and drank in the scent and sight of the land that stretched out before her. She had not expected to be so emotionally affected by the dream. She had meant to tease and tempt him in to yielding to her, and yet he had demonstrated his strength and his power of choice. Was she getting in too deep? Was this mortal man more than she could handle, as her aunt had warned?

He had to come to her. Free choice. She could do her darnedest to seduce him, but the final decision was ultimately his. She wiped the tear from her eye with a quick brush of her hand and stood. She had made her choice. Her intentions were clear. She would not back down. She was a witch. He a mere mortal. She would have him her way. She had invaded his dreams. Now she would invade his senses.

Anybody who was anybody in Washington did not miss a Wyrrd Foundation fund-raiser. It was not acceptable. And besides no one wanted to explain to Sydney Wyrrd why they had been absent from one of her events, which meant that many of Washington's elite returned on Saturday night to D.C. from wherever they were vacationing to attend this special event.

Sydney had put together a remarkable night for the benefit of poor and ill children worldwide. Tickets were a thousand dollars a plate with raffles for extraordinary gifts, and a six-foot-high money tree occupied the foyer, Sydney expecting it to blossom fully by evening's end.

Only the best champagne was being served, and an overflowing buffet table, with a variety of foods prepared by the most talented chefs who had donated their services for the evening, lined the entire length of one wall of the ballroom.

It was a splendid affair, black tie of course, and the men and women mingled, enjoyed, and waited to meet with the eccentric Wyrrds.

Sydney never arrived at one of her events until it was in full swing, and she forbid Alisande to do so. She insisted that people loved anticipation and a grand entrance, and Sydney always made a grand entrance, either alone in some fabulous designer dress or on the arm of an enchanting prince, king, or noteworthy man. Tonight would be no exception.

Sebastian stood amongst the myriad attendees, a glass of bubbly in hand, conversing with a tall redhead. Her name was Tasha, and she was vain and materialistic, though perfect for his friend James, who possessed similar traits.

"Do you know Sydney Wyrrd flew to Paris just so she would have an original designer gown for this event?" Tasha asked in awe of the woman.

Sebastian nodded, attempting to ignore the trivial chatter. He wasn't interested in designer gowns or Sydney Wyrrd. He intended to make himself visible, talk with several important people, and then be on his way. But there was that attractive dark-haired woman James was talking with; perhaps an introduction would spark some interest and clear his head of witches.

In minutes Sebastian had maneuvered Tasha over to

James and the woman, whose name was Lynn. The four talked and shared more bubbly, and when voices fell to whispers, all four pairs of eyes followed the crowd to the staircase.

Sydney Wyrrd stood at the top, a handsome man of perhaps forty on her arm. She looked magnificent. Age seemed to defy time as she descended the stairs in a silver creation that baffled the eye and gave the impression of an ethereal beauty descending from the heavens.

Gasps and whispers followed her and continued as she joined the crowd. Sebastian had to admit the woman didn't look anywhere near her . . . ? He thought a moment. How old was Sydney Wyrrd? Some said possibly fifty, others guessed nearer to sixty, and still he heard one man insist he knew her long enough to make her close to eighty, yet she didn't look a day over forty-five. How many face-lifts had she had?

And where the hell was Alisande? Didn't she want to stop tongues from wagging and catch people's breath with her entrance?

He took a sip of champagne, and as his lips left the glass he spotted her.

Six

Alisande parted the crowd. They moved out of her way cautiously, almost reverently. Men stared in open desire and the women in envy.

The woman knew how to make an impressive entrance.

If Sebastian didn't know any better, he would have thought she floated along the floor toward him, her movements were so gracefully orchestrated. Her black silk dress even appeared to cooperate with her every move, curving here, clinging there and the front slit that disappeared at the apex of her legs parted just enough to arouse the staunchest of men.

He shook his head, his own quick arousal proving his point.

His eyes caught the twinkle reflected off the gold specks that highlighted her hair. She wore it simple, though *simple* was not a word he would equate with Alisande. Her honey-blond hair flowed around her like a lazy river, accenting her stunning features and those mesmerizing green eyes.

''Sebastian,'' she said, gliding to a stop much too close to him. So close that his leg nestled in the slit of her dress and the sensual warmth of her seeped into him. ''How good to see you again.''

His friend James sent him a questioning look, and he

knew James wondered where and how Sebastian had met Alisande and above all why he hadn't informed him that he was acquainted with the notable Wyrrds.

Before Sebastian could respond or introduce Alisande, she turned to James and extended her hand. "Mr. Peters, it is a pleasure to meet you. Your work in genetic engineering is causing considerable tongue wagging. My aunt is impressed and wishes so much to meet with you, a grant I think it was she mentioned."

James couldn't find his tongue; he tripped repeatedly over his words looking to Sebastian for assistance. Sebastian offered it freely knowing James dreamed constantly of having a benefactor who would help finanically further his work. He was also aware that Alisande desired to be alone with him. What was she up to now?

"Why don't you go speak with her aunt Sydney right now," Sebastian suggested.

James looked to Alisande like a puppy looking for permission. "Yes, yes, you must go talk with her immediately." She gave him a little shove.

That left the two women, and he wondered with a grin how she would politely dispose of them.

She turned a dazzling smile on them. "Ladies, I was wondering if you would do me a favor? Our public relations people need a few attractive and exceptionally well-dressed women for photos that will make tomorrow's newspapers; could I trouble you both to volunteer?"

Damn, she was good. Sebastian contained his grin; if he didn't it would have spread clear across his face.

The two women accepted eagerly and were directed to the appropriate people with the wave of Alisande's hand.

"Now for me," he said when she turned back to him. "How will you make me disappear?"

She ran her fingers up and down the lapel of his black

tuxedo jacket. "Darling, I don't wish for you to disappear. I want you."

It took an exceptional amount of willpower to stand there and pretend that he wasn't affected by her ardent declaration. Knowing she was willing, wanting, and waiting didn't help his determination to deny her blatant overtures.

"Behave yourself," he snapped, wondering if he meant the scolding for himself.

Her voice rang in a whisper of erotic chimes. "But I don't want to behave. I want to play naughty with you."

"Damn, woman," he said and stepped clear of her. "We are not exactly alone here."

"Aren't we?" she asked innocently.

Sebastian cast a glance around the large room. All attending were busy in chatter and talk. Not one curious eye was directed their way. It was as if they didn't exist. Sebastian couldn't even manage to catch anyone's attention, except her aunt Sydncy. The woman looked directly at him and smiled.

He turned his attention back to Alisande. "I think your aunt requires your presence."

"She will let me know when she needs me."

"I suggest you go to her now," he said firmly.

"I enjoy being with you." Her insistence was softly noted.

He chose the one weapon she seemed unable to defend herself against, though it was a tactless lie. "I don't want you here with me."

His words stung, but he saw that she recovered quickly, though he didn't. It bothered him that he had senselessly hurt her.

"I will not stay if you don't want me," she said gently and reached for his glass of champagne, sliding her fingers along over his until he relinquished it to her. She pressed her lips to the clear glass, tilted and sipped, then returned it to him.

Her words sang like a spell and weaved around him. "If you dare place your lips to mine, you will taste me there this evening time." Her long red nail poked him in the chest, and she turned and disappeared into the crowd.

Sebastian blinked and focused on the crowd. James was beside him as was Tasha and Lynn. All three were a-chatter about the marvelous event. He stood as he had before Alisande's arrival as though her presence had never been known.

His tall height afforded him a good view of the ballroom, and he hastily glanced around attempting to spot her. He couldn't find her anywhere. He held up his champagne glass and stared at the red imprint her lipstick had left where she drank from his glass.

She was playing a game with him again. A game he had no intention of losing. He turned the glass in his hand and took a sip, her lip imprint mating with his own lips.

He braced himself for a reaction, and when none came he silently chastized himself for even considering that her spell was real. She was no witch. Witches were nonexistent—at least the broom-flying kind.

He deliberately took another sip and joined in the conversation intending to ignore his encounter with Alisande Wyrrd, and then he felt it.

The sensation jolted his senses.

Hell and damnation.

His lips tingled, ached, pulsated, and he shook his head.

Pressure.

Sweet, hot, lustful pressure of a kiss packed with passion.

His knees buckled but he fought to maintain his dignity.

"Are you all right, Sebastian?" James asked with concern. "You seem startled."

"Too much champagne," he joked and patted his friend

on the back, partly as if in jest and partly to maintain his balance.

Lynn suggested they help themselves to the buffet, and Sebastian eagerly agreed, hoping the taste of food would combat the odd sensation running over his lips. Perhaps he had drunk too much bubbly and combined with Ms. Wyrrd's cute poetic phrase a suggestive thought was placed in his already champagne-induced brain.

He quickly disposed of his glass and joined the line of people at the buffet table. He chose a variety of appealing appetizers, popping a shrimp wrapped in bacon into his mouth followed by a mushroom cap stuffed with a crab mixture.

He sighed at the pleasurable flavor that permeated his taste buds and lingered on his lips. He licked at his lips like a young boy finishing a favorite treat.

The sensation hit him full force, and he braced his hand flat on the buffet table for support. He abandoned his partially filled plate in search of water. He found an overflowing fountain near the end of the buffet table and filled a crystal glass with the sparkling clear liquid. The flavor of lemon and lime filled his senses. He drank like a man long in need.

His lips felt refreshed, cold, wet. So wet. Wet from the drink, he convinced himself and snatched a napkin from the table to wipe at his lips. The napkin did little to alleviate the wetness, and he suddenly realized his lips were no longer cold, but warm, tingling warm, and slightly swollen.

He casually ran his hand over them and almost groaned with the pleasure that shot through his arm. He quickly dropped his hand away. He bit at his lips, thinking the harsh pressure might negate the sensual sensitivity. It fueled it, and he realized with dismay it was as if he was in the throes of a kiss.

His glance shot over the crowd, searching for the woman

who had planted the suggestively erotic thought in his mind. Her little mind game was affecting him more than he cared to admit, and he was about to give her a piece of his own mind.

He saw her across the room engaged in conversation with two women and a man. He started toward her and when he was only a few feet away from her, Sydney Wyrrd stepped in his path.

"I have been so looking forward to meeting you, Sebastian Wainwright," she said and hooked her arm in his. "I for one am in need of Champagne. Will you join me?"

Sebastian was about to graciously decline when Sydney smiled and tapped at his chest. "I think you will find my champagne less stimulating."

He sent her a cautious smile along with his nod and followed her to a table where two glasses of bubbly sat waiting. She handed him one and took the other.

"To a future filled with surprise and promise."

Sebastian added his own toast. "And to the beautiful and eccentric Wyrrd women."

The liquid rushed over his lips, and the strange, cold sharpness stung his sensitive flesh, leaving in its wake a refreshing numbness. He felt nothing. Nothing at all.

He smiled as did Sydney. "Do not be harsh in your judgment of my niece. She is special and has special needs. Learn who she really is and understand, only then will you be able to accept the unacceptable."

Sebastian never passed up an opportunity. Alisande's aunt could tell him much. "Tell me about your niece."

The woman laughed, and Sebastian could have sworn the gaiety that lighted her face made her look ten years younger. "No, no, my dear boy, you must discover her secrets yourself. Only then will you have the power."

He leaned down and whispered in her ear. "Are you a witch, too?"

Sydney patted his arm. "Why, of course, my dear, all the Wyrrd women are witches."

Okay, so she wanted to play the game as well. Why not? Maybe he could learn more about the lunacy that ran in the family.

"And how long have you been a witch?"

"Since birth. It is, after all, a hereditary trait."

"Exactly how old are you?"

"Not a polite question to ask a woman," she reprimanded teasingly.

"Appease me."

Sydney laughed, a gentle laughter that spread warmly around Sebastian. "Since you will unite with our family soon I see no harm in you knowing. I am six hundred years old."

"Approximately or give or take a few years?"

Her laughter rippled around him once again. "I like your sense of humor. You will suit my niece well."

"You have a strong sense of humor of your own."

"Most witches do."

"Even the evil ones?"

Her smile faded and she lowered her voice. "Evil exists in all races, creeds, and religions. Love is its nemesis. Remember that and evil will never touch your heart."

He felt as if he had just been taught a heavy lesson, and somehow the thought made him feel more empowered. "I need to speak with your niece."

Sydney reached for the bottle of champagne on the table. "Then I suggest another glass of my special bubbly before you face off."

He laughed and held his glass up to her. "My armor?"

Sydney filled his glass and smiled. "Defend with love and victory is yours."

Sebastian raised his glass and drank, her words echoing

in his thoughts as he took his leave and went in search of Alisande.

Alisande stood looking out at the late-night sky; a thousand twinkling stars lighted the vast darkness. She moved slowly along the brick patio to the stone banister overgrown with lilac bushes, their rich scents heavy in the summer night heat. She reached out and touched the full blossoms, and a few dropped gently into her hand. She brought them to her face and drank deeply of their sweet cologne.

"Thank you," she whispered to the plant.

A soft summer breeze rushed around her, sweeping the petals from her hand and alerting her to the man's presence behind her.

"You dared to taste," she said without turning around.

"I dared to believe."

She turned then with a smile. "I am glad you believe."

He walked up to her and was assaulted by the sweet scent of lilacs rich on her skin. "Do you know what I believe?"

He moved closer to her until the small of her back was pressed against the stone banister and his body was pressed hard against hers. His hands he braced on either side of her on top of the stone railing, possessively imprisoning her.

She answered in a whisper. "That I am a crazy witch."

"Crazy," he corrected.

"Witch," she rectified.

He shrugged. "Little difference." His lips moved close to hers.

"All the difference in the world," she said and ran her tongue slowly over her lips, preparing them for him, tempting him, inviting him.

"Damn," he whispered and leaned down to trace the very path her tongue had traveled with his own. She was wet and warm and tasted sweet, and his tongue savored every inch of her lips before eagerly entering her mouth.

He felt the jolt and relished in it, his arm slipping around her waist and bringing her harder up against him. Hard enough for her to feel how much he wanted her.

She moaned and he understood she wanted more and he gave her more. His teeth nipped down along her neck, over the tops of her breasts, and back up again to her lips. He nibbled along her lower lip until it plumped from his sensual attack. She whispered and he laughed, low and seductively, before he resumed his assault.

He was in control, he commanded her, her seduced her. *He wanted her.*

He drew back from her slowly, keeping a firm hold around her waist until their senses returned to near normal and he could safely release her to stand on her own.

He said nothing. He stared at her kiss-laden lips, watched her chest heave with breathless desire, and imagined the intimate moistness that filled her.

He had only to touch, to reach down and touch her, intimately, knowingly, lovingly.

"Come to me, Sebastian," he heard her say, and yet he could have sworn she didn't speak a word. "Come to me."

Dream or reality?

He turned and walked away, and when he felt the slight tingle on his lips, he turned back around. She was gone. Or was she ever there?

Or was he losing his mind?

"Enough," he warned himself and entered the ballroom in search of his friends. He had had enough. Tomorrow he would begin an investigation and not stop until he found the truth.

The absolute truth.

Seven

"No birth certificate," Sebastian said to himself. "How could there not be a birth certificate?"

He shook his head. His plan to discover the truth was proving difficult if not impossible. He had assigned two highly skilled agents to the case with instructions to dig deep. So far their dig had proved purely surface information. No matter how hard they tried, they seemed to hit a brick wall, a purposely built brick wall.

His own efforts proved just as fruitless. It was almost as though that wall had been built brick by brick along the way, detouring the curious. He had repeatedly checked all his resources, even foreign ones, to locate a birth certificate on Alisande and her aunt Sydney. Strangely enough, he had yet to uncover one. Her aunt Sydney he could understand, probably being born at a time when almost all deliveries took place in the home. Alisande was a different matter. Her age, which he assumed to be in the late twenties to early thirties, meant her birth had more than likely taken place in a hospital. And hospitals kept records. Then why couldn't he locate them?

He ran his hand through his dark hair and mumbled beneath his breath. To say he was frustrated didn't even begin to touch on his annoyance. He had never in all his years working for the government and in his own business run up against such an odd occurrence. Documents of some type, whether school records, immunization records, or religious records to name a few, usually popped up somewhere along the investigative path. And one small lead could start the ball rolling in the right direction.

But he couldn't even find school records for Alisande. Everyone in America had school records somewhere. And she certainly was educated, one only had to converse with her to realize the extent of her education. She was highly intelligent with a quick and calculating mind. Had she been educated abroad?

Even if that proved correct, he would certainly find records of her attendance. And yet when he searched, he found nothing. It was almost as if she didn't exist. If it wasn't for her participation in the Wyrrd Foundation, he would not have located a speck of information on her.

A knock on the door interrupted his confused thoughts, and when his friend and agent Pierce Knowlin entered his office, he was glad for the intrusion.

Pierce joined the Wainwright force only last year and proved to be a definite asset to the company. His average height and looks allowed him to blend easily with the crowd, though his deep sensual voice and well-defined body was a definite attraction to the ladies, not to mention his smooth-shaved head and full mustache.

"I found something, though I don't know if it will help," Pierce said, dropping a sheet of paper on Sebastian's desk.

Sebastian picked it up and curiously scanned the list of names. "What is this?"

Pierce took a seat in one of the two soft gray leather chairs that faced Sebastian's desk. "A friend of mine is nuts about discovering her family roots, and she has researched her family tree going all the way back to the sixteen hundreds. What you have in front of you is a list of births in the colony of Virginia sometime in the sixteen hundreds. The date isn't clear. It can be either 1632, 1652, or whatever, your guess is as good as mine."

"And?" Sebastian asked, not making any sense of the badly faded and barely legible ancient document.

"Read it, Sebastian."

Sebastian did as instructed, though he wondered what in heaven's name—

He bolted forward in his chair.

Pierce smiled. "I figured if we could get a lock on an ancestor, we might be able to trace the heritage to Ms. Wyrrd. Strange, isn't it, that her ancestor should possess the same name as her, Alisande Wyrrd."

Sebastian stared at the name scrawled in barely readable chicken scratch. But nonetheless it was there. A lead, a place to start from, and now they had only to trace it. A formidable task in itself, but a beginning.

"What have you discovered from this?"

"Whoa, boy," Pierce said with a laugh. "I just discovered this little bit of info by sheer accident. Now my work begins. And besides, everyone knows the Wyrrd ancestry goes back at least that far if not further."

"Then why the hell can't I find a damn birth certificate on Alisande or her aunt?"

Pierce shrugged as though the idea wasn't implausible. "We both know the aunt was probably born at home and that midwives often registered births weeks or months after the actual date and some never got registered at all. Who knows, maybe Alisande was born at home. I wouldn't be surprised with the eccentricity that runs in that family."

"I suppose," Sebastian admitted, conceding a point well made. Pierce's explanation was sensible and certainly was possible.

"What exactly is it you're looking for, Sebastian? You

almost seem like you're waiting to uncover a deep, dark Wyrrd family secret.''

''Everyone has skeletons.''

''With a family tree as old as the Wyrrd's I'd say there was a mega amount of skeletons. But do you really want to unearth them? The Wyrrd family has some mighty large clout here in D.C.''

''I want some answers, that's all,'' Sebastian said sternly.

Pierce stood. ''Okay, fair enough,'' he said as he stopped by the office door, ''but you better ask yourself what it is that you question.''

The click of the closed door startled Sebastian, and he jumped out of his seat, ran his hand through his hair, though he felt more like pulling the strands from their roots, and turned to stare out at the capital city he so loved.

His life had been content, normal, sensible, but no more, not since Alisande. She filled his waking thoughts and his nightly dreams. There didn't seem to be a time he didn't think about her, fantasize about her, desire her. She had simply invaded his every thought, and try as he might he couldn't vanquish her from his mind.

She tempted his soul, but then hadn't she said that *magical love* touches the soul? But this wasn't love he was feeling, this was hot, passionate lust.

She spoke about a love affair, and a love affair was a lustful union, not a lifetime commitment. So the real question was why not have an affair with Alisande Wyrrd? She was more than willing, and he certainly wanted her, so what stopped him?

''Practical,'' he reminded with a heavy sigh and a touch of regret. ''You must be practical.''

Alisande believed herself to be a witch, not a mere mortal woman, nor a woman practicing the Wicca religion, but a bona fide, spell-casting, object-floating and who knew what else witch.

And until he could uncover solid, factual information on her, he couldn't take the chance of making love to her. What if she turned out to be mentally disturbed?

He shook his head. He didn't believe that for one minute. She was bright, beautiful, and a highly intelligent woman. Perhaps he had been right all along, and she just enjoyed adding a little spice to her love affairs, and yet he couldn't even find a man she had had a love affair with recently—or at all, for that matter. She certainly had succeeded in keeping her personal life discreet.

"Damn," he muttered. He was going to drive himself insane at this rate. At least Pierce had found a lead no matter how weak. It was a beginning and that was all that was needed to proceed.

"I'm six hundred years old."

Sydney Wyrrd's admission rang clear in his head.

"Nonsense," he said to himself. The woman was teasing him.

Witches, especially six-hundred-year-old witches, didn't exist.

He walked to his desk and hit the intercom button. "Ms. Smithers, do I have many appointments this afternoon?"

"None I can't change if you wish."

He smiled at her astute efficiency. "Good, please reschedule. I will be gone for the rest of the day."

Sebastian left the bookstore with an assortment of books on witches, magic, and Wicca. The material ranged from practice to mythology and to history. He had it all covered. He planned to learn all he could, every aspect. He would have a good working knowledge of the craft, and then maybe he would finally understand Alisande and her deep-rooted interest.

He slipped out of his navy blue suit jacket, folding it over the passenger seat of his Jaguar. He loosened his blue-

and-yellow striped tie and opened the top button of his pale yellow shirt and rolled back the cuff of his sleeves.

It was sweltering today in D.C. The summer heat had hit fast and furious, sending most of Washington into air-conditioned buildings. Those brave souls who tempted fate or those who had no choice looked as though they melted with each step they took in the blazing heat.

Sebastian slid into the smooth leather seat and turned the key. In seconds the car was filled with cool air and the soothing sounds of Mozart.

He drove out of the parking lot with a feeling of relief and headed home. With no traffic to speak of he would make it in no time. He would take a dip in the pool, enjoy a glass of Merlot, and read.

He shook his head as he came to the stop sign. Hell and damnation, how had he taken this turn? He looked at the cross streets in front of him and realized he was in Alisande's neighborhood. But how he had gotten there was another matter. He had no intention of going to see her, or had he? Had his subconscious directed him here?

She had been on his mind for three days, ever since he last saw her at the fund-raiser. And now he had new information he could confront her with—why not go to her?

"Why not?" He shrugged and took the turn to the Wyrrd estate.

The housekeeper once again did not look in the least bit surprised to see him. She directed him to follow her, and he did, though she stopped at the French doors that led out to the indoor pool area and waved him on alone.

A variety of pool furniture in white wrought iron and metal filled the glass-enclosed area, and cushions in solid white touched with veins of gold added the barest of color. A plethora of flowers all in stark white bloom crowded containers surrounding the room, drooped from hanging baskets and sprouted profusely from large white ceramic planters that hugged the corners of the pool.

The sheer boldness of pure white caught the eye and refused to let go until Sebastian noticed the ripple of waves in the clear pool. He watched Alisande rise up and out of the water, and slowly ascend the steps, water beads dripping and licking every seductive curve of her siren's body as she headed straight for him.

She was a sight to behold. She wore a white string bikini, and strings were exactly what held the transparent white material together. The top barely contained her ample breasts, her rosy nipples poking hard at the wet material. The bottom scarcely covered the honey-blond triangle between her legs, and a slim piece of nothing slipped up her backside, leaving her firm buttocks to full view as she emerged from the pool.

This wasn't a swimsuit. This was a piece of seduction.

She stopped only inches away from him. "I'm so glad you came. It's hot out there today. Why don't you join me?"

He was about to say he didn't have a bathing suit, but wisely held his tongue, knowing her reply would be that he didn't need one.

"Perhaps another day," he said to her disappointment.

She wasn't about to concede so easily. "The water is so cool and refreshing."

"I can see," he said and glanced down at her hard nipples.

Her smile was naughty and she reached out, grabbing his hand. "Come join me, you won't be disappointed."

Her hand was cool and warm all at the same time, and the strange combination added to her wet flesh sent shivers racing up his arm.

He fought to maintain control of his mounting emotions. "Perhaps, Ali, I would disappoint you."

Her smile was a slow suggestion of promised seduction. "Why don't we find out?"

She stepped closer to him, her bright green eyes set on his dark ones. She ran her hand in faint strokes down his arm and casually, while keeping her eyes concentrated on his, moved his arm to rest around her slim waist.

He couldn't prevent himself from touching her. It was impossible with her wet skin soaking the sleeve of his cotton shirt. He felt the slight tremor of her body radiating against him with pure unrestrained desire for him, and he couldn't for one sane minute keep his hands off her wet, naked flesh. The touch brought him instantly to life, and he cursed his uncontrollable obsession for her.

His string of expletives continued under his breath as he yanked her wet, near naked body up against him. "You play a dangerous game."

"I play to win," she challenged and bit playfully at his chin, sending his passion over the edge.

Eight

She was wet, so damn wet, and pressed so intimately against him that he could barely think straight, not that he wanted to. All he wanted was to devour her, and his possessive kiss proved his impassioned intentions.

His hand remained clamped tightly around her naked waist and his mouth stayed firm on hers, feeding and flaming the passion racing like wildfire through them both. Her unbridled lust for him astonished and fueled his already raging senses.

Her arms slipped around his neck, and her near naked body moved suggestively against his, sending a shot of pleasure so strong to his loins that he thought he would embarrass himself right in front of her.

He was rock hard and he ached unmercifully for her. Without a doubt he wanted nothing more than to throw her down on the white chaise, rip the bit of seduction she wore off her, and take her fast and furious and to hell with the consequences.

The uncharacteristic thought startled him back to the reality of the situation, and with great reluctance and difficulty he untangled himself from her.

She protested with a whimper as he attempted to disengage her lips from his, and he found himself returning much too often to appease her soft cries of disappointment.

"Who are you, Alisande Wyrrd?" he whispered, biting along her lust-filled lips.

She answered him, her own teeth feeding on his mouth swollen with the taste of her. "I'm a witch who aches for you."

She moved her body slowly against his, and the jolt of desire struck him like a bolt of lightning, blowing all circuits.

He jumped back, pushing her away from him with a gentle shove.

She smiled and crooked her finger at him, her long white nail with traces of gold running through it hypnotic in its insistent summons.

He shook his head as if shaking sense into himself. He prided himself on his control. His control had helped him achieve his success. It had helped him survive difficult missions. Control was his to command and demand at will, and no one could deprive him of his achievement.

No one that is but this *witch* of a woman.

Without a word or acknowledgment to Alisande he turned and walked away with slow and purposeful strides, demonstrating that his departure was his choice and that he was in control of this barely controllable situation.

Ali stood staring in disbelief at the French doors he had not bothered to close behind him.

Aunt Sydney appeared like a breath of fresh air, a white terry robe in hand. She held it up for Alisande, and she gratefully slipped into its warmth.

She felt chilled, not by the pool water still damp on her skin, but from Sebastian's hasty departure.

"I warned you," Aunt Sydney said, pouring them each a cup of raspberry tea from the white china pot on the poolside table.

Ali settled into the chaise, still staring at the door as if expecting, wanting, willing Sebastian to return to her.

"It's no use, my dear," Sydney said, "he may be a mere mortal, but he is a powerful one."

Ali nodded and took the white teacup her aunt offered her, grateful for the hot brew. "You are right. I never considered a mortal's powers. I always felt them inadequate, lacking and ignorant of their own skills."

Aunt Sydney took the chair beside her and enjoyed an occasional sip of her tea as they spoke. "Sebastian is rare in that he has perfected his abilities. You have breached his defenses. You have caused him to lose control, and to him that is unacceptable. You must learn to tread lightly and allow him some rein, or you will lose him."

Tears filled Ali's eyes, and her aunt studied her niece's strange reaction with surprise.

"This mortal means much to you," Sydney said, placing her hand over Ali's trembling one.

Ali nodded. "More than I expected. He is so much a man."

Sydney smiled. "He does not let you control and yet he does not control. He is a rare man."

"I fear I will lose him. My lack of self-control appalls me and yet—" Ali shook her head and wiped a tear from her cheek.

"You want him," her aunt said candidly.

Ali hugged her aunt's hand. "I need him."

"Why?"

"Is this a lesson?" Ali asked with a laugh and another wipe of a slipping tear.

"Yes," her aunt answered honestly. "A very important lesson."

Ali sighed. She wasn't interested in a lesson, she only knew that at the moment she felt empty as though part of her had been ripped away, and the hollow feeling only served to make her more aware of her situation and reflect on the unexpected and profound decision she had made upon meeting Sebastian Wainwright.

"Life is a lesson," her aunt informed. "It is whether we pay attention to the lesson that matters or not. You either learn or you don't. The decision is always yours."

"Not always," Ali corrected, thinking of Sebastian's hasty departure.

"Always," her aunt said sternly. "Think about why you need him. Think about what drove him out of here and learn what it is you were meant to learn or—"

Aunt Sydney stood ready to take her leave.

"Or what?" Ali asked annoyed that her aunt forever proved to be right, and that if she didn't listen and learn she would fail, and somehow failure in this situation just wasn't acceptable.

"Or forever wonder," her aunt said with a smile and walked out of the room leaving Ali to sort out her troubled thoughts.

Sebastian finished his cold shower, slipped into a pair of khaki shorts, and dropped onto the beige striped couch in the gathering room. A name appropriately given since it connected his large kitchen with what was once dubbed a family room.

He thoroughly enjoyed preparing and sharing meals with family and friends but detested spending a good portion of that time alone in the kitchen, so when he had the house remodeled for himself, and with thoughts of the future and added family, he chose the gathering room.

Presently he gathered here alone. The soft neutral tones highlighted by earthy colors and accented with items collected over the years on his various travels gave the room not only an Old World quality but a welcoming appeal, and he often settled here at night to relax.

Unfortunately, he wasn't feeling any too settled. The

cold shower had helped ease his ache but had not helped extinguish his distressing emotions. He could not recall a time when he was so close to the point of losing control, throwing caution to the wind, and to hell with the consequences.

For a moment, a brief flickering moment, he was tempted to do just that with Ali, lose total control, take what he so desperately wanted and what she so obviously offered and to hell with the outcome.

Thank heaven for his sensible side, that practical part of him that maintained his senses and protected him from disaster. He always listened to it, and it never failed to assist him in even the most crucial times.

Then why did he feel so *empty*?

Why did he feel his departure from Ali was a mistake?

He had pondered the curious and troublesome dilemma since his arrival home. He barely knew the woman. They hadn't held an in-depth conversation. Did they even possess any compatible interests? And yet an urgent intimacy existed between them that he had never experienced with another woman.

He had had his share of brief encounters in his younger years. He never cared for them; they seemed only a relief of a need for both parties. An awkward smile and a quick good-bye, and it was over. A memory to recall. A lesson learned.

With most of his lessons well behind him he was now looking for more, needing more than a brief affair. He had been involved in two long-term relationships that didn't work out. In one he wasn't ready to commit, and in the other she wasn't ready.

Now he found himself looking for more in a woman than first encounters provided. Similar interests were important or a woman with new interests that would appeal and enhance his own pursuits.

He longed to share childhood memories, watch favorite movies or chow down a full packed pizza with a pitcher of cold beer. He smiled at the crazy thought.

"And a walk," he reminded himself. "Around the monuments." A favorite pastime of his and the perfect way to shed the added calories of the fat-laden meal.

"You're looking to fall in love, you idiot," he reprimanded himself.

And Alisande Wyrrd wasn't exactly falling in love potential, and yet he felt this insatiable desire for her. How did one figure that equation?

Lust definitely had a lot to do with it, and yet in her own unique, wacky way he found her interesting. How many women would claim to be a witch to seduce a man? She certainly had caught his attention and managed to hold it, driving him near crazy in the process.

He chuckled. He had never been so alert, so on his toes, so to speak, since his government days, and the rush of adrenaline sure felt good.

Sebastian stood, turning on the brass lamp on the oak antique table beside the couch. Rain had fallen along with the night, and fat raindrops splattered in quick succession against the sliding-glass doors.

He walked into the kitchen area and began gathering everything he needed for a Greek salad. He yearned for a full-packed pizza, but that meal was meant to be shared over good conversation.

While he sliced and diced like a professional, he wondered what interested Ali besides her obvious obsession with witchcraft. What had driven her to think herself a witch? And how involved was she with the craft?

He recalled the books he had picked up earlier at the bookstore, and after arranging his salad, a loaf of crusty bread, and a bottle of sauvignon blanc on the kitchen table, he retrieved the books from the foyer bench and seated himself at the table for a good meal and an informing read.

Ali watched the rain from the front porch. It was an incessant downpour that more than likely would release the land from the last few days of sweltering temperatures.

She recalled fondly how when she was little she would run out in the rain and dance barefoot in the puddles, splashing with delight. She would raise her tiny hands to the dark sky and imitate the grown-ups in an attempt to cast a mighty spell.

Her mother warned her that spells were not cast at random or for fun or openly, especially in those early years. She could cause harm even to the innocent if she was not careful. It was a dark time, one of secrets and whispers and hiding in fear of mortals and their ignorance.

But light soon dawned on the dark, and with it freedom. Secrets were still maintained, but witches no longer lived in fear of their lives. Ignorance had turned to curiosity and their craft now thrived amongst the mortals, though it remained misunderstood.

She smiled, wondering what Sebastian was like as a child and if he would have been her friend and kept her secrets of dancing frogs and flying kittens. She loved to play with the animals and they with her. The tiny creatures were her favorite friends during her childhood.

She sighed and plopped down in the wooden rocker, her feet tucked beneath her white ankle-length skirt. She tugged down the long sleeves of the hip-length white cotton sweater she wore and hugged her arms.

This project to find a lover had started out so simply. How had it become so complicated?

It had, when she had made a sudden and life-altering decision. One she herself had not expected to make but at the time seemed a wise one.

Had she been wrong? Had her own desires been too strong for this mortal male? Had she underestimated his abilities and his *own* desires?

It was to be an affair, plain and simple. She would enjoy it and so would he. A whirlwind of pleasure and passion and yet—

She shook her head. What had she done?

Her aunt's question popped into her thoughts.

Why?

Why did Ali feel she needed Sebastian? A good question and one she was sure she had the answer to but was afraid to admit.

It had started with the restoration of her powers. But it had generated into much more than that, and Ali wasn't certain how to handle the magnitude of this unexpected development. She had placed herself in a situation of her own making, expecting everything to go smoothly. She had failed to consider the powers of a stubborn, pragmatic, and much too logical mortal male.

And then there was the surmounting problem of her finding it completely impossible to keep her hands off him, and *he* fought their intimacy at every turn, yet desired her as much as she did him. Why fight it?

Always why?

Why this emptiness? Why this need to know more about him? Why this need to share?

She had family and centuries of friends to share laughter and tears with, and yet she found herself longing to talk with Sebastian about her youth, her dreams, her hopes for the future, but would he understand? Would he accept her for who she truly was? A three-hundred-year old witch.

She had few mortal friends who were aware of her true origin. And their families had been connected with the Wyrrds in some way or another over the years.

Truth be told, when she planned this sexual escapade,

she had expected Sebastian to find her story amusing, her enchanting, and then nature would take its natural course. She had never considered him rejecting her. Her powers must be at their lowest ebb if she couldn't charm a mortal male into her bed.

But then she had never taken a mortal male to her bed—or a man of magic, for that matter. She had been tempted on many occasions and had broken many hearts, but she had always only allowed intimacy to go so far. Why?

She often wondered herself. Many a man proved interesting, charming, and sincere, but none enthralled or challenged her.

Not until Sebastian.

Nine

The doorbell rang twice before Sebastian heard it. He shook his head. He had read half of the interesting and informative book on the history of witches last night, and after Saturday chores and errands he had plopped down in the chair to finish off the rest of the book. He was on the last pages of the chapter on the persecution of witches. The material disturbed him. Like most people he had a minimal amount of knowledge concerning witchcraft. And of course the movies had filled many a head with nonsense. He was shocked to learn the brutal facts and wondered just how many innocent people were wrongly persecuted because of ignorance.

He yanked open the door and was surprised and in a way strangely pleased to see his very own witch standing there.

His very own?

When did he begin to think of her as his own?

And a witch?

At least this time she was fully clothed, and he had to admit he liked her diverse style; she always managed to appease and tease. She wore white wide-leg pants with a white and gold embroidered button-down vest. Her honey-blond hair was fashioned in a simple braid that hung almost to her waist, and she wore large gold hoop earrings, and dozens of gold bracelets chimed at her wrists. His glance purposely drifted to her feet tucked in gold sandals; the tiny bell sparkled in the sunlight.

"Are you going to invite me in, or do witches intimidate you?" Her smile erupted into a soft laughter.

Her nature was mischievous, her grin contagious, and at that moment with his own smile broadening he wondered if she hadn't actually cast a magical spell over him.

He moved aside.

Her step was light and followed by a whimsical chime, her bracelets to be sure, he convinced himself, trailing behind her.

She made her way to his gathering room and made herself comfortable on the striped sofa.

"Iced tea would be lovely," she said.

He stared at her and gave a brief shake of his head. He had thought of asking her if she cared for iced tea, but had he verbalized his query?

He nodded, went to the kitchen area, poured them each a glass, and returned.

"I am here to talk, not tempt," she informed him after accepting the tall frosted glass.

He sat on the opposite end of the sofa bracing himself in the corner so he could easily watch her.

Ali sipped while admiring the snug fit of his faded jeans. They curved and hugged in the best places, and his pale blue knit shirt defined his excellent muscle structure so very nicely. When she met his dark eyes, she saw amusement mixed with pleasure.

"I like what I see," she admitted.

But wasn't he about to ask her that? He had thought it, but had he voiced it? No, he was sure he hadn't.

"You're a mentalist," he said with sudden realization and relief.

"One of my many abilities."

"I wasn't aware that witches read minds. I thought they cast spells and followed rituals."

"Real, honest-to-goodness witches have many unique powers."

"You mean you could turn me into a toad if you so pleased?" He laughed.

"I don't waste my inherent ability on adolescent tricks, and besides," she said, reaching for the book on witches that lay on the coffee table, "you should be more aware, or knowledgeable, shall we say, on the subject."

"I was curious," he confessed.

"About me?"

He could tell she wasn't teasing, she was serious. "About what you claim to be."

She returned the book to the table. "You won't find the answers you are searching for in books."

"Are you saying these books are not factual?"

"To a point they are," she conceded.

"What point?"

Her smile turned provocative. "That we exist. We are real."

"Then prove it," he challenged. "Float an object, cast a spell, show me you are who you claim to be."

She sighed. "I wish I could, but unfortunately my powers have dwindled considerably, and I cannot perform any such magical feats, though in my prime I could move you across the room with a crook of my finger."

He laughed, he couldn't help himself. He found her antics delightful. "And that is why you need me."

She hesitated briefly, and he wondered over her fleeting misgiving. "Yes, Sebastian, I need you."

It sounded like a whispered plea, almost as if he were her salvation. The odd sensation unnerved him.

"But," she cautioned, "you must want this union, this

coming together of our souls, this uniting as strongly as I do.''

Crazy as it seemed, or as she was, he probably wanted it more, or at least at the moment he felt that way. His one consuming thought was to unbutton the row of pearly knobs that ran down her vest, slowly spread the intrusive material aside, and gently release her ample breasts from the confines of her silky garment. Then he would taste and tease her nipples until they grew hard in his mouth, then he would feast on her.

Her moan brought him back to reality and the fact that she could read his mind. Her face was flushed a faint red, and he was certain if he ran his hand across her breasts, her nipples would be rock hard.

''I'm sorry,'' he said, though not convincingly.

She answered in her candid way. ''I'm not. It proves just how much you do desire me.''

He laughed softly. ''You're crazy, but I am attracted to you. That I will not deny.''

She moved closer to him. ''Then why deny us at all?''

He could smell her familiar scent so rich and potent it assaulted his senses and ignited his need. Her arms slipped around his neck, and her mouth inched closer to his own.

He remained still, his one arm braced on the back of the couch and his other resting on the cushioned arm. He sat open and vulnerable, and she moved in with the lithe and grace of a skilled predator.

Her lips met his with a tender touch, and her body maneuvered against him ever so gently, though erotic enough to excite and entice.

Her kiss was pure magic, her lips feeding along his in gentle pressure, her tongue eager in its pursuit, and her entrance shockingly stimulating.

He fought to maintain control of his senses, his desires,

but she worked pure, hot undeniable magic on him, and he was soon lost to her enchanted touch.

His control slipped from his grasp, or perhaps it was stolen, he wasn't sure and at the moment he didn't care. He wanted her as much as she wanted him, maybe even more. His hands shot out, gripping her, turning her until she lay beneath him and he took command. Gentleness vanished and in its wake followed pure, carnal passion. His tongue thrust in her mouth like a warrior bent on revenge, and yet she met his lusty thrusts not defensively but with eager anticipation.

His fingers went to work on her buttons, popping one or two in his hasty attempt to free her. He pushed the material aside and snapped the clip on her bra, and when her breasts fell free to his gaze his breath caught.

“My beautiful witch,” he whispered and caught her nipple with his teeth, teasing it to hardness and her to wetness before his mouth captured the rosy pebble whole.

Her fingers gripped his arms, her long nails dug into his flesh, and her lustful moans filled his ears. All sensible thought vanished in the wake of heated passion. His mouth fed on her, his hands roamed her body, and her sensual cries speared his soul.

He wanted nothing, nothing more than to be inside her, feel her hot and wet around him, hear her cry out for him, feel her climax along with him.

“Tell me you want me,” she said. “Please, Sebastian, tell me you want me, need me like I need you.”

Need.

This was all to satisfy a need, a lustful need. Was that all he wanted from her? His body ached, swelled with desire for her, but what was it he really wanted from her, *needed* from her?

“Sebastian?”

He gently tasted her nipples once again and reluctantly

withdrew his lips from her silky flesh and brushed a soft kiss across her lips.

"I need to think about this before we take the next step," he said and sat up, his hands going to her breasts to help cover her.

She pushed his hands away. "I'll do that."

He shoved at her hands. "No, *I'll* do that."

His demanding tone warned her not to argue, and she bit back her retort, realizing any argument would prove futile.

Two top buttons were missing from her vest, and after he helped her to sit up, he went in search of them.

She was about to inform him that his search was unnecessary, that she had extras, but she understood that the buttons provided the distraction he momentarily needed.

Ali straightened herself as best she could, though ignoring her raging hormones was a different matter entirely. She ached horribly for him, the pain was so palpable that she thought she would die for the want of him. She crossed her legs and stifled the moan that rushed to her lips.

Instead she smiled when he handed her the two pearl buttons and frowned when he turned his back and moved to sit in the large oversize chair across from the couch.

He had put a safe distance between them, and she could sense that he meant to keep it.

"I didn't mean for that to happen," she said, not wanting him to believe her only reason for coming here was to seduce him.

"Didn't you?" His expression was stern, his voice cautious, and his intent gaze roamed to her vest and the area where the two absent buttons left the tops of her full breasts exposed.

"Want it, yes, plan it, no," she admitted.

Sebastian respected her frankness; now if only she would drop this farce of a story and confess her true intentions. He decided a change of conversation in the direction of securing valuable information might prove beneficial for them both. And besides, if he didn't get his mind and eyes off her, he was definitely going to do something he would regret.

He reached for his glass of iced tea that was anything but cold right now.

"Let's get to know each other better." He instantly regretted his foolish remark.

She laughed and moved her foot enough to set the tiny toe bell to ringing gently.

He silently cursed himself and swore that one day he would get his hands on that little bell of hers and—

He shook his head. He damn well didn't need to think of what he would do with that toe bell.

"What is it that you want to know about me, Sebastian?"

That teasing erotic tone of hers could tempt a saint. Ignoring it the best he could he said, "Let's start with where you went to school."

"I was privately tutored at home."

That would account for the absence of early childhood education records, but not the later years. "For how long?"

"Until a teenager, then I attended an exclusive and very private school in Europe."

Suspicion put him on alert and his dark, studious eyes widened just a fraction. "Where in Europe?'

"Ireland," she volunteered, but with what Sebastian felt was a definite reluctance.

"Where in Ireland? I have visited the country often and found it quite enchanting."

"Oh, that it is," Ali said with a laugh, recalling her years of lessons with others like herself. Learning from the fairies in the woods, casting spells with the masters, chanting, listening to stories and languages of the past and plans for the future, but how did one share such knowledge with a mere mortal?

She sensed he waited impatiently, and he would continue to wait until she felt he was ready. "My lessons were diverse," she said.

She was leading him away from where he intended to go, but then people often attempted that diversionary tactic on him, it never worked.

"Your favorite lesson?" he asked, confident of answers.

Ali's smile was bold and beautiful and for a moment stole his breath. "Do you really want to know?"

He managed to nod, his breath still locked in his throat and his heart beating like castanets in his chest.

"Remember, you asked," she warned, intending to be honest even if she risked seeming more insane to him.

He nodded, though he briefly wondered if it was a wise decision.

"I simply adored playing and learning with the fairies in the woods."

All right, he would play along with her little game. "The woods were enchanted?"

"All woods are enchanted. Nature thrives in abundance there, and therefore the fairies thrive," she answered as if he was a student and she a teacher.

"What did these fairies teach you?"

"Secrets," she whispered and pressed her finger to her lips.

"Secrets that you cannot share?"

"Not with mortals."

"And yet you tell me fairies exist: isn't that against the witches' rule book?"

"Do you believe in fairies?"

He was about to laugh and admit he didn't when he caught the seriousness of her expression.

"Such a pity," she said sadly.

He sat forward in his chair. "Isn't there some kind of rule that stops you from reading my mind?"

"You only need ask," she said with regret.

He was about to snap at her when he sensed her disappointment with his reaction, and gently he asked, "Would you please stop reading my mind?"

"As you wish," she said, "but if you change your mind, you will let me know?"

"I will advise you of my wishes immediately."

Her smile once again brightened. "And what was your favorite subject in school?"

"All subjects interested me. I couldn't get enough knowledge."

"But one, one in particular must have challenged you, compelled you to seek its wisdom. One you found more interesting than all others."

He laughed then, a robust laugh as if what he recalled churned up happy and startling memories. "My aunt insisted I take a particular course in the prep school I attended. I thought it foolish and a waste of my time, and yet it taught me more than I ever thought possible."

"What was it?" she asked, anxiously.

"Fencing," he admitted without reluctance.

"Oh, I love to fence."

"You know how?"

"I was taught by—" She quickly stopped herself. How do you explain being taught by a man that was dead two hundred years. "—a wonderful man."

"In Ireland?" he asked, wondering over her brief pause, and besides, he wanted to get back to that school she attended and finally get a name.

"No, in England," she said and reached for her iced tea.

"You attended a school in England as well?"

She did, but that was one hundred years later. "Yes, and I always missed Wyrrd house when I was away. You know it has been in the family since the sixteen hundreds."

He was well aware of her attempt to change the subject, but now was as good a time as any to find out where she was born.

"It is a stunning place, and your family has preserved its past splendor while blending it with the modern amenities quite well. Have you always lived there?"

"I was born there."

"In the house?"

"Right upstairs in the large master suite."

That might account for the lack of a birth certificate, though a doctor had to be in attendance and he was required to fill out documentation. There had to be a birth certificate somewhere. It was required as proof for so many things today.

He decided to be blunt. "When is your birthday, Alisande?"

"The winter solstice," she said with pride.

"December twenty-first of what year?"

She laughed. "Are you trying to find out my age?"

"Yes," he admitted.

"I'm much younger looking than I am."

Maybe she was in her thirties, though she looked twenty-seven or -eight tops. "Not going to tell me?"

"Someday, Sebastian, you will know my age and more. Until then let's say I'm probably a wee bit older than you."

He didn't think that was possible. He was thirty-six and she didn't look anywhere near that age, but he would humor her for now.

"I like older women. They are intelligent, confident, and bring so much more to a relationship."

"Yes, the years can teach you much," she said, thinking of the three hundred and so years she had lived thus far.

He stood, marking the end of their conversation and obviously her visit. He didn't trust himself to spend any more time alone with her. There was a hungry need in him for her, and he sensed the same in her for him and that disturbed him. He had been attuned to women before but never anywhere near to the degree he felt with Alisande. It was as if she were part of him and he a part of her and that type of close involvement frightened him. He had intended, wanted that with the person he would spend the rest of his life with, the woman who would have his children, who would grow old with him and who would love him forever.

He walked her to the door. "I'll speak with you soon."

She stood only a short distance from him and yet he was aware of every part of her so alive and vibrant with passion. It radiated from her like a pulsating energy. He was about to take a step back away from her when he thought he heard her cry out in disappointment.

Her distress was so tangible to his senses that it forced him forward, his arms wrapped protectively around her, his mouth reached down for hers, and they were soon lost in a kiss that robbed their senses and blended them together as if they were one.

This time Alisande brought their kiss to an end and with reluctance but haste she ran out the door without looking back.

Ten

Ali sat in the solarium deep in thought. Troubled thoughts, to be more exact, and of course the trouble was Sebastian. She had not stopped to consider that he owned a security firm and therefore would be more suspicious than the average person. The personal questions he had plied her with the other day when she visited him confirmed his skeptical nature.

She worried how far he would go to uncover information on her. If one dug long and hard enough one could possibly find a minuscule amount of information that would eventually lead to further discoveries. She wanted him to believe her, to accept who she was, a witch. If he could accept her heritage, then perhaps he could also accept her true age.

''Mortal trouble, my dear?'' Aunt Sydney asked, entering the solarium and pouring herself a hot cup of honey lemon tea from the silver serving set on the table, then joining her niece on the wicker settee.

''He asks too many questions,'' Ali said with a sigh.

Aunt Sydney studied her niece over the rim of the delicate china cup as she slowly sipped her tea.

Ali shifted uncomfortably against the cushion, feeling unsettled and more than a little upset. ''What if he finds the answers before he understands?''

"What does he need to understand?"

"Who I am!" she snapped and instantly regretted her sharp response. "I'm sorry—"

Her aunt interrupted. "No need to apologize, my dear, I can see this plan of yours has encountered some obstacles."

"He won't cooperate," Ali said, annoyed, and stood, the gold silk caftan she wore shimmering around her and falling to cover her bare feet as she nervously paraded back and forth in front of her aunt.

"I warned you of mortals."

Ali stopped, her hands going to her hips. "Well, this mortal is certainly different from the ones I have met through the centuries."

"Which means he is strong, keeps in control of his mind, and won't let you dictate to him," a deep rich voice said with a laugh.

Ali spun around and her eyes lighted with joy. She ran for the outstretched arms of the handsome man standing in the doorway.

"Dagon!" she shouted cheerfully.

He caught her up in a huge hug, lifting her off the ground and spinning her around.

Once settled back on her own two feet, Ali took a step back from him, though her hands remained firm on his arms. "When did you arrive, and why didn't you let Aunt Sydney and I know you were coming?"

"An unexpected business matter brought me to D.C., but that is unimportant. I want to hear about this mortal male who is causing you such distress." Dagon cast Ali a suspiciously amusing glance and added, "Or is it you causing the mortal distress?"

She playfully slapped his arm and sauntered away from him. "I am merely looking to mate."

"With a mortal?" he asked incredulously. "And are you allowing this, Sydney?"

"She does have a mind of her own," Sydney reminded. "Now come give me a proper welcome, dear boy."

Ali sighed silently, watching Dagon, her friend since childhood, walk over to her aunt. The man was stunning, heartbreakingly stunning. His tall height, his graceful, fluid strides, his long shiny black hair, his fit body and sensual voice all combined made him simply . . .

Ali laughed to herself. He was simply to-die-for, that was what he was. And then there were those outrageously sexy eyes of his. One look from those dark intense eyes, and a woman was completely lost, swallowed up whole, forever captivated by his compelling spell.

She had been when she was younger, but a strong intuitive sense warned her that he would better serve as a friend than a lover and he had. She and Dagon's friendship grew to be more like a trusted brother and sister relationship, and she was pleased. Over the years they had often laughed and cried together, and knowing he was always there for her made her feel that much safer and loved.

Dagon gave Sydney an affectionate kiss and hug and sat beside her on the settee.

"Tea?" Sydney offered.

"Yes, please. A cup will do nicely while Ali informs me of this mortal male she has mistakenly thought to mate with."

"This is not a mistake," Ali defended.

"Dear heart, any witch who mates with a mortal is making a disastrous mistake," Dagon insisted in that irritatingly arrogant tone that all but announced he knew better.

Ali had frequently argued a point with him especially where mortals were concerned. Dagon tolerated them, claiming them mindless fools. He repeatedly voiced his opinions that witches belonged with witches and mortals with mortals. To prove his point he constantly made reference to the old witch trials, eagerly reminding them all that not one genuine witch was executed. Only innocent mortals suffered and by mortal hands.

Ali defended her decision. "This mortal is different."

"How?" he asked, his smile challenging.

Ali never backed down from a challenge, least of all from another witch.

"Don't tell me," Dagon said before she could respond. "The fool doesn't believe in witches."

Ali sent him a scathing look.

Dagon laughed. "Dear heart, your energy is much too low to contest me."

"Precisely why I need to mate and why I have chosen Sebastian Wainwright."

Dagon was out of his seat in a flash, sending the china cup toppling. Sydney saved it from crashing to the floor with a quick crook of her finger. The cup sailed gracefully through the air to land safely on the table.

"You foolish girl!" he yelled in her face, his hands pushing aside his European-styled black sports jacket and settling abruptly on his slim waist.

"*Woman,*" she corrected, standing firm and planting her own hands on her hips.

Sydney sipped her tea and watched the delightful antics of the two witches as she so often had done over the years.

"A *woman* who has not a lick of intelligence. Sebastian Wainwright has an impeccable reputation. How long do you think it will take a man of his talents to piece together the true history of the Wyrrds?"

"He will be mine before then," she said confidently.

"Yours?" he said, turning to Sydney. "She intends to keep him?"

Sydney looked surprised. "Is this true, Alisande? I thought he was only to be a lover, not permanent."

Ali hesitated, fighting with her own emotions and her reluctance to admit the truth. They wouldn't understand;

heaven only knew she didn't understand it herself. "My lover until I say otherwise."

Dagon and Sydney glared at her.

"I know you too well, Ali, and you don't sound as though you are certain of your intentions," Dagon said, shooting her a sharp look from those intense eyes that warned her he knew she was up to something.

"I agree," Sydney said, adding her own concern.

Ali shrugged, skirting the real issue and focusing simply on the response. "I find I enjoy his company, and I wish to keep him around for a while."

"Then don't mate with him," Dagon advised candidly. "For without a doubt if you do and your powers return full force, he will never be able to cope with your magical abilities. Have your fun, play your games, torment if you so please, but in the end find yourself a witch for mating."

"I want Sebastian and I am old enough to make my own decision," Ali insisted, a bit more sharply then she intended.

"Even if that decision will cause you heartbreaking pain?" Dagon asked gently.

Ali felt the fight go out of her. She cupped Dagon's face in her hands. "Have not some of your choices caused you pain?"

He sighed. "When did you grow so wise and yet remain so foolish?"

Her reply resounded with the truth of the matter. "When I saw a picture of Sebastian Wainwright. His eyes told me all I needed to know about him."

Dagon took Ali's hands in his and turned to Sydney. "Will he hurt her heart?"

"This is not for me to say; I can offer guidance only."

"You have the sight, you know," Dagon said.

"And you are well aware that with that sight comes a responsibility. Only Ali can decide her fate; the choice is hers. She decides what will be. I offer guidance if asked."

"Fine, then guide," he said. "Tell her she makes a mistake. The mortal will break her heart."

"I have expressed my concern, the rest is up to her."

Dagon looked at Ali. "And still you intend on pursuing this mortal?"

"Vigorously," Ali said with a grin.

"And when he breaks your heart?"

"I will come crying to you, Dagon," she said and kissed him gently on the cheek.

Dagon stepped back from her, executed a perfect bow, and announced dramatically, "And then, my lady, I will slay the beast for you."

Ali curtsied, the gold caftan shimmering in the wake of her graceful dip. "Thank you, kind sir."

They smiled, recalling the past and all the imaginary beasts Dagon had slayed for her and the tears he had wiped from her eyes. But this time was different. Sebastian was real, and if he hurt Ali, made her cry, she knew Dagon would see that he suffered.

"Sebastian is a good mortal," she said, needing Dagon to know the truth about this mortal of hers.

"Let us hope so, dear heart."

"I think lunch is just about ready," Sydney said, standing. "You will join us."

Dagon held his arm out for Sydney to take. "Always the diplomat."

"Not an easy task with you two," Sydney reminded.

"I take exception to that," Ali said, following behind the pair as they strolled out of the solarium.

"But of course, my dear, you take exception to almost everything," Sydney said with a laugh.

"You're right about that," Dagon agreed.

"And you're right about everything," Sydney said in the same teasing voice.

"Now wait a minute," Dagon argued.

"When she's right, she's right," Ali said, hooking her arm with Dagon's free one and smiling.

Sebastian sat in the meeting in the large conference room, his mind anywhere but on the topic. His development staff was detailing the results of some new high-tech equipment that had been installed a few months ago. If it proved successful it would be a big boon to Wainwright Security.

The video surveillance equipment was undetectable and microscopic in size, making concealing possibilities mind-boggling.

"That's the only glitch, and for the life of me I don't know what happened," Bert Simmons, the project engineer, said. "We picked her up entering the building, but right after that she disappeared. We can't pick up an image of her anywhere in the building following her entrance, and none of the security guards recall ever seeing her."

Sebastian's interest suddenly peaked.

"Out of video range," Herb Walters, project assistant, suggested, jotting down notes in his leather notebook.

Bert shook his head. "The cameras are strategically placed to cover the entire front entrance of the building, scanning all areas right up to the elevators. Nobody enters Wainwright Security or leaves without being caught on video."

"So how do you explain the blonde's vanishing act?" Ann Davis, engineer consultant, asked.

"Magic?" Herb suggested with a laugh.

Sebastian remained silent, carefully listening to the exchange. He had not bothered to view the videotapes the day Alisande had entered the building and his life. He had foolishly disregarded the tape's value, but hearing this changed his mind.

"When did the video camera first pick her up and when did it lose her?" Sebastian asked.

Bert answered his boss. "As soon as she entered the building. We have a good shot of her as she approaches the reception desk, and the next thing you know—*poof*—she's gone."

"Like magic," Herb offered once again with a teasing smile.

"Not funny," Sebastian snapped, and the room grew instantly silent. "We are a high-tech security company with an impeccable reputation. How do you think this will look to our clients, not to mention our competitors?"

"Maybe she's a spy for one of our rival companies," Ann said.

Bert shook his head again. "No, research checked her out. Alisande Wyrrd, Wyrrd Foundation, mega money. We assume she was here to speak with Mr. Wainwright regarding the foundation's work."

"Did she have an appointment?" Ann asked.

"No," Bert said. "But it's common knowledge that she and her aunt drop in on important people unexpectedly and always walk away with a hefty donation."

All three pairs of eyes settled on Sebastian.

"Why she was here is unimportant," he said firmly. "How she managed to gain access to my private office and leave without a trace is extremely important."

"It's the equipment," Herb said in disgust.

"But we triple-checked everything," Bert argued, "and we can't find anything wrong. And since the incident we haven't had a single problem."

"Check it again," Sebastian ordered.

Bert nodded. "Fine, but I—"

"Just do it," Sebastian said. "If you find nothing once more, we'll continue to run the equipment here for a few months; if no problems surface we'll go with it."

Bert smiled, relieved and pleased by the decision, and they all stood to leave.

''Bert, a word with you,'' Sebastian directed as the other two left the conference room.

Bert remained standing beside his chair as Sebastian approached him. While Bert wasn't a short man, standing almost six feet with his shoes on, he always felt short next to his boss. The man simply exuded confidence and power, and he intimidated in the most unobtrusive ways.

''Do you have the surveillance tape with you?''

Bert detected a hint of annoyance in the deep voice. ''Yes, I do.'' He slipped it out of his briefcase and handed it to Sebastian.''

''I'll make certain this is returned to you.''

''No problems, I made copies.'' And with a polite nod Bert turned to leave.

''Bert.''

The man halted midstride and turned back around, his nerves causing a fine film of perspiration to break out on his upper lip.

''You've done exceptional work on this project. I want you to know how much it is appreciated, and of course it will be reflected in your pay.''

Bert relaxed instantly. ''Thank you, Mr. Wainwright, and you can be sure we will have this worked out in no time.''

''I'm confident you will.''

Bert left with a smile of satisfaction.

Sebastian went directly from the conference room to his private office across the hall, instructing Ms. Smithers he was not to be interrupted.

He inserted the tape into the VCR and pushed the play button. He took a few steps back, crossed his arms over his chest, and stared intently at the screen. He resembled a man prepared for a confrontation.

After a moment of static and snow Ali appeared on the

screen, and he smiled, admiring the sensual sway of her hips and the swell of her full breasts that peeked out from the white silk jacket. He hastily wiped the grin from his face and cast a quick glance around his empty office as if fearful he had been caught fraternizing with the enemy.

He watched as another camera picked her up from a different angle. The white silk skirt hugged her firm backside and accented her slim legs, and his emotions rebelled. All he could think about was her naked in his arms, the soft and gentle feel of her against his hardness, and the sweet liquid taste of her on his lips.

While his lustful thoughts ran rampart, his practical eye caught her hand movement. He shifted his mental focus with difficulty and rewound the tape.

Her hand dipped into her jacket pocket, she withdrew it with a flourish, and if he hadn't looked quickly enough he would have missed the glittering specks that descended down around her. Then in the next instant she vanished.

He replayed the tape again and again. What had she done? What had she concealed in her pocket that she used to remove or block her image from the camera?

Whatever it was he intended to find out and confront her.

Magic?

He shook the ridiculous thought away and laughed. "Fairy dust, she'd probably tell me."

Then he recalled a passage from one of the books he had read on witchcraft.

Fairies conceal themselves from human eyes with sun dust. The early morning dew is dried by the sun and turned into dust which the fairies gather and use as protection against prying eyes. A small sprinkle will render a human incapable of seeing the fairies. A larger amount will cause the human to completely forget that they even exist.

Sebastian shook his head again. Was he going crazy? Fairy dust? Absurd. Ridiculous. Possible?

Her words replayed in his head.

I simply adored playing and learning with the fairies in the woods.

He refused to shake his head again. He refused to believe such utter nonsense. He was a practical and sensible man, and he would use his intelligence to solve this puzzle.

And when he did?

Suddenly there was no doubt in his mind. He would take Alisande to his bed and make love with her, but not, absolutely not, until he discovered the truth about her.

Eleven

''Were you ever truly in love, Aunt Sydney?'' Alisande asked, stretching out on the clear plastic raft that drifted aimlessly in the pool.

Sydney sat poolside sipping raspberry iced tea and enjoying the scones Adele had freshly baked. ''Several times.''

Ali dipped her fingers into the cool water, sprinkling the refreshing liquid over her bare midriff. She wore a striking yellow bikini that covered and curved in all the right places.

''No, true love can be but one love,'' Ali said with a soft sigh.

Sydney smiled knowingly. ''And why is that?''

''Simply because you can only truly give your heart once.''

''I have loved many times over the years, my dear.''

''I have no doubt you have,'' Ali said, ''but truthfully how often have you given your heart?''

''Once, my dear,'' Sydney answered softly.

Ali cast her aunt an inquisitive glance. ''True love?''

''Yes,'' Sydney said with tears tempting her eyes.

''Tell me about him.''

Sydney reached for her glass of iced tea. ''Some memories are better left as just that: memories.''

Ali knew better than to pry, though she would have loved to have heard about the man who had once captured her aunt's heart.

"Why do you ask about love, Alisande? You know the difficulties of losing your heart to a mortal."

"Yes, all too well," Ali said irritated. "Mother, among others of our kind, drummed the fact into my head that mortals do not fully understand the true meaning of love and therefore they are not capable of maintaining the cherished emotion."

"Well, at least you paid attention to their wisdom and advice," her aunt said, "but do you intend to take heed?"

Ali slipped off the raft and swam in measured strokes to the steps. She walked up and out of the pool slowly, as if her response weighed heavily on her mind. "You agree then that mortals fail to fully comprehend the true meaning of love?"

Sydney offered her a large white terry cloth towel. "Love is an easy emotion to define, yet humans cannot seem to grasp its simplicity. They dissect it, debate it, fight over it, but understand it? I think not."

Ali patted herself dry. "So what you are saying is that a mortal can never experience the depths of love that we do?"

Sydney reached out for her niece's hand and grasped it in hers. "Do these questions pertain to your involvement with a mortal male?"

Ali lowered herself to the chaise beside her aunt. "I thought this would be so simple. Introduce myself to him, explain my need, and let nature take its course. And yet Sebastian refuses to cooperate."

"How so?" Sydney asked seriously.

"He obviously wants me, I can feel it. He can feel it. We both are engulfed by an overpowering passion whenever we are together and yet—" She shook her head.

"He refuses to act on his emotions?"

"Refuses? Ha, he's downright adamant about not satisfying my simple request."

"You did cast a spell on him when you first met?"

Ali hesitated and with reluctance said, "Yes."

Sydney's posture stiffened. "What spell did you use?"

"A good one," Ali insisted.

"Alisande Wyrrd, I will not ask you again what spell you cast on this unsuspecting mortal."

Ali knew better than to defy or disrespect her aunt, and besides she needed to confess her rash actions to someone. So her answer was forthcoming though with a bit of trepidation. "The magical love spell."

Sydney gasped and collapsed back in her chair. "Do you realize what you have done, child?"

Ali held her chin defiantly high, her bravado a mere mask to cover her own misgivings. "Yes, I made an important life decision. And I hope you respect my wisdom enough to support my choice."

Sydney spoke with love and concern. "You should have discussed this decision with an elder."

"And they would have attempted to talk me out of it." Ali insisted.

"Are you prepared to face the consequences of your rash actions?" Sydney asked her tone sympathetic.

"I tell myself I am, but when the time comes I wonder if I will be able to live with the outcome," she admitted honestly, her worry finally surfacing.

"Do not doubt your abilities," her aunt cautioned.

"What abilities?" Ali laughed with disgust. "I am almost powerless."

Sydney smiled and offered her own wisdom. "My dear, what better way to win a mortal than by his own rules? Perhaps you have not allowed yourself to truly understand his ways. Remember, you must know your opponent even better than you do a friend.''

''I don't think of him as an opponent.''

''You have waged a battle for him and for a dear price,'' Sydney warned. ''I would suggest you do all that is in your power to win him, or you will learn the true meaning of sorrow.''

''Another lesson for me,'' Ali said with a hefty sigh.

''A lesson that you have chosen, and may I suggest you keep in mind a favorite mortal expression,'' Sydney said.

''Which is?''

''Look before you leap.''

An hour later Sydney left Ali sound asleep on the chaise. She retired upstairs to her comfort room, a small room off her private quarters. It housed her precious collection of books and memorabilia, which she had collected over the centuries. Here is where she took tea, continued her studies, basked in the solitude, and listened to the silence. It was also a room where many sought comfort from her and advice.

''I expected you sooner, Dagon,'' Sydney said, sitting in a petit point cushioned rocker near the window that looked out on the grounds of the vast Wyrrd estate.

Dagon stepped from the shadows in the corner of the room, and after an acknowledging nod from Sydney, he sat in the chair opposite her.

''What are you going to do?'' he demanded and softened his tone when she sent him a chastising glance.

''You heard?'' she asked, though the query wasn't necessary.

''You were fully aware of my nearby presence at the pool. I half expected you to scold me in front of Ali for eavesdropping.''

''Nonsense,'' Sydney said, ''you did it out of love for

her, not deceit. You care and therefore worry over her."

He smiled. A wicked grin that usually sent all the ladies' hearts a fluttering. "I cherish her as if she were my sister. We played with fairies, rode dragons, and skinned our knees together. I have only the fondest of memories of growing up with her."

"Yes, you two were always inseparable when young."

A frown robbed Dagon's smile. "Ali always had a dream she would never surrender. She would tell me of this man who would be her life mate for eternity. She would know him, she insisted, when she first laid eyes upon him, as would he with her, and once united they would never part. Time would stand still and they would be as one."

Sydney shook her head. "Magical love."

"You must do something, or she will most certainly be hurt."

"She has cast the spell. There is nothing I can do," Sydney said helplessly.

Dagon stood, his shadow spreading over the room along with his temper. "I refuse to stand by and watch her be hurt. I swear on my family's honor that if this mortal hurts her, he will pay dearly."

"You cannot interfere, Dagon," Sydney reminded firmly.

"If asked I can."

"Ali would never ask you. She is proud and wants this mortal on her terms."

"But if requested by either party involved in the spell, I may help," he said, yet looked to Sydney for confirmation.

"Yes, if asked for help, you are permitted to give it."

"I will keep that in mind," he said, almost as if he already knew how he would use it to his advantage. "In the meantime I think we should look into this mortal's background and see if he fits well with our Alisande."

Sydney smiled brightly and motioned for Dagon to sit

down, which he did. "You always looked before you leaped, dear boy. A marvelous trait."

"I always felt it was better to be at an advantage than a disadvantage."

"Exactly," Sydney agreed, "which is why I have had a thorough background check done on Sebastian Wainwright."

"By which methods, may I ask?"

Sydney grinned. "Need you ask, Dagon? I wanted pertinent information, not statistical facts."

He leaned closer to his aunt and spoke in a conspiratorial tone. "And do you plan to share them?"

She winked. "Oh, I have a plan, all right."

Ali dozed in and out of sleep, her restless state disconcerting. Her aunt's words resounded in her head like a litany.

What better way to win a mortal than by his own rules.

Her eyelids grew too heavy for dozing, and wrapped snugly in her terry robe and curled comfortably on the lounge, she fell into a deep slumber.

She stood in Sebastian's kitchen, a stranger in a foreign land. The place glowed in cleanliness. The countertops shined, the appliances bore no smudge marks or fingerprint stains, and yet the scent of freshly baked blueberry muffins from breakfast still permeated the air. The kitchen may have been kept spotless, but it was also well used and enjoyed.

What was that antiquated mortal saying? Ali thought, her finger tapping at her lips in concentration.

The way to a man's heart is through his stomach.

She smiled triumphantly. "I will bake him a cake as mortals do, with my own two hands. A chocolate one with nuts and cherries and a deliciously sweet and sinfully tempting chocolate icing."

Ali glanced down at herself. A yellow bikini wasn't exactly baking attire, but it would have to do.

Armed with enthusiasm, she anxiously searched the cabinets. With little difficulty she located a cookbook, and perusing the pages, she found the perfect recipe for a chocolate cake she could easily adapt to her own taste.

She tucked the cookbook in the holder that cradled it at an angle that allowed easy reading, and silently praised mortals for devising gadgets that made their lives easier.

She set to work gathering the baking tools she felt were necessary to complete her task. She bubbled with excitement when she discovered an extra-large mixing bowl in a bottom cabinet and used it as a basket to hold all the other items she collected along the way.

With a light step and a tuneful song on her lips she placed the full bowl on the extended, sand-colored countertop and went in search of the baking goods.

''Eggs, milk, chocolate, baking soda, baking powder, sugar, nuts, and cherries, too,'' she sang, ''this is so easy and exciting to do.''

Soon she was busy measuring, mixing, and chopping. Mortals made it relatively simple to bake with all their measuring contraptions and precise directions, though she relied more on taste adding a bit more of this and a little less of that and lots more cherries. She loved cherries.

When all the ingredients were thoroughly mixed, she cast a skeptical glance at the dark mixture, and deciding it was too dark of a chocolate, she decided to add more flour. She dipped her hand in the flour canister, grabbed a handful, and dropped it into the bowl.

Without thought she wiped her hand across her bare stomach, and then swatted at an itch on her nose.

''Sugar,'' she said, liking sweets sweet. ''A handful.'' She plunged her hand into the sugar canister and deposited a good amount into the bowl.

She blew at the loose strands of hair that fell on her forehead, and when they refused to budge she brushed them aside with her fingers.

The mixture was more difficult to blend than she had imagined, so she grabbed milk from the fridge and added it until she was satisfied with the consistency. Bunches of cherries and chopped nuts followed.

When it was all done she smiled with satisfaction and went in search of baking pans. It took four pans to hold the entire mixture, and while it cooked she got busy on the icing.

She wasn't prepared for the difficulty of melting chocolate, and soon she found that her hand had left smudges of chocolate on her yellow bathing suit.

She scratched at her chin and rubbed her cheek and released a long sigh, deciding spells had their advantages.

Ali worked hard creating her own cherry-chocolate icing, and it wasn't until she caught the scent of burning cake that she realized the oven was smoking.

She yelped, swung the oven door open, coughed at the smoke that rushed at her face, and let out another yelp before grabbing the oven mitts and rescuing the charring cakes.

Ali stared in abject horror at the burnt and shriveled cakes, at the wretched mess that covered the counters, and at the chocolate icing spread over almost everything but the cake.

Where had she gone wrong? Mortals did this every day. Why couldn't she?

Tears pooled in her green eyes as she stood in complete awe of the mess she had made of everything.

Sebastian arrived home from work worn out. He was looking forward to a light supper, a good glass of wine, and hitting the sack early.

He found Ali standing in his kitchen—at least he thought it was his kitchen. He wasn't certain if she had laid siege to the place or the kitchen had waged war against her. He had to admit that he certainly admired her war gear. One look at her in that yellow bikini would cause any fighting man to surrender. The chocolate smudges on her chin and cheek resembled war paint, as did the spot of flour on her nose and the streaks of flour running across her flat stomach. She was certainly decked out in full war paint.

But it was the sparkle of sugar granules glinting in her hair that caught his attention, reminding him of their first meeting. She was even more bewitching now than she was then.

He blinked a few more times to make sure he wasn't in the middle of a damn good dream. Then he caught the mist of tears in her eyes, and he instantly forgot everything. He dropped his navy suit jacket to the couch and rushed to her side.

He wrapped her protectively in his arms and kissed the flour on her nose and the chocolate on her cheeks and slowly savored with his tongue the dark chocolate that streaked across her chin.

"Don't cry, Ali," he whispered. "Don't."

She sniffled. "I wanted to bake you a cake."

"Witches don't bake, they use their powers," he teased and pressed a gentle kiss to her lips.

She returned his kiss and sniffled again before she said, "I know, but I thought if I attempted to be mortal, you—"

He silenced her with another kiss. "I want you to be you."

Ali eagerly slipped her arms around his neck. "I am a witch."

"My witch," he whispered and his warm breath rushed over her neck and sent a shiver of pleasure racing through her.

"I like that response." He teased her lips with half kisses, half bites, and full passion.

His hand wandered around her bare waist, slipped over her backside, and gently squeezed her bottom.

"This has to be a dream," he murmured against her mouth and continued to meet her eager kisses with his own.

"I am a witch, Sebastian, a witch," she said frantically, moving her mouth away from his and tilting her head to the side for his lips to have free rein of her neck.

He kissed the silky column of her throat until he thought he would go mad with desire. "Damnable witch," he mumbled. "Snared me with your spell and now I can't escape."

"No," she whispered softly. "No, you must want me—me."

"Damned if I don't," he said, and his hands grabbed her face, holding it perfectly still for his lips to claim hers. And they did with an urgent passion that fueled her soul and woke her senses.

She returned his kisses with the same urgency, and when his hand moved to her bikini top and unsnapped the clasp, releasing it to fall away, she moved her mouth off his stubborn, unrelinquishing one, raining kisses on his cheek and to his ear.

"Come to me, Sebastian, come to me," she urged in a whisper.

She placed gentle kisses on his eyes, forcing them closed, and with the small amount of power she still possessed, she waved her hand, returning the room to its previous sparkling clean condition, and vanished.

Ali woke with a start on the lounge and cast a quick glance around the pool area to make certain she was alone. She sighed and swatted at the strands of hair that fell in her face. Sugar sprinkled over her. She ran a hand over her face and came away with a mixture of flour and chocolate smudges.

"Oh, no," she cried. "I saw to the kitchen but forgot—"

Her eyes widened in realization, and she peeked down inside her terry robe. "Oh no," she repeated and collapsed in disbelief back on the lounge.

Twelve

Sebastian woke with a start. His eyes widened as he attempted to focus on the digital clock on the nightstand beside his bed. The numbers finally cleared and he jumped off the bed.

"Seven A.M.?"

Why had he slept so late and why hadn't his alarm gone off? And what the hell was he doing in his clothes?

He raced around his bedroom, stripping off his wrinkled navy trousers and white shirt. He remembered wanting a drink, wine to be exact, when he arrived home, but he didn't recall having one. Had he collapsed exhausted on his bed and dropped into a deep sleep?

Work had been consuming a good portion of his time, but long hours was something he was accustomed to. To fall asleep fully clothed and sleep straight through the night was not a habit of his.

Not until Alisande.

He cringed at the thought and the too-cold water that greeted him when he stepped into the shower.

"Admit it, you idiot," he said to himself, adjusting the water temperature. "You think about Ali all the time. There isn't a moment in the day—"

He stopped talking, stopped washing his hair, and stood frozen in place, memories assaulting him.

His kitchen. The yellow bikini. Good God the, yellow bikini!

Shampoo trailed down into his eyes, and he turned his face to the warm spray and let it rain over him.

Had it been a dream?

He shook his head. He didn't know the difference between a dream and reality any longer. This whole matter was driving him absolutely crazy.

He grabbed the soap and started scrubbing, annoyed at himself. There was a perfectly reasonable explanation for last night.

Exhaustion. Overwork. Reading too many books on witches.

His exhaustion coupled with his subconscious managed to produce—

"One hell of a dream." He laughed, attempting to convince himself.

How could he think for even a brief moment that Alisande Wyrrd would be standing in his kitchen in a yellow bikini, smudged with flour and chocolate in an attempt to bake him a cake?

Like mortals do.

He shook his head, a common habit these days. He was going crazy, completely insane. He probably should admit she was a witch, make love with her, and end the torment once and for all.

He shut the water off and grabbed the beige towel off the brass towel bar as he stepped from the shower.

So what was the problem?

He found her attractive not only on a physical level but an emotional one. And the emotional part is what disturbed him the most. He didn't understand enough of what he felt to make a sensible judgment, but his interest in her ran deep. Deeper than he cared to admit.

He went into his bedroom and dressed, his thoughts remaining on the crazy woman who made him crazy.

No, crazy was asking her out on a normal date and getting to know her, really know her.

His fingers stilled on the shirt button he was about to secure. Why not ask her out?

Like a mortal.

So far their encounters had been just that, encounters. How would she react to a normal date? Would she accept? Would she still claim herself a witch? Would she float dishes or cast spells? He laughed as he finished tying his gray tie.

The phone rang and he had no doubt it was his secretary calling to see how late he would be. It was almost eight and he was always to the office by seven; if not he would call.

He was surprised when she mentioned nothing about his tardiness and even more surprised with her reason for calling.

"You have been issued a command appearance by Sydney Wyrrd for lunch today at one. Ms. Wyrrd was certain you would clear your calendar for her and is looking forward to speaking with you. Ms. Wyrrd did not give me the chance to decline or confirm, but she was aware of your luncheon date with Senator Billings, and she assured me the senator wouldn't mind rearranging his schedule to accommodate her. And frankly, sir, no one turns down Sydney Wyrrd."

Sebastian smiled. "I am well aware, Ms. Smithers, that a Wyrrd does not take no for an answer."

He finished dressing and was headed out the door, deciding he would have coffee at work, when he suddenly stopped, backtracked, and took a hasty peek in the kitchen.

Spotless.

"A dream," he mumbled and rushed out the front door almost colliding with Thelma Barns, the woman who kept his house sparkling clean.

"Sorry, Thelma," he apologized and stepped aside for her to enter.

"Running late?" she asked, returning her key to her purse.

"Running way past late," he confirmed with a wave and in a rush rounded the front of his car, jumped in, and within seconds was down the driveway.

Thelma shut the door and went directly to the kitchen. She always brewed a fresh pot of coffee for herself when she arrived.

She was about to fill the glass pot with water when a bright piece of material on the floor caught her eye. She leaned down and scooped up the yellow cloth that partially peeked out from beneath the cabinet.

She smiled, stretching out the yellow bathing suit top in front of her. The woman who wore this was obviously well-endowed. Mr. Wainwright must have had a good time in his kitchen last night.

Thelma took the top to the laundry room to add to the wash. She would discreetly place the item in Mr. Wainwright's closet so when he came across it he would simply think that the lady forgot her top and no one would be embarrassed or the wiser.

Sydney Wyrrd never demanded attention or respect, she simply received it. She was treated like a beloved queen by all, and the special attention didn't amaze Sebastian. It actually seemed appropriate given the generosity and love she spread so freely.

When she requested to speak with the chef, the man immediately rushed out to see her. He listened intently while she detailed the way she preferred her crab salad prepared, and if he wouldn't mind seeing to it for her she would be grateful.

The chef guaranteed her food would be prepared strictly to her instructions.

When the fussing subsided and they were finally alone, Sydney settled an appreciative smile on him.

"I am ever so grateful to you for meeting with me on such short notice."

"I never turn down a meal with a beautiful woman."

Sydney reached across the table and patted his hand. "Then you should ask my niece to supper."

"I was thinking the same thing myself," he admitted without reluctance.

Sydney appeared surprised, though pleased. "And here I thought you were running away from my niece."

He laughed, a deep rumble. "I couldn't run far or fast enough, she even invades my dreams."

Sydney sighed knowingly. "Ali is a determined one."

"That is an understatement."

Their meal was served with style and grace of years gone by, and Sebastian had to admit he was impressed.

"Tell me, Sebastian," Sydney said with great care. "What do you really think of Alisande?"

"Are you certain you want me to answer that?"

"By all means," she encouraged.

He didn't hesitate. "She's willful, spoiled, crazy, independent, beautiful, charming, unpredictable—"

He stopped short, placed his fork on his plate, and looked her directly in those stunning Wyrrd green eyes that seemed to contain age-old wisdom and strength. "Why does she insist that she is a witch? And why do you encourage it? Are all Wyrrd's crazy?"

His candid question did not upset her in the least. She

spoke without a trace of irritation. "You don't believe in witches?"

"Modern witchcraft per se or those who practice Wiccan, but the broom-flying, spell-casting kind?" He was shaking his head before he finished.

"So witches are a figment of the imagination?"

"Overactive imagination," he amended.

"Then where do you think witches originated?"

Sebastian ignored his food, finding the interesting conversation stimulating. "From what I have read so far, I would say that their origins took root in a harmless secular group based on and around nature."

"What today is referred to as Wiccan?" Sydney asked.

"No, I would say Wiccan took some beliefs from this ancient sect but deviated from the original."

"Interesting perspective."

"Consider history," Sebastian said. "Fear and ignorance bred by radicals who practiced tyranny contributed to the demise of many old religious and secular beliefs. Think of what was lost to the world because of the frenzy to dominate the masses. What better way to instill fear than to create the illusion of evil."

"So what you are suggesting is that witches never existed, they were created to inspire fear and thereby be used as means to control by those in places of power."

He nodded. "Created supposedly by intelligent men whose beliefs were based on good and evil and greed."

"And anything that wasn't understood was evil."

"Right. Say this ancient sect was a highly evolved race who understood the energy of nature, their crops flourished, their health flourished, their knowledge expanded. Yet those around them suffered from disease, starvation, and such. Wouldn't it make sense to think that those who did not suffer but were fortunate made a pact with the devil?"

"Why not just offer their knowledge to the less fortunate?"

"Because the less fortunate are innocent and they are made to believe by those who wish to propagate ignorance and domination that it is the devil's work and that he is attempting to coerce them to the side of evil."

"And this highly evolved group of people, do you believe them capable of possessing—" She paused a moment. "Certain abilities?"

"I suppose you mean the broom-flying, spell-casting kind?" he asked with humor.

Sydney answered with a nod and a smile.

"An intelligent race would have no need for such antics."

"Antics?" Sydney said indignantly.

"Why cast a spell when a matter can be settled intelligently?" he asked. "Take your niece for instance. She is a beautiful, alluring woman. Why insist she is a witch?"

"Honesty is important in a relationship."

"Precisely," he agreed and cast a suspicious glance at Sydney. "Do you honestly expect me to believe Ali is a witch?"

"Have you ever for one moment suspended your belief in the obvious, the practical, and looked beyond?"

"There is always a sensible explanation for everything," he insisted, his opinion strong on the subject.

Sydney spoke softly. "Like that time you were a little boy, no more than four, and you were lost in the woods that surrounded the cottage your parents had rented in Ireland for the summer."

Sebastian stared at her in disbelief but remained silent. Any good security firm could dig up basic information on him, and he was certain Sydney Wyrrd had not wasted a minute in hiring the best—or second best, since his firm was number one. And he planned on finding out who was responsible for invading his past so thoroughly.

Sydney continued. "You began to cry. You felt frightened and alone and feared you would never see your parents again. Do you remember what happened?"

He nodded. "Distinctly. My father found me."

"By the edge of the woods near the cottage," Sydney confirmed.

"That's right."

"But how did you get there? You wandered a considerable distance into the woods."

Sebastian stiffened. "I was lucky."

Sydney smiled. "Come, my dear boy, admit the truth."

"What truth?" he asked with reservation.

"Beatrice." She said her name as if she were familiar with the woman.

Sebastian had not heard the name in years. He had put it out of his mind, relegated it to childhood fantasies or dreams. No one knew about Beatrice. How could they? She wasn't real.

"Beatrice saved you," Sydney said, offering his hand a comforting pat. "Beatrice is like that. She loves children, but then all forest fairies do. When she spotted you sitting on that rotted stump sobbing and your knees skinned from a tumble, her heart went out to you. Normally the forest fairies will direct the lost child home without them realizing it, but she sensed you were special and so she appeared to you."

"On my shoulder," he said almost in a whisper. "Wearing that lopsided flowery wreath on her head, fluttering her crooked wing and sporting a wide magical smile.

Sydney's own smile widened. *Magical.* There was hope for the dear boy yet.

"Beatrice promised she would help you find your way home. And of course she did. Fairies never lie. She remained on your shoulder all the way to the edge of the woods.''

''Chatting incessantly along the way.'' He laughed, recalling her endless, nonsensical string of chatter whispered softly in his ear.

''To keep you calm,'' Sydney said, ''though she can go on at times.''

''At the edge of the woods she instructed me to call out to my father. She told me that she could go no farther.''

Sydney nodded. ''The woods protect the fairies. Once past them they are in danger of being discovered.''

Sebastian continued, the long-ago memory vividly returning. ''I asked her who she was and she told me, Beatrice. Then she disappeared.''

Sydney's smile faded. ''And when you told your father, he didn't believe you.''

Sebastian shook his head. ''No, he didn't.'' He stared suspiciously at Sydney. ''How did you find out? No one knows that story but me and my father, and my father passed on years ago.''

Sydney's smile returned. ''You are an investigator, you figure it out. Now, are you going to ask my niece out?''

Subject changed meant subject closed. She would leave him hanging. Give him food for thought. Sebastian smiled at the older woman's cunning. ''Do I have a choice?''

''I think, my dear boy, that your choice has already been made.''

Sydney sat alone at the table having explained to Sebastian she would wait for a friend she was to meet.

With a gracious kiss to her cheek, Sebastian thanked her for a most interesting lunch and suggested they meet again soon.

She had promised him they most certainly would.

"Daydreaming or devising, Sydney?" Dagon asked as he joined her at the table.

"A little of both," she admitted. "Sebastian Wainwright is extremely intelligent. He came terribly close to understanding the history of our heritage."

Dagon raised a concerned brow. "How did he manage that?"

"Logical deduction from various facts he had gathered. But his logical, pragmatic mind refuses to accept anything out of the ordinary. Actually, I don't think he believes anything exists out of the ordinary."

"Meaning he will never accept Alisande being a witch."

"If he can rationalize it he might," she suggested, "though I have a feeling logic will fly out the window as he becomes more involved with Ali."

"And how is he to do that when he keeps his distance from her?"

Sydney smiled with joy. "He is going to ask her out."

Dagon shook his head in disgust. "What good will that do? Ali will not deny her heritage, and he will not acknowledge it. He is destined to hurt her."

Sydney disagreed. "I think not. I sense he has feelings for her. Feelings he has yet to understand or deal with."

Dagon laughed. "How wouldn't he be having difficulty? The little minx is probably invading his dreams and tormenting him senseless."

"She can only do so much," Sydney reminded. "Remember the spell she cast."

"She always ran headfirst into things never giving thought to the consequences, always believing all would turn out well."

"And you always managed to catch her if she should fall, softening the impact."

Dagon sighed with resignation. "I don't want to see her

hurt. If she wants this mortal, heaven forbid, then I will do all I can to help her."

"That's what I was counting on," she said. "There is nothing like an extra wheel to upset the applecart."

Dagon's sinful smile elicited several gasps from the women at the surrounding tables. "Is it time for us to put your plan into action?"

"I have managed to set it in motion," she admitted. "It won't be long before you are called into action."

"Good," Dagon said, rubbing his hands together, then stopped and dared to direct a finger at Sydney. "But I warn you, if this plan doesn't resolve the issue, I will take matters into my own hands, and you know what a temper I have when someone I care for is made to suffer needlessly."

Pushing his wagging finger aside she said, "I am counting on it."

Sebastian rode the elevator to his suite of offices on the top floor, thinking of his conversation with Sydney Wyrrd.

Damned if he wasn't annoyed that she uncovered that incident in his youth. And who had she hired to research his past? Being in security, he had taken certain precautions to guarantee his privacy. So how did Sydney breach his security? He would have to look into this himself, and when he found the source he would make certain he hired him. The person was good. Damn good to have uncovered that bit of personal information on him.

Sebastian informed Ms. Smithers that he had an important case to work on and she was to hold all calls. He then spent the remainder of the afternoon investigating. It wasn't until Ms. Smithers announced she was leaving for the day that he realized that no one had breached his defenses. No one had done a legal or illegal background check on him. At least not through normal channels.

Then who had related the story to Sydney?

Sebastian relaxed back in the large soft leather desk chair, resting his head, closing his eyes, and remembering.

He had been so frightened when he realized he was lost. he didn't know what to do except cry, as any terrified four-year-old would do. The towering trees, the thick high bushes, the odd sounds were like strange creatures closing in on a small lost boy. He had thought for sure a wood monster would appear and swallow him whole.

But instead of a monster he got a fairy.

Beatrice appeared on his shoulder. She attempted to dry his wet eyes with the sleeve of her white and pale blue gauze dress. She was plump, cheerful, and had the prettiest face framed by the blondest hair Sebastian had ever seen. But it was the lopsided flowery head wreath she wore and her crooked wing that he would always remember. The wreath sat tilted on her head until it almost covered one eye, and she was forever pushing it up only to have it fall down again. And her crooked wing caused her to fly or flutter in place on an angle so that she appeared off balance more often than not.

She chatted endlessly, though to him reassuringly, in his ear as she directed him through the woods. And she walked along his shoulder, sat on it, even leaned against his cheek several times to wipe his trailing tears. If it hadn't been for her?

He slowly shook his head. What was wrong with him? His father had explained that she was only a figment of his childish imagination and that his own good senses got him out of his predicament. After all, he had walked himself into the woods, he was certainly capable of walking himself out. But he had liked Beatrice and he had so wanted to believe she had been a real fairy.

Think logical, boy.

His father's words rang in his ears. *Apply logic and sound reasoning, and the answers will appear.*

"Okay, Dad," Sebastian said aloud. "If I didn't tell Sydney Wyrrd and you didn't tell her, then who told her about the woods?"

Beatrice.

The thought had him shooting out of the chair, raking his fingers through his hair, and pacing in front of the row of windows.

He was losing his mind. He had to be if he believed in wood fairies.

His glance went to the phone.

Ask her out and get some answers.

He walked to the desk and reached for the phone.

Thirteen

The restaurant was a small, intimate place outside of D.C. The menu was tastefully selected, the wine list exceptional, and the atmosphere discreet. It was the perfect place for a lover's rendezvous.

Ali had no doubt Sebastian chose it with privacy in mind, and the thought pleased her. Just as it pleased her to know he couldn't take his eyes off her. And she owed his rapt attention to the wisp of white silk she wore. The dress was designed to tantalize, leaving just enough to the imagination to tempt and torment. She wore no jewelry so as not to distract, and her hair was fashioned in an intricate twist with falling strands accenting her neck and face. A minimum of makeup, a touch of color to highlight her lips, and pearl white polish on her nails complimented her attire. She had chosen wisely for this evening's liaison.

But then, so had Sebastian. He looked simply delicious. His clothes were obviously tailored to fit his athletically built body, and she liked his choice of the contrasting navy and tan colors of his sports jacket and trousers.

And his aftershave? She sighed and quietly murmured, "Sexy."

After she took the seat he held for her, he leaned over her shoulder and whispered in her ear, "Seductive."

Her smile turned to one of pure pleasure mixed with excitement.

Sebastian took the seat opposite her at the round, cozy table, and their eyes instantly met and held.

The waiter, obviously accustomed to discretion, left the menus and quietly disappeared.

"You wore that dress on purpose," he accused in a low whisper.

"*For* a purpose," she corrected with a look that promised more than an intimate dinner.

He leaned nearer to her. "Behave."

She moved closer herself. "Do you really want me to?"

What a question to ask him. Damn if he didn't want her to be just who she was: a passionate, audacious and seductive woman.

He cringed at his own answer. "Yes."

Her laughter sounded like soft chimes drifting on a gentle wind. "I am who I am, Sebastian."

"Who are you?" he asked, suddenly in need of knowing, really knowing her.

"A woman who wants you." She said it without hesitation or coyness.

Direct and honest. He liked that about her. And she had not mentioned one word about being a witch. She was simply a woman who wanted him.

"Why?" he asked, enjoying this exchange of normal conversation.

Ali remained silent as the waiter discreetly approached them with a bottle of wine. He poured a sample for Sebastian, who tasted it and nodded his approval. Once he filled their glasses, he vanished.

Sebastian waited for her answer.

She tasted the red wine, approving of its rich, dry flavor with her own nod and then responded. "I am attracted to you."

The waiter lingered a short distance away, waiting for a signal from Sebastian.

"Let's order, then we can talk about this *attraction.*" He motioned to the waiter.

She ordered the pork with baked apples, and he ordered the chicken with artichokes and sun-dried tomatoes in wine sauce, each offering to share a taste with the other.

"Now, where were we?" he asked.

"You were about to tell me why you find me so irresistible," Ali said sweetly.

Irresistible. She was certainly that. And different in a way he was unable to clearly summarize. She was secure and confident with herself and with her actions. Perhaps, too, it was that she dared to be different. Dared to think magically instead of logically.

He responded candidly. "You fascinate me."

"How so?"

"You are like a puzzle, so many pieces that don't seem to fit, and yet the more complex the puzzle becomes, the more engrossed I find myself."

"And what do you do with all those pieces that don't quite fit?"

He shook his head and smiled with arrogant pride. "I always make the pieces fit."

"And how do you do that?" she asked.

"Deductive reasoning."

Salads with balsamic dressing were placed in front of them along with warm sourdough rolls. They began to enjoy the meal and eagerly returned to the conversation.

"You believe everything can be settled through deductive reasoning?"

"Of course, why wouldn't it? If you find a starting point and work forward or backward, you begin to establish a pattern and background. And like a puzzle, once you have all or even most of the pieces, the puzzle begins to take shape, and from there it is only a matter of time before the puzzle is complete."

"Were you this analytical as a child?" she asked with a teasing smile.

He laughed. "I was a terror."

The idea of him being a hellion intrigued her. "Who did you terrorize?"

"Anyone who didn't see things my way."

"Which I take it was often?"

He nodded and grinned over forgotten but happy memories. "I forever questioned in my attempt to understand. My mother blamed my father and my father strutted his pride in my inquisitive nature."

"Don't you mean stubborn?" she corrected.

"That would depend on who you asked."

"Did this reign of terror extend to your teachers?" she asked, delighted at learning all she could about him.

He cringed at the memories. "I was relentless on them. I demanded to know why. Always why. There was a reasonable explanation for all that existed in the world and I wanted to know. I researched and studied, then researched and studied more."

"And your inquisitive nature landed you a position in government security?" She knew the answer. She knew much about Sebastian Wainwright, but she wanted to learn more. Especially that part of himself *he* had yet to learn about. The part that would inevitably connect him with her.

"While in college I was approached by a division of the government that dealt with top security," he admitted, realizing his background check would have shown his work with the government but not the exact agency, and he wasn't about to detail classified information.

"They liked the fact that you researched so thoroughly."

A reasonable conclusion for her to reach, he told himself. "Impressed with my talent and tenaciousness for finding answers. They offered me a position that I accepted, and that led to my present business.''

End of that discussion, she thought. He intended to supply her with only so much information, but that was all right. She knew all about his days with *The Department.* She wanted to know more about him.

Their meals were served quietly and graciously, and after the waiter made sure of their comfort and satisfaction, he left them to enjoy the appetizing fare.

Ali discovered she liked watching Sebastian. The simplest, most common movement he made intrigued her, though his movements were more orchestrated than common. He possessed a style and confidence that she admired. He was secure and accomplished in who he was, and it showed, especially in his hands. Those long lean fingers sliced, cupped, and stroked like a man at ease and sure of his every motion.

She wondered if he possessed the same confidence in bed, though if his kisses were any indication, he had long ago mastered the art of making love.

''I warned you to behave,'' he whispered. ''Those sexy green eyes of yours are raging with passion.''

She sighed like a petulant child denied her favorite treat. ''Won't you satisfy my rage?''

Damn, if he didn't want to do just that. To hell with the meal and the intimate atmosphere. He wanted nothing more than to make passionate love to her for hours on end. But he needed to understand her. Understand why she claimed to be a witch.

''I'm tempted. That is why I want to get to know you better.''

Her sigh turned to disappointment. ''My need for you isn't enough.''

''I'm looking for more than need.''

She perked up instantly, and with a seductive voice that

melted over him like warm honey, she said, "Detail 'more than need' to me."

He didn't bother to slip the piece of chicken off his fork, his tongue was too busy salivating over her delicious wet mouth and that tiny pink tongue that licked suggestively at her lips.

Focus, he warned himself.

"I have had my share of affairs," he admitted.

Yes, and I know about each one. Passing fancies, nothing more.

"They leave an empty sometimes bitter taste in one's mouth. I decided that I wanted more from the next woman I take to my bed."

"And what is more?" she asked, as if not knowing his answer.

"I want the promise of a lifetime together," he said and waited.

Her green eyes grew brilliant and pooled with tears. "You search for love."

"Yes," he conceded. "Don't you?"

She blinked back her tears and nodded. "Yes, but love cannot be easily defined, and it is often evasive when tenaciously sought. Love knows no discretion. It reaches out and grabs hold of the heart and then—"

She smiled and reached across the table to tap at his temple. "Reasonable deduction flies out the window."

He returned her shrewd smile. "Sound reasoning and understanding would make for a more solid and more permanent marital foundation."

"What about passion?" she asked and placed her arms on the edge of the table, leaning forward, eager for his answer.

She could easily intimidate, especially with those exquisite green eyes that penetrated the surface and touched within. But he was prepared. He was always prepared—well . . . almost always.

"Passion doesn't last forever."

She smiled like a patient teacher instructing a pupil who had difficulty learning his lessons. "You are wrong. Passion is everlasting."

"Not possible," he argued confidently. "It is fleeting, coming and going with emotions."

She challenged him further. "Passion is emotions."

"Obsessive emotions."

"Zesty," she contested.

He grinned, enjoying their debate. "Yet manageable when one is practical."

Her green eyes grew brilliant with excitement in their startling color, and her smile turned softly sensual. "Then you have never known true passion."

A shiver rushed over him, sending goose bumps racing up his arms and down his spine. Damn, but she could tempt.

"A debate better left for another day," he said, knowing the conversation would soon become too heated for further discussion.

Finished with their meals, their plates were removed, and coffee, tea and cognac were served along with a selection of miniature pastries and fresh fruit that simply could not be ignored.

Turning the conversation to a safer topic, he asked her about her childhood, and they were soon lost in tales of childhood memories.

"You were fearless," he said after learning of her solitary adventures in the woods that bordered her family's home in Ireland.

She shook her head and chose her words carefully. She had purposely avoided any mention of being a witch. She had convinced herself that she would attempt this evening out with him as a mortal. She did not wish to lose her own unique identity, only to better understand him, so he may eventually better understand her. A starting point as he would recommend, a place to proceed from.

"Not really. I possessed a strong sense of myself."

He had no idea what made him say it. He wasn't even thinking about his disastrous adventure in the woods. Perhaps it was because he was recently reminded of the incident, or perhaps he wished to witness her response.

"When I was very young I thought I saw a wood fairy. But my father made me understand it was my fear and overactive imagination that made me *think* that I actually saw a fairy."

"How sad for you," she said with genuine sorrow.

"How so?" he asked, touched by the concern in her voice.

Ali could no more deny the existence of fairies than she could deny herself a witch. Fairies did wonderful work and were the most loving and giving creatures she had ever met. And it was incomprehensible to think a father would deny a child the privilege of meeting one.

"To believe in fairies takes courage. To see a fairy is a privilege. Why would your father deny you such a wonderful experience?"

Sebastian immediately defended his father. "He spared me the embarrassment of telling a tale that people would find amusing."

Ali had long ago grown accustomed to mortal peculiarities. Particularly to their logical natures. If they would be illogical for only a moment, they would discover such wonders.

"I believe in fairies."

He smiled. "Somehow I thought you would."

"Do you think I am crazy?"

"Eccentric."

She leaned forward and whispered, "What if I told you there was a fairy sitting on your left shoulder this very moment?"

Sebastian turned his head to look.

"You do believe," she said with excitement and a clap of her hands.

He shook his head in disbelief. "I can't believe I fell for that trick."

"It's no trick. If you did not believe, you would not have looked. There is hope for you yet."

He studied her with intense eyes for a long moment and said, "I don't believe in fairies."

She shook her head, her eyes registering her sadness. She understood what he was telling her. He not only didn't believe in fairies. He didn't believe in witches. What was she to do?

They drove home in silence. Both understanding that their relationship was now at an impasse. He was a practical mortal. She was a witch. What ever would become of them?

Sebastian helped her out of the car after coming to a stop at her front door. Logic would have her invite him in for a cup of coffee, but somehow he doubted she would end their evening on such a logical note.

She stood beside him at the bottom of the steps to the front porch and turned her head to look out over the surrounding grounds. The warm night air drifted over them with the thick scent of honeysuckle, and thousands of stars glittered like diamonds in the dark night sky.

Ali raised her hand to stroke his cheek, so warm and soft and yet so hard and unyielding in the set of his jaw. She balanced herself on her toes to reach her mouth to his and kissed him lightly on his lips. A fleeting kiss, followed by another and another until she softly whispered, "Come to the woods with me and meet the fairies."

He realized she was asking him to believe in more than

fairies, and he wasn't sure he could make such an impractical commitment. What would people think? He the CEO of the largest security firm in Washington, D.C., venturing into the woods after midnight in search of mythical creatures.

"Another time," he whispered, not wanting to completely deny her request, just place it on hold for a while.

She nodded, though her eyes spoke her disappointment.

He kissed her then, tenderly, lovingly, and their arms wrapped around each other. She clung to him and he to her, holding on tightly, not wanting to let go, not wanting to surrender this night.

They parted reluctantly and without a word being spoken, and as Ali watched him drive off she feared as only a mortal could that she might never see him again.

Fourteen

"I am no good at these mortal games," Ali said and plopped herself down on the chaise lounge next to the one her aunt occupied near the indoor pool.

Sydney reluctantly closed the mystery book she was reading after tucking the bookmark inside and placed the book on the table beside her. She then turned her full attention on her disgruntled niece. "A problem with your date last night?"

Ali nodded, slipping out of the terry beach robe she wore and throwing it over the bottom of the chaise. Needing the warm healing rays of the sun on her skin, she had worn the barest of bikinis.

"That, my dear young lady, is indecent," her aunt scolded with a firmness that made Ali feel contrite.

"I know. I didn't buy it with the intention of anyone but myself seeing it."

"Make certain that you don't let anyone see you in it," her aunt reprimanded. "Especially Sebastian. One look at you in that scrap of nothingness, and he would lose what little sense he has left."

Ali smiled. "Really, you think so?"

Sydney shook a warning finger at her. "You cast a serious spell, Alisande Wyrrd, and there will be no interfering with the results."

Ali's smile instantly faded. "I am fully aware of my actions."

Sydney's voice softened. "Why did you choose the magical love spell?"

Honesty was a virtue Ali long respected in others and herself, so she spoke truthfully and from her heart. "I feel as if I have waited forever for that *special* man, mortal or witch. And when my powers began to diminish, I realized a serious choice must be made. Mate briefly or mate forever. I sensed that briefly would not fulfill me, so I decided to make a choice."

"A serious choice," Sydney reminded. "You do understand that Sebastian must want this union of his own free choice. If you mate without his full acceptance, the spell will fade and consequences will result. It will take many many years to heal your heart. That is why the spell is seldom cast without first discussing it with an elder."

"I was never one to follow rules," Ali said with a smile that betrayed her concern.

"Our rules protect us, Alisande, and you have seriously failed to consider the second more profound part of the spell. Do you doubt he will be able to fulfill it?"

Ali sighed her frustration. "I felt so confident, so sure of myself and my abilities to convince him."

"He is too practical. He cannot believe in the unbelievable. And if he cannot believe, then . . ."

Sydney shook her head. She couldn't speak the words, couldn't hear herself tell her niece that the man she was falling in love with would be lost to her forever.

"I was aware of the consequences when I cast the spell." Ali laughed lightly, though her heart felt heavy. "I was not aware of his stubborn practicality."

"I assume he was practical last night?"

A sigh rushed past Ali's lips, and she slowly shook her head. "The evening started so wonderfully. We talked, teased, shared stories, and learned much about each other."

"The way lovers should," Sydney encouraged.

"Mortal lovers."

Sydney nodded her understanding.

"He chose a perfect romantic setting, looked perfectly appealing, smelled exquisitely sexy, and sounded perfectly mortal."

"Which is how you were to sound in return. What happened?"

"He tested me."

"And you tested back," Sydney said, knowing her niece all too well.

Ali nodded. "I thought if I could just get him to open his eyes and truly see, he would understand—"

"You?" Sydney finished.

One single tear was followed by another down Ali's cheek. "I want him to know *me*."

Sydney reached out and grasped Ali's hand, squeezing it. "You want him to *believe* in you."

Ali wiped at her tears with her hand and Sydney reached for the box of tissues on the table beside her, offering one to Ali.

"He loves you, you know," Sydney said, sensing her niece needed to have her suspicions confirmed.

"Thank you for the reassurance," Ali said, blotting at her wet cheeks. "Strangely enough I never really doubted the fact that he would love me. I think that is what made me cast the spell in the first place. When I entered his office and my eyes met his, I instantly recognized the passion that existed between us. A passion not only born of pleasure but of love. I think that is what made me cast the special spell."

"Then you had not planned on using that particular spell."

Ali shook her head. "Honestly, no. It wasn't until I stood beside him and began my chant that I realized no other spell would do. I made my choice then and there."

"So in a way, you looked briefly before you leaped," Sydney said with a laugh and an earnest understanding.

"Very briefly, but I leaped with no regret."

"Then you have no choice but to pursue your decision with your usual tenacious verve."

"True," Ali admitted with a confidence that had been briefly lost, but which her aunt had so generously helped to restore. "I'm just not sure which route to take. Playing at being mortal was fun for the moment, but I found it was hard to quell my audacious nature."

Sydney laughed, a full-hearted, robust laughter. "Darling, your audaciousness is as much a part of you as being a witch. You are who you are, Alisande, and you cannot deny your nature nor your heritage."

"What you are saying is that I will not, nor would I ever, change who I am."

"Precisely."

"Then I cannot expect Sebastian to change his nature."

"Precisely."

Ali shook her head completely confused. "Then how in heaven are we going to get together?"

"By accepting each other for who you are, not what you want the other to be."

"Practical, stubborn, logical, with no thought to the magic of life, this I should accept in Sebastian?" Ali asked, her confusion turning to annoyance.

Sydney's tone was serious. "If you cannot accept him as he is, how do you expect him to accept who you are?"

Ali pondered her question. "He is tenacious just like me."

"That he is."

"And passionate." Ali grinned wickedly. "He is so very passionate."

"Like you," Sydney reminded.

Ali nodded vigorously, her grin growing wider. "And he is searching for a permanent love, not just a brief affair."

"A reasonable and wise choice."

She recalled his words. "He wants the relationship built on a solid, practical foundation."

"A good place to begin. A good foundation offers sturdy support during the most inclement times."

"He does possess many good qualities."

"Like you."

Ali's grin turned satisfying. "I suppose we are more alike than I first thought."

"An astute observation," her aunt remarked. "Now, what do you intend to do about it?"

Ali didn't hesitate in her response. "Continue my pursuit."

"How exactly?"

Ali's green eyes twinkled with delight. "Practical, reasonable, logical, and"—she threw her hands up and laughed, the tinkling sound raining down upon them—"with a sprinkle of magic."

"If it is a sprinkle of magic, then there is only one place to obtain it," her aunt said with a wink.

Ali sat straight up, gripping the arms of the lounge and staring wide-eyed at her aunt. "Do you think I dare?"

"It is not for you to dare, my dear. It is a mere favor you request from an old friend."

"Do you think she would do it?"

"For you and Dagon, Beatrice would do anything," Sydney assured her. "You two imps were always her favorites."

"Sebastian told me he thought he saw a fairy in the

woods when he was a young boy. He would be so surprised to see one now as an adult.''

Sydney smiled pleasantly. ''You have no idea just how surprised.''

''But Beatrice is in Ireland,'' Ali said disappointed.

''I think we can arrange a quick transportation.''

''Do you think he will share his experience of seeing her with me?''

''It doesn't really matter,'' her aunt assured her. ''It will give him food for thought, and that is what he needs, to open his mind to other possibilities.''

''What possibilities?'' Dagon asked, stepping from the French doors out to the pool area to join the two women.

''Endless possibilities,'' Ali said, reaching for her robe and covering up.

''Good move, dear heart,'' Dagon said with a wink and pulled a chair nearer to Ali.

Ali leaned over and kissed him on the cheek. ''Guess who is coming to visit?''

''Who?'' he asked and looked past Ali to Sydney.

She smiled and nodded. ''Beatrice.''

''Going to put Wainwright in his place, is she?'' he teased.

Ali playfully slapped him on the arm. ''She's going to offer her assistance.''

Dagon tapped her nose. ''She's going to teach the mortal a much needed lesson.''

That got Ali's dander up and brought her to her knees on the chaise, her finger jabbing at his chest. ''She will help.''

''Hah,'' Dagon said, tapping at her nose again. ''She will put him in his place.''

''She will help,'' Ali repeated with further jabs to his hard chest.

''She will teach him a lesson, as you need to be taught

one,'' Dagon said with a confident grin that irritated Ali all the more.

''Who's going to teach me that lesson?'' she challenged, placing her face directly in front of his.

''Alisande, dear,'' her aunt interrupted. ''Your powers are weak.''

''I don't need powers to handle her,'' Dagon bragged.

Ali got to her feet, though even at her five-feet-six-inch height Dagon still towered over her. ''Going to lower yourself and use mere mortal tactics?''

He grabbed her chin. ''Since you have been playing with mortals, you should well understand their games.''

''I do,'' she said defiantly, yanking her chin from his grasp and placing her hands on her hips in an I-dare-you stance.

''Good, then you will expect my next move.''

Before she could respond, Dagon had lifted her effortlessly into his strong arms and proceeded to walk toward the pool.

''Don't you dare,'' she warned, kicking her feet wildly while her hands failed miserably in their senseless attempt to pummel his very hard, muscled chest.

He laughed. ''Wrong response.''

He held her over the pool and with a smug smile said, ''Enjoy the swim.''

Not one to be bested, Ali reached out and grabbed tightly around his neck. He stumbled attempting to stop them both from toppling head first into the pool.

He wasn't successful.

Sebastian sat in the chair staring at the phone on the table beside him. He had been staring at the blasted thing for the last thirty minutes. All day his thoughts had focused on Alisande. He had to admit he had thoroughly enjoyed last night with her. Her last request, to meet fairies, had disturbed him, but giving it more rational thought in the bright light of day, it didn't seem so unreasonable.

People were believing in all sorts of improbable things nowadays. Angels. Trolls. Fairies. If it made someone feel good to believe in mythical creatures, why not? Hadn't he pretended to slay Dragons when he was a young boy. And didn't everyone have a guardian angel? So what if Ali chose to believe in fairies?

He quickly reached for the phone and dialed her number. Surprisingly, a man answered with a curt hello.

Sebastian requested to speak with Alisande, attempting to keep a pleasant timbre to his voice and to ignore the disturbing sensation in his midsection that the man's unexpected presence had caused him.

"Alisande is presently indisposed."

He didn't like the sound of that or the brusque way in which it was delivered. "Is she all right?"

"As well as can be expected after suffering a much deserved dunking," Dagon said sharply.

"You deserved it, damn you." Sebastian heard Alisande call out. Her agitated voice brought him out of his chair in a flash, his hand clenching in a fist at his side.

"Put her on the phone," he demanded of the stranger on the other end.

There was a brief moment of silence before Dagon spoke. "I don't take well to orders."

"I don't give a damn what you take well to, put Alisande on the phone now," Sebastian said, his voice rising steadily.

"Sorry, pal, but since she's standing here stark naked, I think it would be best if she called you back." With that the phone went dead.

Sebastian stood staring incredulously at the receiver still gripped in his hand. His first thought was to go storming over there like an enraged lover. . . . But he wasn't her lover. And what if she knew this man? Was familiar with him? And why the hell was she standing naked in front of him?

He slammed the receiver down and stormed out of the gathering room, out onto his deck that ran almost the full length of the back of the house. He marched back and forth, mumbling to himself.

He wanted so badly to drive over to Alisande's and punch that guy in the face.

Impractical.

He shook his head. He hadn't even gathered all the facts, and here he was resorting to violence. He was a grown man, not an adolescent in the throes of juvenile irrationality. He was a man who researched, gathered information, and made a reasonable evaluation of a situation before deciding on the wisest course of action.

He shook his head again. Then why did he still feel like punching the unidentified man in the face?

He took a deep calming breath, grasped the top rail of the deck, and released his breath slowly.

He didn't like the idea that Ali could be standing naked in front of any man but him. The thought drove him crazy, so completely insane that logic disappeared and male pride ruled.

He had no right to think of her as his, but he did. Where was the rationality in this?

He stopped himself from shaking his head again. His thoughts hadn't been rational since Ali walked into his life.

He wandered down the steps and toward the stone path that led to his wildflower garden in the woods. It was his place of solace. Where he went to think, relax, and settle his thoughts.

A decision was necessary concerning Ali and their relationship. He had to face his feelings and the consequences that inevitably would follow.

He walked a good distance into the woods and sat on a bench, an old, sturdy wooden one that had seen one too many refinishings and looked to be on its last leg. The sturdiness and courage of the old piece caught his eye, and he had bought it to the surprise of the antique shop owner who had used it to display his wares.

It was his special bench he shared with no one. He would sit on it when he was most weary or confused and absorb its strength.

He sat now, stretching out his jean-clad legs and folding his arms across his chest, covering the remaining letters on the blue faded shirt that once announced he was "thirty and proud" and now read "rty and oud."

"I am in love with a crazy woman," he announced to the wildflowers, who appeared to be standing in rapt attention waiting to hear his declaration.

A soft summer breeze blew over them, and their blossomed buds nodded in unison.

"Oh, and I can't forget that she is also a witch." He shook his head. "I'm in love with a crazy witch."

The wildflowers nodded enthusiastically.

But where was the breeze?

He refused to shake his head again. "I'm going crazy. The next thing you know I'll be seeing fairies."

"You call and I'm here, me boy," the soft voice said in his ear.

"I'm not going to look. I'm not," Sebastian said to himself.

"And why not, when I traveled so many miles to see you?"

Sebastian sighed and reluctantly looked to his left shoulder.

Fifteen

''Damn you, Dagon,'' Ali said, dialing Sebastian's number for the third time in fifteen minutes and once again getting his answering machine. She didn't bother leaving a message. She wanted to talk with him, not a machine. She wanted to clarify this huge misunderstanding, but most of all discover the reason he had phoned her in the first place.

Dagon sat with a terry towel draped around his lean hips while his hands were busy rubbing dry, with a thick towel, the dark hair that fell over his broad shoulders onto his chest.

''He had no business ordering me about,'' he snapped with irritation.

''So you tell him I am naked?'' Ali all but shouted at him.

He pointed an accusing finger at her. ''With that thing you call a bikini, you might as well be naked.''

Ali tucked the large terry towel more securely around her. ''Now what will he think of me?''

''It is not what he is thinking of you that matters. It is what he is thinking of Dagon.''

Both heads turned sharply toward Sydney, who was pouring wine for them all at the poolside bar area.

Sydney continued. ''Mortal males.'' She paused a moment and cast an intense glance at Dagon. "And male witches as well are notoriously jealous creatures."

"I am not the jealous type," Dagon protested adamantly.

"Then you have never truly been in love," Sydney informed him and sent him a look that dared him to repudiate her statement.

Ali childishly stuck her tongue out at him.

"Brat," he retaliated.

"Are you two quite finished acting like juveniles?" Sydney asked calmly and handed them each a glass of wine on their approach to her.

They nodded, looking repentant.

"Now, I think this whole situation can be easily resolved and to Ali's advantage if handled properly," Sydney explained.

Dagon and Ali, after slipping into beach robes, followed Sydney to the poolside table shaded by a large umbrella.

Dagon took a seat only after holding out a chair for his aunt and then Ali. Proper manners were a trait his aunt insisted he maintain at all times.

"Does this plan include helping Ali win Wainwright?" Dagon asked skeptically.

"This plan assists Ali in implementing steps that must be taken to see if her spell will prove successful," Sydney answered, patient in her response but firm in her explanation.

"And if it isn't successful, will you be able to accept the consequences?" Dagon asked Ali with obvious concern.

Her chin and stubborn pride went up. "I will have no choice. I will survive the outcome no matter the results."

Dagon softened his tone and reached out to give her hand a comforting squeeze. "I will be there for you, dear heart, no matter what the circumstances."

"I never doubted that you wouldn't be," Ali said and leaned over to give him a grateful kiss on the cheek.

"Now that you two have finally made up and grown up, we can proceed," Sydney announced like a schoolmistress ready to begin a lesson. "This is what we are going to do."

Sebastian stormed into his office the following morning shouting orders. "I want my full research staff in the conference room five minutes ago, Ms. Smithers."

The woman wasn't the least bit ruffled by his abrupt manner. She did as directed, and within seconds people were filing anxiously into the large conference room adjacent to Sebastian's office.

Sebastian stood staring out the window of his private office. He was as usual impeccably dressed. He wore a smoky gray suit, pin-striped shirt, and a power tie that caught the eye and demanded attention. He was clean shaven and wore an aftershave that was subtle. The only difference in his appearance was that his dark hair, though stylishly groomed, was a tad longer than he normally wore it. He had not had time for a haircut recently. He had not been on time for meetings recently, and he had not slept a good, solid night's sleep without dreaming recently. Recently being Alisande Wyrrd.

But this weekend ended all that. This weekend was the icing on the cake, and he was about to get to the bottom of it once and for all. Even if it took every last dime he owned, and he owned a substantial number of dimes.

"The staff is all here, sir," Ms. Smithers informed him over the intercom.

Sebastian entered the conference room, all eyes turning on him in rapt attention. He cringed, recalling the wildflowers in his garden.

He didn't bother to take his seat in the comfortable leather chair at the head of the long table. He stood and got directly to the point.

"I want a complete and thorough background check

done on the Wyrrd family's various businesses and holdings."

Whispers and mumbles rushed around the table.

"I also want you to find out what firm was responsible for the background check done on me."

That statement really caused grumblings.

"I'll handle the check on you," Pierce Knowlin volunteered.

"I appreciate that, Pierce, and I also have something else I want you to concentrate on."

Pierce nodded.

Debra Carter, a middle-aged woman with a quick mind and a sharp tongue, spoke. "This is going to cause a stir."

"She's right," Jim Cheevers agreed. "The Wyrrds are important people, and it isn't going to look good for business if we start poking around in their business."

Sebastian grew irritated. "Correct me if I am wrong, but we are a security firm that deals with people who insist on discretion above everything. After all, this is Washington, D.C."

They all laughed.

"I'm not asking for trade secrets to be divulged. I am interested in simple business matters. What do they own and have partnerships in. An easy request and one that should not take you long."

They were all aware that he meant this was to be given top-priority handling.

"If any of you have any questions or doubts concerning this case, see me, but presently this is all you need to know. Thank you for your attention to this matter, and, Pierce, I wish to speak with you privately."

Everyone departed quietly, each wondering what was going on—but each knowing better than to ask.

Pierce followed Sebastian into his private office, where

Ms. Smithers had fresh coffee and muffins waiting for them.

Pierce sat on the couch helping himself to a cup of coffee and an apple muffin.

Sebastian paced in front of the glass-top cocktail table that held the mouthwatering fare. He got right to the point. "I need you to find out if any of the Wyrrd enterprises are engaged in experiments with hallucinogenic drugs."

Pierce gulped down the mouth full of coffee he had just taken. "What the hell are you talking about?"

Sebastian ran his hand through his hair. "I can't explain the whole matter to you. I just need to know if they have access to drugs that can cause hallucinations."

"Are you sure about this?"

Sebastian raked his hair with his fingers again. He wasn't sure about anything. How the hell did he explain that he sat in the woods for over an hour yesterday and talked with a fairy named Beatrice who sat comfortably on his shoulder the whole time? And that she even had him laughing. If that wasn't hallucinating, he didn't know what was.

"Look, Pierce," he said, finally sitting in the chair opposite the couch. "I don't know what's going on, but I need to get to the truth, and right now my practical side tells me to do what I do best. Research and deduce the information."

"The Wyrrds are a bit eccentric from what I hear."

Sebastian laughed. " 'A bit' is putting it mildly."

"Though I must admit, I have heard only good things about them and the work their foundation does," Pierce said.

"I must agree with you there. The Wyrrd Foundation has helped many a needy person, family, and institution. So I can count on you being discreet?"

Pierce smiled. "I'll knock on their business doors, and they won't even know I'm there."

Pierce finished his coffee and two muffins before their conversation drifted to an end with Pierce promising he would have something for him by the end of the week.

Finally alone, Sebastian sank back in the gray tweed chair and closed his eyes. He had barely slept last night, his thoughts shifting from Alisande to Beatrice as he attempted to make sense of a senseless situation.

He hadn't been drinking, so he couldn't even blame the incident on alcohol. Of course, he had been on edge and concerned about Ali, so perhaps that could have brought on the vision.

Vision.

Now he was having visions. Visions of fairies.

His first thought after returning to his house had been to pick up the phone and call Ali. He felt excited, almost as excited as he had felt as a child when he first met Beatrice.

He shook his head. How had this tiny imp of a creature become so real to him?

But he knew the answer. She had become real as soon as he opened his eyes and saw her standing on his shoulder, her flower head wreath slipping down over her eye, her crooked wing fluttering, and her wide smile lighting her stunning face.

And he couldn't forget her voice, so soft and soothing. He relaxed as he recalled their conversation.

''You have grown into a fine man,'' Beatrice said, walking along his shoulder to tap him on the cheek with her tiny finger. ''What's this I'm hearing that you don't believe in fairies?''

Sebastian closed his eyes.

''Don't think you'll be denying me by not looking at me.''

He opened his eyes quick and looked directly at her.

''That's better,'' she said and plopped down on his

shoulder to sit, swinging her small feet back and forth. "Now tell me the problem."

"You are not real."

That got her dander up, and she pushed at the wreath that sat cockeyed on her head. "What am I, then, if not real?"

"An illusion?"

"Is that a guess or fact?"

He had to smile. She was too precious not to smile at.

"You believed in me when you were just a small boy."

He nodded. "It is easy to believe in fairies, dragons, and such when you're young."

"And have you grown so old and cynical that you don't believe anymore?"

"I have grown older, wiser, and more practical," he admitted, though it sounded more like an excuse than an answer.

"Do you want to believe in me, Sebastian?" she asked, her tiny feet still now and her delicate little hands folded in her lap.

"Yes, I do," he responded without hesitation.

"Then why stop yourself?"

He spoke as if reciting text out of a book: "Fairies are mythical creatures created long ago to entertain children. They do not exist."

"If I don't exist, then who are you talking with?"

He shook his head. It was useless. He had gone completely crazy. His mind had snapped. Rationality was a thing of the past.

Beatrice stood and walked along his shoulder until she came to rest against his face. She patted his cheek softly. "Did you ever stop to think that maybe mortals are the mythical creatures the fairies created to entertain them?"

She walked back along his shoulder, waving her hands in the air. "The woods are my home and the woods have been around far longer than mortals. I am real, Sebastian, and I offer you guidance as I did once before. Do you remember?''

He nodded. ''You told me to follow my heart because my heart would lead me to those I loved and those that loved me.''

''You listened to me then and you found your way home.''

''An impossible task if it wasn't for you.''

Beatrice smiled. ''Because you listened when I told you to. Listen to me now, Sebastian. You are lost again, but one who loves you calls out. Listen and follow, for therein lies your destiny.''

''I'm not lost,'' he insisted.

''You are lost in your own sensibility. Shed it and discover the wonders and mysteries of life,'' she urged with a wide smile and a playful poke to his cheek.

Sebastian opened his eyes, returning himself to his office. What had seemed like an all-too-real visit near twilight on a hot summer's day faded with the dawn of a new day.

Part of him wanted desperately to believe in fairies and witches and, another part warned him against such illogical reasoning. He was no longer a little boy with a childish imagination. He wondered if he ever had been.

A gentle knock on the door brought him fully to his senses as Ms. Smithers quietly entered his office.

''I tried the intercom, but you didn't answer,'' she said, offering an explanation for her intrusion. ''You have an urgent phone call from Sydney Wyrrd.''

Sebastian was out of his seat in a flash and grabbed for the phone on his desk as Ms. Smithers quietly shut the door behind her.

''What's wrong?'' he asked, ignoring formality.

''You must come to the house immediately,'' Sydney informed him quickly and paused, taking an audible breath before saying, ''Alisande is in danger.''

Sixteen

Sebastian entered the living room of the Wyrrd house, acknowledged Sydney's presence with a curt nod, and went straight to Ali, who stood looking out of the French doors that led to the terrace.

His arms circled her waist, and before she could step back into his embrace, he yanked her gently back to press firmly against him. He needed to know she was safe here in his arms where no harm could come to her.

He leaned his head down, pressed his cheek to her temple, and whispered, "Are you all right?"

Her answer sounded more like a whispered plea than a simple yes. And she shivered, not from fear, but from the closeness of him. His strength wrapped around her, his warmth rushed over her, and his concern filled her heart. She snuggled against him, content in his protective embrace.

She sensed he had no intention of letting her go, and she didn't want him to. She fit so perfectly with him that the thought frightened her. They had been made for each other. Two pieces that fit as one.

He felt her shiver, the slight tremble of her body running along his own and his arms tightened around her, wanting to chase away her fears.

She fit so perfectly.

The thought flashed in his mind like a message. A message he didn't need to be reminded of; he already knew all too well that she fit with him. If he were honest with himself he would admit that she had tempted his sensibilities from the first day she had walked into his office and cast her strange spell.

If a love spell it truly was, then it had worked, for at the moment he could think of nothing but how very much he loved her and would do anything to protect her from harm.

"Tell me what's wrong," he said.

"Perhaps I'd best explain," Sydney said, walking up beside them.

Neither Sebastian nor Ali made any attempt to separate and their tenacious clinging brought a smile to Sydney's face.

"Whether you believe in the existence of witches or not, I expect you to listen with an open mind," she said and waited for Sebastian to agree to her terms.

Sebastian nodded. He had faced many strange and frightening situations during his time with *The Department.* He had no doubt he could handle this one.

Sydney continued. "Ali had a visit from an old friend, a powerful male witch named Dagon. He is looking to mate and has chosen Ali. She rejected his proposal, but he has warned her that he will not take no for an answer. He is adamant, stubborn, and entirely too used to having his own way."

Ali almost laughed at the accurate description of Dagon.

Sebastian remained silent for a moment, digesting the information. How was he to handle two women who believed themselves witches with a warlock on their heels?

"This warlock, Dagon—"

Sydney immediately corrected him. "Dagon is no warlock. Warlocks practice the black arts. They are evil in thought and deed, and true witches will have nothing to do with them.''

''Forgive me, I am not familiar with all the particulars of witchcraft.''

''You will learn,'' she said as if she had just decreed it. ''Now I think what would be best is for Ali to stay away from the house for a few days. Someplace where Dagon won't be able to find her. He will grow weary of searching, since he has no patience—''

This brought a grin to Ali's face.

''—and will take himself off to find another more agreeable witch to mate with.''

Sebastian offered a different solution. ''Why don't I have this Dagon thoroughly checked out.''

Ali stiffened in his arms, and he turned her around to face him, his long lean fingers resting intimately on her narrow hips.

''My suggestion disturbs you?'' he asked her.

''No,'' she reluctantly admitted, for if Dagon discovered that Sebastian intended to research his background, there would be no holding his temper. ''I just don't think you will find anything worthwhile.''

''It will make me feel better and give me a better understanding of who I am dealing with,'' he said. He would never place himself in a situation he had not first thoroughly investigated. That would be giving his opponent the upper hand, and that he refused to do.

''By all means, Sebastian, check him out,'' Sydney offered to Ali's surprise. But then Ali realized that her aunt must have been prepared for this turn of events or she would have never agreed so willingly.

''While I am investigating this man, I will have one of my top men assigned to protect you,'' Sebastian said, already calculating in his mind who he would use and a safe place to take her.''

''Oh, no, no, that won't do at all,'' Sydney protested, vehemently. ''You are aware of our unusual background, and we trust you. But a stranger protecting a woman unaware that she is a witch or that a powerful male witch is after her? No, no, that will not do at all. You must protect her yourself. You must not let her out of your sight.''

The thought had crossed his mind but briefly. The consequences of being in close proximity with Ali day and night could not be ignored. And while he had no doubt he loved her, there was still this issue of her being a witch that needed to be addressed and settled once and for all.

Ali ran her hand slowly up his shirt, getting his attention quickly. ''No mere mortal is a match for Dagon. His powers transcend mortal strength.''

Sebastian laughed. ''Are you telling me that I'm no match for this man?''

''Witch,'' she corrected. *Say it, please say it. Admit that witches are real. Admit you believe.*

''Whatever,'' he said, annoyed that she should think so little of his own strength and courage, and sounding as though she actually admired this man who was on a hunt for her.

Ali sensed his hurt and it pained her that she had caused him to suffer. Her love for him was growing strong, so strong that she was attuned to his every emotion.

''You are a strong, capable mortal, but he is a *witch*,'' she said, attempting to make him understand and openly admit that there was a difference between them.

Sebastian held his tongue. Witches didn't exist. They were not real. So why all this high drama? What were these two women really up to?

Sydney finally interrupted with a demand. ''I must insist you take my niece home with you at least for one night and protect her. I will pay you for your services.''

Sebastian sent her such a scathing look that she actually

took a step back. "Don't insult me, Ms. Wyrrd. I will protect Ali because I care for her, not for money."

Ali beamed with joy and hope. *Perhaps things would turn out all right after all.*

"Forgive me," Sydney said sincerely and with a knowing smile. "I did not mean to offend you."

"Your niece is welcome to stay at my home tonight. In the meantime I will personally run a background check on this Dagon. But tell me, are you safe from him?"

Sydney laughed. "Dagon wants nothing from me, only from Ali. And witches respect age and the wisdom that comes with it. He would never harm me."

Sebastian had to ask. "How old is this Dagon?"

"Around three hundred years, give or take a few," Sydney answered.

"He should have an interesting history to track down," Sebastian said with a tone that held a note of skepticism to it.

"His most interesting history you won't find in any files or records," Sydney said. "But Ali can tell you about him; they grew up together."

That statement brought a swift turn of his head toward Ali.

"I better pack a bag for the evening," she said and gave him a quick kiss on the cheek before scurrying out of the room in haste.

Sebastian couldn't help but notice her bare feet. He could have sworn he heard the tiny tinkle of her toe bell, and he knew then and there he was in serious trouble.

Upon Ali's exit the housekeeper entered with a large silver tray. Mint iced tea, finger sandwiches, and miniature pastries were served.

Sebastian joined Sydney on the soft blue and ivory silk striped couch and graciously accepted the Waterford crystal iced-tea glass she had filled for him.

"The truth, Sydney," he said calmly when they were finally alone.

"She needs you," she answered bluntly. "And since I am being candid, you need her."

"I won't deny that, but there still remains a problem."

"That you refuse to accept who she is, a warm, loving intelligent—"

"Witch?"

Sydney was all too aware of the perimeters of the spell, and she dared not step beyond them. They were already too tenuous.

"You said you care for Ali."

"Very much," he assured her.

"Why do you care?"

He looked at her strangely.

"It is not an odd question. If you care or love someone, there is usually something special that attracts you. What is special about Ali?"

"She's different from any other woman I have known."

"How?"

He smiled. "She's audacious in everything she does."

"Like walking into your office unannounced?"

His smile spread to a grin. "She really threw me for a loop that day."

"Couldn't get her out of your mind, could you?"

"No, she haunted my dreams day and night."

Sydney nodded. "She has a way of doing that."

"She fills my thoughts constantly."

"And do you think you feel this way because of the spell she cast on you?" she asked.

Sebastian stared at her incredulously. "You've got to be kidding. No one can make another person love them simply by chanting a few words." *Could they?*

"Then why not accept her for who she is?"

"That's just it, who is she?" he asked. The question so simple, yet the answer so elusive.

"You have two choices," Sydney said. "You either believe she is who she says—"

"A witch."

Sydney nodded. "Or you believe she is a crazy eccentric. The choice is yours and yours alone, Sebastian."

"And this Dagon?"

"Again the choice is yours. Whatever you choose to believe about Ali, you believe about Dagon."

"So he could be a crazy eccentric, too."

Sydney shrugged. "The decision will be yours." She reached out and lightly squeezed his hand. "Whatever you do, Sebastian, listen to your heart, for then and only then will you know the truth."

He felt a tingle of apprehension run over him. "Are you telling me to avoid being reasonable in this matter?"

"Reason will not help you when it comes to Ali. Opcning your heart is the only way you will see the truth."

"Love can often blind," he said.

She laughed softly. "True love never blinds, it reveals all."

"I'm ready," Ali announced, entering the room with a bulging tote bag in hand.

Sebastian stood and walked over to her, admiring her long slim legs partially covered by white shorts and a cropped white knit top that he wouldn't dare allow her to wear out in public if she was his wife. Her long hair was pinned up, her stunning face was clear of makeup except for a rose blush that tinted her lips, and she wore simple white sandals.

She was out to get him, and with that battle gear she just might get him to surrender.

He took the bag from her hand and leaned down to whisper in her ear. "You're not going to behave are you?"

She licked her lips with that sweet little tongue of hers. "Do you want me to?"

"What if I said yes?"

She laughed and shook her head, several long blond strands falling free around her face.

"That's what I thought," he said and grabbed her hand and wondered how the hell he was ever going to handle her tonight. With great care or with great passion?

He turned his attention to Sydney. "I'll be in touch."

With quick goodbyes they were off.

Ali suggested they stop at a grocery store so she could pick up a few things and cook him supper.

Recalling his dream of her in his kitchen and taking another look at her outfit, he shook his head. "I'll cook."

"I can cook," she insisted, confident that she had practiced the chicken recipe well enough with Adele that she wouldn't make any mistakes.

"Another time. Besides, I want you to tell me all you can about this Dagon fellow. Concentrate and think on it and don't leave anything out. Even the smallest scrap of information could prove vital."

Ali didn't want to talk about Dagon and had no intention of talking about him, but then she was confident she could easily distract Sebastian, starting now.

She casually kicked off her sandals and crossed her legs, resting her foot with the toe ring near his knee. She pretended to study the passing countryside as if she had not a care in the world while she slowly bounced her foot up and down, grazing his knee every now and then.

He knew what she was up to and he tried, lord how he tried to ignore that slim leg, trim ankle, and toe ring that tinkled with each deliberate bounce.

But he was a man, a mere mortal at that and she? She was a captivating witch bent on seducing him.

He loosened his tie and turned up the air-conditioning. That brought a smile to her face, and she moved her foot just a fraction closer.

They hit a bump and he cursed his driving and her as her foot rubbed along his thigh. And still she looked out that damn window pretending innocence.

A few more streets and they would be home, just a few, not many, and then they caught a stoplight and Sebastian against his better judgment glanced down at her leg.

Long, slim, smooth with a delicate splatter of freckles along her slender ankle. His hand slowly reached out and was just about to trace the swirling freckles when a blast from the car horn behind him jolted him back to his senses, and he looked to see the light had turned green.

He mumbled a curse beneath his breath and refused to look at her. When they arrived at his home, she followed a grumbling Sebastian inside. He stormed down the hall into a room and tossed her tote on the single bed.

"This is where you will sleep." he instructed sternly.

She smiled, shook her head, turned, and with a sway to her hips he could only term lethal, she walked away from him.

Seventeen

Sebastian sat staring at the image on his computer screen. This Dagon fellow was not only a good-looking man, but a powerful businessman of immense wealth. He owned various companies on the East and West coasts and quite a few overseas. He was of Celtic descent, and as with Ali, Sebastian could find no record of birth, though his educational history was available and impressive.

The few phone calls he had made confirmed most of the information he had discovered through his computer and through an intricate search system Wainwright Security had implemented.

Sebastian saw nothing in the information that would lead him to believe that this Dagon was anyone other than who he appeared to be, a wealthy businessman. Which meant the key to this whole issue was Alisande.

He left his home office and went in search of her, the one person who could provide him with the pertinent information concerning Dagon.

He found her in the gathering room, snuggled comfortably on his couch reading a mystery. She still wore that temptress outfit and her feet were bare, though tucked partially beneath her. At least that blasted toe ring wasn't visible.

He had changed out of his suit into khaki shorts and a white knit shirt. A casual and relaxing attire. And he liked the picture of the happily married couple that they portrayed. It made him think how nice married life could actually be, though with Ali he wondered if it could ever be normal.

"I thought we would barbecue," he said, entering the room. Information was more easily disclosed when a person was relaxed, and besides he found the idea of spending a casual evening alone with her appealing.

Casual and alone?

The two words were not synonymous. He needed to ditch the *casual* and concentrate on the *alone* because he somehow got the feeling that the word would go well with *temptation* and possibly *surrender.*

Ali smiled her approval. "How delightful."

While she had attended many functions where barbecues took place, she never participated in the actual barbecue itself, but there was always a first time. "Can I help?"

He gave that question serious thought, thinking where in the kitchen she would cause the least chaos. "Can you make a salad?"

"Yes," she said, excited. Adele, after countless attempts at trying to teach her how to cook, had insisted she learn to make a good salad, explaining that she could make a passable meal if she could make a basic salad. Bless her.

Sebastian was impressed by her enthusiasm over such a simple chore. "Good, you can make the salad while I prepare the chicken and potatoes for the grill."

To Sebastian's surprise and bewilderment, Ali helped him gather all the necessary items with the ease of someone who was familiar with his kitchen.

He took great care to keep a safe distance from her, though she managed, with surprising innocence, to brush intimately against him several times or reach around him or downright torment the hell out of him with her teasing and deliberate actions.

He decided a good conversation about Dagon just might take the wind out of her sails, and he was pleased to see her respond exactly as he expected. "So tell me about Dagon."

Her hands stilled in the process of tearing the lettuce leaves and she sighed. It was a soft, fleeting sigh, barely audible, but he heard it.

"What do you want to know?"

Sebastian shrugged his shoulders as if it didn't matter, though it did. He wanted to know everything, including how she felt about this questionable man.

He continued to prepare the honey-based marinade and decided on a simple question to start. "How do you know him?"

"Our families have long been friends."

"So you were childhood friends?"

"We spent some time together in our youth," she admitted. *One hundred years to be exact.* But she couldn't very well admit that.

He was on top of her every response. "Which means you attended school with him in Ireland."

"Only part of the time," she said. "Mother and father love to travel, and Dagon's parents often looked after me, especially if Aunt Sydney was off on her own adventure."

"Was he always a bully?"

"Dagon never bullied, he intimidated," she said, happy memories bringing a smile to her face.

"You admire him," he said, surprised by her obvious respect for the man.

"He is special to me."

"Then why not mate with him and solve your problem and his?"

Ali was surprised and pleased by his irritated response,

and her reply did little to alleviate his annoyance. "Dagon has never lacked for female companionship, and his powers presently far outweigh mine."

Sebastian attacked the potatoes with the peeler taking his frustration out with every jabbing stroke. "So he wants to jump-start you?"

Ali laughed at his analogy.

Her amusement irritated him all the more, and he continued to unmercifully attack the potatoes.

She tilted her head to study him, so intent in his actions and yet so removed from them. The fading light of early evening spilled softly through the windows and across his strong features.

He was simply stunning. His jaw was taut, his lips pursed, his brows angled in annoyance, and his nostrils flared ever so slightly in anger. His temper and jealousy, though contained, were a compelling sight to behold.

"You haven't answered my question," Sebastian said and looked directly at her, causing their glances to lock.

"What question?"

"Why Dagon wants you."

"He just thinks he wants me," she said and took a step away from him, needing space, needing to catch her breath and control the rapid beating of her heart.

"What does he want?"

She walked around the counter and calmed her breathing before answering him. "What you want."

He looked at her oddly, dropping the peeler to the sink, and washed and dried his hands. "What do I want?"

She stepped into dangerous yet necessary territory with her answer. "Love."

He walked slowly toward her, rounding the counter in measured strides. "So Dagon and I search for love?"

Control. Where was her control? Her heart hammered,

her stomach fluttered, and her voice sounded barely audible. ''Dagon will find love soon enough.''

Sebastian stepped forward, placing himself a mere inch away from her. ''You know this for a fact?''

She knew for a fact that the intimate nearness of him was going to make her do something completely outrageous if she wasn't careful. But then, she hated being careful.

''Aunt Sydney is a powerful seer. She is well aware of Dagon's future. He will love, but not love whom he expects.''

She felt the sudden relief that flooded his emotions, and the intimate sensation ran over her like gentle fingers stroking her bare skin.

''And does she know your future?''

Ali shook her head, fighting the urge to reach out and touch him. ''She cannot see mine.''

''Why?''

''I took my future in my own hands when I cast the spell on you. She cannot interfere with that spell.''

Sebastian reached out and tenderly brushed a stray strand of hair off her face, his fingers faintly whispering across her cheek.

Ali felt the shiver clear to her toes, the tiny toe bell responding with a faint chime.

''We have much to discuss, Alisande,'' he said, his hand slipping to the back of her neck to draw her close to him as his mouth reached down to meet hers.

Before she could reply, his lips descended on hers softly, patiently, and powerfully. He stole what little breath she had, released her briefly, sighed with satisfaction, and then descended on her lips once again.

His taste was pure magic, his tongue mating in gentle demand with hers. He took complete command and she freely surrendered to his enchanted skill.

His lips ran anxiously over her chin, down her throat,

and back up again, and as he nibbled hungrily on her lips he whispered, "I can't get enough of you. I always want more and more."

"Then take me, Sebastian, take me for who I am," she pleaded, her need for him so strong that she felt the empty ache down to her soul.

His hand remained firm on her neck, and he slowly rested his forehead against hers. "Who are you?"

"Who do you think I am?" she asked, hopefully.

"A crazy woman who believes she is a witch," he said with honesty.

Ali stepped away from him. "And who are you, Sebastian?"

He shook his head and smiled. "A man who wants to believe in crazy witches."

At that moment Ali sensed if she reached out to him, he would surrender to her, but she needed him to understand more. She needed him to understand her and the consequences of their actions. This was one time she did not intend to leap without looking.

"I'm hungry," she said.

His smile grew wicked. "So am I."

One step and she could be in his arms. One simple step and she would have—what? His love of a crazy woman who thought herself a witch?

She wagged a finger at him. "I'll light the barbecue."

"With your finger?" he asked with a laugh.

She stuck her tongue out at him as she walked out the sliding-glass doors.

He shook his head again. Damn, but he had to stop doing that, and walked around the counter to get the striker he used to start the grill.

"Here," he said, joining her on the deck and stopped short.

"All done," she said and blew at her finger as if it had emitted a flame and needed extinguishing.

He was about to shake his head and thought better of it. "This is definitely going to be an interesting evening."

Dusk covered the land, the last faint glows of the sun fading away reluctantly. Dagon sat with Sydney on the terrace enjoying a glass of white wine while they waited for supper.

"Ali loves him," he said.

Sydney agreed. "Yes, she has wanted to love for a long time now."

"That is why she waited to mate."

"Ali never wanted to settle. She wanted someone special. Someone to love and accept her for who she is."

Dagon nodded his understanding. "That is why she used the magical love spell. All or nothing."

"Does Ali do anything any other way?" Sydney said with a laugh.

"In a way I can't blame her," he said, his envy obvious in his tone. "To have someone love you faults and all is a rare quality."

"Is that what you look for, Dagon?"

He laughed and shook his head slowly. "I intend to find a female witch as strong or stronger in power than myself. I will settle for nothing less."

"No mere mortal?"

He laughed even harder. "Never. I could not tolerate a mortal woman. They cry, demand, and are weak-willed. I want one of my own kind. Strong in nature, wise, and passionate. There is nothing like a passionate witch."

Sydney laughed this time. "Be careful of what you wish for, my dear boy."

"I am not wishing. I intend to have what I want."

"Like Ali?"

He grew annoyed. "I will not place myself in a precarious position such as she has done."

"She has taken a chance."

"Chance?" Dagon said raising his voice and almost jumping out of his chair. He paced back and forth on the flagstones in front of Sydney. "She was foolish, absolutely foolish."

Sydney defended her niece. "She felt love would conquer all."

"Hah."

"You don't believe love is so strong it conquers?"

He stopped in front of her. "Ali believes that this mortal male will love her so much that he will accept who she is, a witch. A witch with extraordinary powers. And they will live happily ever after."

"And you don't believe in happily ever after?"

Dagon closed his eyes briefly as if holding back the inevitable. "He will make love to her, of that I have no doubt, but when he finally sees and admits who she truly is, I fear he will not be able to accept her uniqueness. And then all will be lost to her."

"She made the choice."

He nodded. "A foolish choice. According to this ancient spell, she will never be able to love another so strongly, and he will be lost to her forever. She will not even be a faded memory to him. She will be erased from his mind and his heart."

"The choice will be his, Dagon. If he truly loves her, then his love will conquer the spell. If not, then he never truly loved her at all. Ali aches for such a powerful love and would be satisfied with nothing less."

"The fool will probably think that it was the spell that made him fall in love with her."

"Let us hope he is wiser," Sydney said, "and realizes that the spell is cast to test the power of love."

"She should have mated with this mortal, enjoyed him, and moved on."

"That is not love," she argued.

"Love is impossible to hold on to," he insisted.

"Love should never be imprisoned."

"Love is painful."

"Love is joy."

"Love is damn hard to find," he said frustrated.

"Love finds you."

Dagon returned to his chair and looked to Sydney for an answer to a question that had long disturbed him. "Does everyone find love?"

"Yes," she said with a patient smile, "but too often many are blind to it."

"Not so Ali," Dagon said with envy. "She knew love when she saw it and allowed nothing to stop her from getting it."

"She is a stubborn and determined one."

Dagon laughed and held his glass up in a salute. "Then here's to Sebastian Wainwright. He is going to need all the help he can get."

Eighteen

Ali sat tucked in the corner of the couch, finishing a cup of honey-lemon tea. Supper had gone well. Conversation had been kept to the ordinary. She now needed to step beyond the mundane and take a chance. A chance that could cost her dearly.

An oak end table separated the couch and chair where Sebastian sat, his thoughts on Ali.

"It is time we talked," he said, "and strangely enough I sense you feel the same."

If only he would rely more on his senses, but then, would he understand what he felt? Would he fully comprehend this connection between them, or would he seek a reasonable answer?

She nodded her agreement. It was all or nothing, she could wait no longer. "Yes, Sebastian, the time has come."

She made it sound so final, as if their actions this night would decide their fate. And the strange thought that he might lose her filled him with a sudden dread.

"Do you believe in destiny?" she asked.

His brief smile betrayed his skepticism. "Destiny is merely an accumulation of foolish or unwise decisions."

"A sensible response."

With a slight bow of his head Sebastian graciously accepted her compliment. Sound reasoning had its advantage.

"And what is your destiny, Sebastian?"

He didn't hesitate in his answer. "To believe in crazy witches."

"Do you believe?"

This time he did hesitate. "A few short weeks ago my belief system was firmly rooted. Now I find myself questioning the impossible."

"Have you found answers?"

"I think the question should be, have I found any sensible answers?"

Ali laughed and put her empty mug on the coffee table. "Perhaps you search too hard."

He looked directly at her. "Perhaps I don't search hard enough. You sit here before me, a woman in her late twenties possible early thirties, yet have no birth certificate to confirm you were ever born. You are clearly highly educated, and yet no record of an extensive education exists. You come from a wealthy, eccentric family whose heritage dates back to the ancient Celts, and yet certain documents confirming this are unattainable. So as I asked you many times before, who are you Alisande Wyrrd?"

The truth. He wanted to hear the truth as much as she wanted him to accept the truth. The truth would decide the outcome of this spell. The truth would bind them together or separate them for all eternity.

She held her head up with pride and answered with honesty. "I am a witch born of a witch. My heritage is ancient and my powers great. Can you accept this about me?"

A chill raced over him and he stood, pacing the floor in front of the couch until he stopped and his dark, troubled eyes met hers. They questioned, they pleaded, they loved. "You actually believe you are a witch?"

"I am a witch, Sebastian," she said patiently.

How did he respond to that? How did he accept what he

thought impossible? And most of all, how could he feel this passionate about a crazy woman?

"I am not crazy, Sebastian."

He glared at her. "My thoughts are private."

"Not now. Not when we need to understand each other. I read your thoughts clearly because I care so deeply for you. That is why you are able to read mine—"

"I cannot read your thoughts," he protested. The idea was simply preposterous. Outrageous in its presumption. He had no such abilities, nor would he ever.

"You can and you have. Still your thoughts, listen, and you will have your answers."

Sebastian remained silent and heard nothing but endless silence. He was about to shake his head when he thought he heard a whisper. He closed his eyes and focused on the soft sound, not straining to hear, simply listening.

We are part of each other, you and I.

His eyes popped open and he stared at her. "You play tricks, Alisande."

"No, I open myself to you."

He felt her disappointment in his rejection, and it hurt him to know he caused her pain. It was a strange sensation being able to connect so strongly with her emotions. Strangely passionate.

"This is ridiculous," he said, his practical side rearing its intolerable head.

"Why? Does it frighten you to be so intimately connected with a person that you can feel their every emotion?"

"It is an intrusion," he insisted, once again his sensible side answering.

"You cannot intrude where you are welcome."

She had an answer for everything, which disturbed him all the more since she made sense in an odd sort of way. Which led him to say, "Start at the beginning, Alisande."

She nodded and smiled, taking this chance to once again make him understand and accept. "I am a witch who needed to mate to restore my dwindling powers. I chose you, and when our eyes met I knew that only a special magical spell would do. You resisted at every turn, fighting the dreams, fighting your attraction, fighting what you did not understand. Dagon provided me with an opportunity that would cause a confrontation and a decision. Are you ready to make that decision?"

"Dagon was a ploy? Never your nemesis? Never your destiny?"

Alisande stood and walked over to him. "Need I remind you of your own words? Destiny is an accumulation of foolish or wise choices. I have chosen wisely. I have chosen you. Have you chosen?"

"I think I am about to," he whispered as she stopped directly in front of him.

She looked up at him, her green eyes brilliant in their intense color. "In your choice lies your destiny."

"Nothing like a bit of pressure to help the decision process," he said teasingly.

She ran her hand in a light, yet tempting touch down along his arm, to his hand, taking it in hers and bringing it to rest against her breast over her heart. "You have my heart, but our souls are yet to touch."

She raised her lips to his but his hand gently grasped her chin. "You have tormented me since we first met."

"The choice was and still is yours."

"I want more," he murmured and brushed his lips over hers.

"I will give you all I can," she said, her mouth yearning for his.

He would not allow her to taste him, not yet. "I want magic. I want to feel it all, share it all, and I want the same from you."

"I think you ask for the magic of love," she said softly.

He ran his lips across hers lingering, teasing, tempting. "Are you willing to give it?"

She eased her chin from his grasp and whispered as her lips skimmed across his. "You have always had it."

"I must be crazy to even consider—"

"Taking a witch to your bed?"

He grasped her by the arms and gave her a gentle shake. "You will cast no spells, sprinkle no dust, wag no finger."

"Magical love requires no such help."

He shook his head. "I must be crazy."

She stepped back and held her hand out to him. "Feel what I feel, Sebastian."

He took her hand without question. Her touch was gentle and warm, and a tingle rippled up his arm spreading slowly, patiently, like a ripple often does until it encompasses all it surrounds. Heat followed, a tender warmth that tickled his skin and turned it hot. So hot that every sensation in his body was magnified. His heart raced wildly, his pulse beat erratically and his breath caught in his chest, leaving him almost breathless. This was Ali's passion. This is what she was feeling.

An involuntary moan escaped his lips, and he pulled Ali against him, his arms locking around her. "This is what you feel for me?" he asked incredulously.

She buried her face in his chest, attempting to control the unbridled desire that ran through her. "This is how *you* make me feel."

"It hurts," he said, his breath short and rapid.

"Then end my torture," she pleaded, tilting her head back to look into his dark eyes filled with her unrequited passion.

Denying himself was a brief consideration, denying her was not an option. He swung her up into his arms and with a quick, urgent kiss to her waiting lips, he carried her off to his bedroom.

He set her down by the bottom of the king-size bed and stepped away to turn on the single light next to the bed.

"No," he said abruptly, seeing her about to undress. "I want to take your clothes off piece by piece. You are a gift I will enjoy unwrapping."

He walked over to her, ridding himself of his shirt and tossing it to the chair as he went.

"I don't get to unwrap you?" she asked, disappointed, her eyes admiring his taut chest and her fingers anxious to free him of his shorts.

He shook his head and slowly ran his hands beneath her white top. "You are *my* gift."

"And you're mine—" she gasped when his fingers unsnapped the front of her bra and gently cupped and squeezed her full breasts.

"One gift per person, per night," he instructed, playfully, his thumbs teasing her nipples.

Speech was difficult, though she attempted a response. "Then tomorrow night—oh!" She gasped again, his tongue having replaced his thumbs.

He pulled her shirt over her head, tossing it aside along with her bra. His tongue continued its erotic play while his hands worked on the button and zipper to her shorts.

Her short gasps and lingering moans heightened his already raging passion not to mention the taste of her nipples so warm and responsive against his tongue.

He moved his mouth over hers in a rushed kiss, giving her no time to taste him. Instead his lips brushed near her ear, and his whisper sounded like a harsh urging so great was his own need for her. "I'm going to touch you intimately."

With that said his hand stroked down along the band of her shorts, past the open zipper, and beneath her white silk panties. Slowly his fingers moved along her stomach and down over her soft mound to come to rest between her legs.

"Are you ready, Ali?" he murmured, his breath warm against her face.

Anticipation raced goosebumps across her sensitive flesh, and she found herself speechless, her answer coming in the form of a shiver.

He laughed with a teasing softness as his finger gently worked its way inside her, his free hand tenderly forcing her legs to part wider for him.

His breath grew rapid in her ear and matched her own wild breathing. "So wet. So beautiful. I want to feel more of you."

And with deliberate slowness, yet exquisite skill, he inserted another finger.

Ali couldn't think, could barely breathe, especially when his thumb explored and discovered her tiny nub of intimacy, coaxing the little bud to life.

Her head collapsed on his chest, and after several more strokes that turned her legs to jelly, he stopped, lifted her in his arms, and gently laid her on the bed. He then proceeded to divest her of her shorts and panties.

She lay naked, subdued by passion. She watched him discard his remaining clothes and she sighed at the naked sight of him. He was simply magnificent. He possessed tight, round buttocks, firm, sturdy legs, a slim waist, a defined chest, and a manhood that brought a wide smile of admiration to her lips.

"You drive me insane," he said, moving over her.

His skin was hot and his arousal hard against her. His passion raged on the brink of explosion, and she sensed the battle he fought to control it so that he could bring her pleasure.

"I want to feel *you*," she said with a soft urgency.

He obliged her without question, raising himself slightly off her and rubbing intimately against her.

She lifted her body in invitation, and his strokes grew bolder.

He dropped his mouth to hers, capturing a fleeting kiss.

"You torment me!" she cried as he pulled away before she could taste him.

"I like to play, *punish*, pleasure," he said with a wicked grin and reached for her mouth again.

A swift taste was all she got before his mouth descended on her nipple. Quick nips, a lingering tongue, and the sensitive bud disappeared entirely into his mouth where he continued to have his way with it.

Ali moaned with pleasure, and wanting to give the same in return, she slipped her hand down his body, exploring slowly and teasingly until she grasped a firm, intimate hold on him. And then she squeezed.

He groaned and swore savagely at her tenacious capture.

She laughed and nipped lovingly at his slim lips swollen with passion. She relished in the lust-filled taste of him.

"You will pay for that, you witch," he said and kissed her with a harshness bordering on punishment. A punishment that they both favored.

Their passion surged, their touches turned frantic, demanding, impatient. Their need so long denied had turned into a driving force that knew no boundaries. Their bodies soared beyond reason, past sanity, to the brink of magic.

And before they could take that step beyond, Ali had to make certain he understood who she was.

She whispered breathlessly in his ear, "I am a witch."

Sebastian took her mouth with an angry hunger, but not before saying, "I know. You're *my* witch."

Nineteen

My witch.

The words echoed in her thoughts briefly. There was no time to comprehend his meaning. She was lost in passion, in her love for this mortal man.

He moved to lock her fingers with his and she protested.

''I want to touch you as you enter me,'' she said, her hand making its way down his waist to once again rest intimately over him.

He shook his head. ''Not a shred of sanity do I have left.''

She grinned, her hand stroking him and her body moving invitingly against him.

He indulged her and himself with brief, short strokes until she reiterated with a demand of her own.

Passion warring, he reached down, firmly placing his hand over hers. ''Playtime is over.''

With his hand locked over hers, he forced her to join him as he slowly moved to enter her. They moaned simultaneously, their fingers locking and sliding away together from where their bodies continued to join as one.

The magic took over from there. Magic as old as time. Magic that consumed and devoured. And soon reason and sanity were completely stripped away and they found themselves lost. Lost in the magic of love.

Time lost all reality. There was only the two of them forever united by this special union. Their bodies blended as one, their tempo frenzied, their desires raging.

Her head tilted back, her fingers dug into his arms, and she cried out her release with his name spilling in agonizing pleasure from her lips.

He joined her, their elated cries circling above them and bursting to rain down over them as they spiraled like mating eagles to the earth and back to reality and the consequences of their union.

Ali lay replete and complete in his arms. Sebastian had rolled off her and pulled her against him, their breathing still rapid and their bodies damp and exhausted.

She relished this quiet moment in his arms. Words weren't necessary. His touch was and he gave of it freely, his hand stroking her arm and his leg draped over her. She was content to lay like this—

The surge ran through her like energy gone wild, and her body jolted against the surprise attack.

"What's wrong?" he asked, concerned, his hand rushing down over her stomach. "Are you in pain?"

"No," she lied. "A sudden chill."

He wasted no time in seeing to her need. He reached down, dragging the sheet and blanket that had been shoved to the end of the bed up and over them.

"Better?"

"Much," she said, snuggling back in the crook of his waiting arms. And waiting, this time prepared for the second wave of energy that would hit her momentarily.

She had completely forgotten about her returning energy. She should have been prepared, but then she hadn't expected the surge to be that powerful, at least not the first time.

Their union had generated more energy than she had anticipated.

The second surge started with a tingling numbness in her feet and rushed like a bolt of electricity straight through her.

She smiled with the joy it brought her, and she cuddled closer to Sebastian. He had given her more than he would ever know tonight, and she was forever grateful and forever in love.

The surges would continue for the next few hours until the last one, which would feel more like a gentle lapping wave, and then it would be done. Her powers would be fully restored, and she would once again be herself. An empowered witch.

Sebastian turned, rolling Ali on her back. He looked her directly in her stunning green eyes, their usual brilliance softened by their lovemaking, and he slowly ran a finger gently down her cheek. "You are not only a beautiful woman, you are an extraordinary lover."

His sincere words brought a smile of pleasure to her lips. She raised her hand to stroke his brow, caress his cheek, and skim his lips. "You, my dear man, are unique."

"How so?" he asked, capturing her finger with his lips to taste briefly and release it.

She grinned at his playfulness and at the surge of energy that raced over her. "You make magic."

"And magic is special."

"You learn quickly," she said, hoping he spoke the truth, hoping he believed.

His tone turned serious. "I know what we have is special."

"Very special," she agreed.

He had not expected this tenacious possessiveness to take

such a powerful hold of him. He only knew that he wanted Ali forever and always. He had never made love and felt so completely connected with a woman. It was as though she were part of him and he part of her and that neither could survive without the other.

Was this true love? This feeling of need so compelling it bordered on pain? Or was it as Ali said, *magic*?

That word returned him with a sharp suddenness to the reality of the situation.

Ali took his face in her hands. "Tonight, Sebastian, there is only you and I. The world doesn't exist."

She was asking him for one night. One night when nothing mattered but them.

He smiled and whispered in her ear, "Let's make magic."

They were sitting on the floor naked, Sebastian's back braced against the end of the bed and Ali resting comfortably between his legs, her back against his chest. A bright yellow tablecloth was spread out in front of them, and the remanent of a well-enjoyed snack of chunks of various cheeses, an assortment of fruits, and a loaf of French bread sat on plates. A bottle of Merlot sat empty as the two lovers sipped the last glasses of the fine wine.

"Are you always so hungry after making love?" he teased. "Because I'll be certain to keep my refrigerator full."

She playfully pinched his leg. "It takes energy to make magic three times in one night." She was afraid to admit to him that her resurgence of powers also generated her outrageous appetite.

He laughed, discarded his empty glass, and slipped his hands around her waist to slowly run down her stomach and settle intimately between her legs. "The night is still young."

Ali cuddled back against him, wishing she could hold on to this one night forever. The last few hours had been magic. They made love, laughed, napped, ate, joked and never once spoke of reason or witches. They lived in a magical world where only they existed. And they had a few precious hours left, she didn't want to waste a minute.

"Only two in the morning."

"So much time," he whispered, nibbling along her neck.

"All the time in the world," she agreed and gasped when he began to intimately explore her.

Ali lay sleeping against him, her naked body damp and blushed from their recent bout of lovemaking. He had not been able to get enough of her. With each fiery climax he thought himself finished, replete, and then she would touch him, kiss him, or he would touch her, and all would be lost once again.

He had surrendered his soul to this woman and she to him. He loved her more than he ever thought possible, more than he believed was ever possible, and he knew, actually felt, her intense love for him. It was crazy but wonderful.

But what if—

He refused to think about *what-ifs.* Tonight was time for magic, not logic. Tomorrow would be soon enough to face reality. But practicality reared its impatient head, and he allowed himself to reason for a moment, only a moment. If she was a witch—a preposterous idea but one he considered—then her powers would have been restored from all their frantic lovemaking. Yet here she lay quietly sleeping. No flying objects, no flying people, no strange occurrences, so reason would lead him to believe that perhaps she was a bit eccentric. Eccentric he could deal with.

He looked at her and smiled, feeling relieved.

She stretched; she did that often in her sleep, slow like a cat, each limb reaching out, her back arching.

He groaned. Damn if he didn't want her again. He ordered himself not to touch her. They had made love so many times, she was sure to be sore and yet . . .

His hands itched to touch her, stroke her. Once. Just once. His hand reached out, starting at her throat and working his way slowly, lovingly down her responsive body.

"Sebastian," she sighed softly.

"Yes, love?" he asked, kissing her gently while his hands continued to explore her.

"Not fair," she protested with a groan. "I want my turn on you."

"Tomorrow, love. Tomorrow I'm all yours," he promised with a kiss.

"Tomorrow," she repeated in a whisper and surrendered to his exquisite touch.

It was near five in the morning when Ali slipped out of bed. Her energy had been completed restored, the last wave of power filling her only an hour ago. She was fully charged to say the least and needed to balance and ground her energy before it took charge of her.

She quietly left the bedroom, leaving an exhausted Sebastian to his deep slumber. It was better he didn't know, better to wait and introduce him to her skills slowly so he could accept more easily.

She stopped still in her tracks halfway across the gathering room.

Practical.

When had she begun to reason and think with a logical mind. Time was a commodity she didn't have much of if the spell were to work to her advantage. Either he accepted who she was or he didn't.

She shook her head. Acceptance had nothing to do with it. Love was the key to the spell. How strong was his love for her?

She hurried out the sliding-glass doors, making certain to disengage the security alarm first. She rushed down the deck and rejoiced when her bare feet touched the grass.

She raised her hands to the heavens and called down a white light to swirl in circles around her, clearing and defining her energy. It filled her with delight, this presence of being welcomed home. This uniting of energy that solidly connected her to the Mother Earth and to the richness of life.

When she finally felt full, complete, and renewed, she sent a prayer of thanks to the Mother Sky.

With that done she plopped down and rolled like a child in play in the green, healthy blades of grass, their nutrients nourishing her and grounding her even more to the Mother Earth.

It felt so good, so refreshing. It felt as if she had returned home to a loving family's eager arms. She giggled and laughed and rolled over and over, the strong, green blades poking, prodding, and tickling her.

She settled on her back and stretched her arms up to the dark night sky, her fingers eagerly plucking at the faraway stars as if in an attempt to capture one.

She giggled and laughed like a child at play thoroughly absorbed in the energy of the Mother Earth and her worldly magic.

Sebastian stood at the sliding-glass doors watching her. He had been startled out of a sound sleep by a sharp voice that ordered him to wake up. When he saw Ali was gone, he immediately went in search of her. And he had found her almost by instinct. He knew where she would be. How he knew? That was a confusing revelation to him, but he knew she would be outside.

He had spotted her, the distinct light from the half-moon shining down as if in a spotlight upon her. She rolled with joy in the thick carpet of green grass as if she had not a care in the world. It mattered not to her that she was naked in his backyard. And hadn't he bought the property with privacy in mind and for a similar reason? He had given thought to swimming naked with his future wife in his indoor pool, and the surrounding woods provided him with just such privacy.

Of course making love on the grass under the stars was another matter. A matter of feeling free enough to dare such a tempting stunt.

Free.

Ali possessed a freedom many searched for but few found. And at the moment he wanted nothing more than to join her in that autonomy. Tomorrow was soon enough to think of his actions. To recall that he, Sebastian Wainwright, CEO of Wainwright Security, walked naked out onto his deck at five in the morning and cavorted with the woman he loved in the grass. He quietly opened the sliding-glass doors and stepped out.

Ali felt his presence, had known instinctively he had stood watching her, and had continued to frolic in delight.

Her hand made a quick stab at the sky. "Gotcha."

Sebastian descended the few steps, aware that his presence was known to her.

She turned her head toward him and held out her closed hand. "A gift."

He stopped beside her, her outstretched hand almost touching him, and looked down at her. "What is it?"

Running a quick glance of admiration over the man she so desperately loved and who filled her with endless delight, she said, "It is a star to wish upon."

She waited, anxious to see if he would deny her offering.

He didn't hesitate. He placed his hand over hers and carefully accepted her gift, grasping it in his hand.

"Now make a wish," she urged. "A special wish, Sebastian. A star that falls far enough down from the heavens to be captured holds great magic.''

He needed all the magic he could get. He loved this crazy woman who believed herself a witch, who believed in fairies, who made magical love, and who captured stars from the night sky. He loved her with his heart and soul and wanted to spend eternity with her.

''Hold it close to your heart and wish and know your wish will be granted,'' she said softly.

He brought his hand to his heart, pressed it to his chest, and closed his eyes. *Please, please let me believe.*

Ali smiled as a small burst of white light erupted in his closed hand and spread over his chest fading away as he opened his eyes.

''Did I do well?'' he asked, releasing his grasped hand to fall to his side.

''Perfect. Now you only need to believe, and the wish is forever yours.''

A chill ran over him even though the night was hot and humid. He shook his head slowly, raising it to the night sky, sending a silent prayer for help to the heavens, and turned wide, wanting eyes on her.

She held her hand out to him. ''Come to me, Sebastian.''

He recalled his first dream of her and how she had drifted away from him when he most wanted her. Tonight she would not drift away. Tonight she was his.

He heard the tiny bell chime as his hand slid in hers and he smiled. He lay beside her, her body cool and damp from the grass and so refreshing against his parched skin.

''That bell has driven me crazy,'' he admitted in a teasing whisper.

''That tiny bell has special powers,'' she said, running her leg along his, the little bell chiming softly against his skin.

He played along, but then he loved her strange beliefs, her magic. ''What kind of power?''

''The chime stimulates the senses.''

''By mere touch?''

She shook her head slowly and moved so that she could more easily run her foot along his thigh. ''By command,'' she whispered and slid her foot between his legs.

The tiny bell chimed an erotic note and sent a shaft of pure pleasure shooting through him, though it could have been from the way Ali worked her toes so intimately over him, or a combination of both, or that she simply knew how to drive a man wild with her foot, not to mention the feel of the bell rubbing against his . . .

He moaned. Whatever was the case he didn't care. He didn't care about a damn thing but the tiny bell that chimed a seductive tone in his ears and fired his blood.

His hands frantically grabbed at the blades of grass alongside him, tearing them out from the roots. He told himself he should be touching her in return, driving her as insane as she was driving him. But he couldn't move, couldn't think, could barely breath.

Then he felt her tongue on him, and all was lost.

Night bid welcome to morning as the first rays of daylight began to appear in the sky. Sebastian lay in the grass attempting to regain his breath, his strength, his senses.

Ali lay spread over him listening contentedly to the rapid beating of his heart.

''You are a witch,'' he managed to say. ''And I will repay you in kind for what you did to me.''

She raised her head, smiling with delight. ''Promise?''

He placed a soft, lingering kiss on her lips. ''Promise.''

''I will hold you to that promise,'' she warned.

He had a warning of his own to deliver. ''I must caution you.''

She looked with wide, worried eyes at him.

"Keep that damn toe ring hidden, or I swear to you that I'll ravish you on sight."

She laughed and held up her leg, jiggling her foot. The tiny bell remained silent, and Sebastian stared at her oddly.

"I don't understand? I clearly heard it last night."

"Its powers are mine to command."

He shook his head. "It only chimes when you instruct it to?"

"That's right," she admitted proudly. "So I can drive you crazy whenever it pleases me."

"Where do I get one of those things?" he asked seriously.

"It was a gift from a special person," she explained with a yawn.

He wanted to learn more about this special gift, but the long, sensuous night had finally caught up with them. He felt exhaustion slowly creeping over him.

"We need sleep," he said, gently rolling her off him.

She agreed with a nod and another yawn.

He stood, reached down, and scooped her up into his arms. They entered through the sliding-glass doors, and Sebastian asked her to engage the alarm while he held her.

She did and as he made his way to the bedroom, he realized that he had never told Ali the alarm sequence, yet she had instinctively known it. How?

He yawned as he placed her on the bed, following her down to lay beside her after pulling the covers over them.

He would ask her about the alarm later this morning. He would ask her many things, but he would also tell her . . .

"How very much I love you," he whispered in her ear as he drifted off to sleep.

Twenty

Sebastian woke first, his arms wrapped protectively around Ali. She snuggled comfortably against him as if she had always been there in his arms sleeping, waking, loving.

He didn't stir. He didn't want to disturb her or this magic moment. He smiled. When had magic become so much a part of his life? The answer was simple. When Ali entered it.

Love was truly magical. The entrance of Ali into his life had changed him forever. He could not think of a day without her sharing it. She was part of him, an intricate part whose absence was unthinkable and frightening. He didn't want a life without her.

She had given him a taste of freedom, and he seriously doubted he could ever live his life as rigidly as he had before she stepped into it.

Practical.

There was that side that persisted, but then he could not run his business without being practical. And with Ali possessing such an eccentric nature, she would need some logic in her life. They would do well together. He and his eccentric witch.

She sighed in her sleep, rolled away from him, stretched, and then buried her head beneath her pillow.

He placed a gentle kiss on her shoulder, slipped from the bed, covered her, then started his day with a brisk shower.

It was ten by the time he started the coffeemaker. Being Saturday, there was no need to rush. Faded jeans and a black T-shirt was his casual dress for the day, especially if he planned to work around the house.

He stepped out onto the deck grinning at his thoughts. Today he planned to work on Ali.

It was hot, the sun bright, the air humid, but then, it was mid-August. Too hot outside for his morning repast, not to mention the scandalous memories of his early morning romp on the grass, he decided to return inside to the cool air-conditioned house.

He turned and saw her standing at the sliding-glass door, wearing nothing but his faded blue T-shirt. Her hair was mussed, her skin faintly blushed, and her lips wore a petulant sensual pout that punched him square in the gut.

She pressed her hands flat against the glass. He walked over to her, connecting his hands with hers, the glass warm to his touch.

Feel me. She mouthed the words and yet he heard. Heard as clearly as if she had whispered in his ear. And feel? He felt the cool tingle of her palms against his. He felt the quivering sensation slowly spread up his arms, to his chest, and stab playfully at his heart.

Come to me, Sebastian.

He heard her. Heard her clearly and ignored the fact that he had not seen her lips move. He slid the door open and stepped inside, closing it behind him.

She kissed him softly on one cheek and then the other, and then she kissed him gently on his lips.

"Mmm," she said, sniffing the air. "Hazelnut coffee, my favorite."

He smiled and shook his head.

"Sit and I'll get us some," she said, pushing him into the large overstuffed chair.

He did as she requested, watching her hurry off. He caught a glimpse of her bare backside and shook his head again. This was going to be an active day for them both.

She returned shortly with two mugs, handing him one. "Light, no sugar."

He wasn't going to ask how she knew; by now he accepted the fact that she possessed the uncanny ability to read minds and that was fine. He would do research on the subject to better understand it and in turn understand her.

He took a sip of coffee and almost spilled it all over himself when she casually though eagerly joined him in the chair. Not next to him but nestling her bare butt in his lap and wiggling her feet to wrap her legs around him.

"There, that's comfortable," she said, snuggling her bottom in the crook of his jeans.

"For who?" he asked, his body instantly reacting to the intimate position.

"For us both." She grinned and drank her coffee. "Actually, I think we should share our coffee like this every morning."

"I would never get to work on time."

"We could get up early."

"You have an answer for everything."

"I have solutions."

He placed his coffee cup on the end table beside the chair. "What solution do you have for this?" He cupped her bottom with his hands and moved her slowly, rubbing her bottom over the thick bulge in his jeans.

She smiled and laughed, discarding her mug next to his. "I think you have the solution."

"No, I have the problem," he corrected.

She rested her forehead to his. "Then I have the solution."

"Show me," he said, his breath short and his heartbeat rapid.

"My pleasure," she said, reaching for the zipper to his jeans.

They floated naked together on the yellow raft in his indoor pool.

"I have never spent so much time naked," he said, feeling more relaxed than he ever had.

Ali sprinkled a handful of water over his chest and gently massaged his wet flesh. "Are you complaining? We could always put clothes on."

"No," he said quickly and with a laugh. "I like being naked with you."

"Good answer."

"Honest answer," he said, looking into her eyes.

With her powers restored, she could see much more if she allowed herself to. She had not truly looked and at the moment she didn't want to. Time was precious, but so was his acceptance of her.

Love held the key to their future, and the word had yet to pass either of their lips. Though she knew his love for her was as strong as hers for him. She was actually counting on the power of his love.

"Troubled thoughts?" he asked, his hand coming to rest over hers on his chest.

Part of her urged her to face the inevitable, and another part warned to proceed with caution. She warred with herself, and yet her honesty would not allow her to dismiss the issue.

"Concerned."

"With?" he asked.

His anxiousness assaulted her senses and disturbed her all the more.

"The future," she admitted reluctantly.

He brought her hand to his lips and kissed her palm. She braced herself prepared for his doubt and worry to flood her; surprisingly it was a commanding aura that invaded her senses and brought her relief.

"We need to take one step at a time. I told you I wanted more than a brief affair and I meant it. We have time—"

She attempted to interrupt him, warn him in some subtle way, but he pressed his finger to her lips.

"No, we will not rush."

"Do you believe in magic, Sebastian?" she asked, needing at least to know that much.

He grinned, a playful, mischievous grin. "You taught me to."

But how much did he really believe? She tapped at his chest over his heart where emotions sprang eternal. "Do you believe with all your heart?"

He saw the concern in her green eyes, felt the tension in her body, and understood, clearly understood, how important this was to her.

He leaned up and over her, the raft rocking precariously in the cool water. He cupped her face in his hand, and his eyes met hers with a bold honesty that startled her.

"You taught me the true meaning of magic, and the true meaning can only be felt from the soul."

Tears rushed to Ali's eyes. She was right about this man. This special mortal of hers. His love for her was strong, his courage solid, and he would face the most difficult of spells and emerge the victor, winning the magic of eternal love.

"Don't cry," he said, kissing at her eyes. "Don't, Ali, please. I love you so much it hurts me to see you cry."

Her breath caught in her throat, her heart skipped several beats, and time suddenly ticked faster.

He eased them off the raft and took her into his arms, kissing her over and over. "I love you," he said again and again. "I think I have loved you forever. I was waiting for you. Waiting for you to walk boldly into my life."

Tears streamed down her eyes. "I love you," she said simply and almost in a whisper. Afraid now, very afraid, for with his open acknowledgment of his love for her, his acknowledgment of his belief in her must follow. If not, all would be lost.

He lifted her chin and captured her mouth in a demanding kiss before once again announcing. "I love you so very much, Alisande Wyrrd."

Please. Please love me that much, Sebastian.

She pressed her lips to his gently and whispered against them, "I love you, Sebastian, forever and always."

"Not long enough," he said roughly and lifted her up against him, kissing her with an urgency that fired their souls and sent them hurdling into the vortex of passion.

Ali arrived home after ten that evening. Sebastian had urged her to stay, but she insisted a night of rest was necessary for them both, and that was impossible if they remained together.

He acquiesced reluctantly and made her promise that she would join him tomorrow evening for supper and of course to remain the night with him.

She agreed and they had parted with the reluctance of newly united lovers.

"So it is done."

Ali looked up to see Dagon walking down the curving foyer staircase. Splendidly tailored in white slacks and a white silk shirt, his long dark hair lay in startling contrast over his shoulders.

Her first instinct was to run to him and the reassurance of his comforting arms, but she restrained herself. His tone held disapproval, and at the moment she needed solace.

She placed her tote bag aside to take upstairs later and

walked with her head high to the atrium. Dagon followed.

She discarded the white sandals she wore and the purple fringed shawl she had tied around her waist to the stone bench just inside the atrium. Her pale blue dress gave way at her waist to fall straight to her ankles. She reached up and released the combs she had artfully secured in her hair, giving the long blond strands freedom with the shake of her head.

She was about to ease herself down on the wicker settee when she felt his hand on hers. She looked up into those dark eyes that knew all her secrets and loved her still the same, and she was lost.

Dagon had her in his arms before the first tear shattered on her cheek. "I swear I will kill him."

She shook her head between sobs. "I love him."

"Does he love you?" he asked, holding her tightly, attempting to ease her pain.

She nodded vigorously. "Yes, yes, he does, very much."

He held her close as he sat down with her on the settee. "And he has accepted who you are?"

Ali wasn't sure how to answer. Sebastian had accepted the magic of their love, but her being a witch? Her special powers? They was still very much an issue.

Dagon sighed. "He still doesn't realize who you are, does he?"

"I thought I might have some time," she admitted, feeling foolish.

"You thought to keep him from admitting he loves you?" He pulled her away from him to cast a stern glance on her. "He is mortal."

"He is different," she insisted and moved back into his arms, not wanting to see the concern and sympathy for her in his eyes.

Dagon took a deep breath, a sure sign to Ali that he was attempting to control his temper.

"You have a few weeks at the most; if he doesn't openly accept who you are, then you will begin to fade from his memory."

"I don't need reminding. I cast the stupid spell."

"No, you were stupid to cast the spell."

She pulled away from him and sent him a scathing look. "I saw a chance for true love and took it."

"Then fight for it," he ordered sharply. "You always fought for what you felt was important to you."

Tears clouded her eyes once more. "I know, but this love is so strong it fogs my senses."

"You have your powers," he reminded.

"And when he sees what I am capable of, what will he do?" she asked fearfully.

"That will depend on his love for you."

"He is practical and logical."

Dagon laughed. "Of course, he is mortal."

"You make it sound like he has a disease."

"A weakness," he corrected. "Show him true strength and courage."

She sighed. "He possesses both in abundance."

"Then perhaps there is hope for him after all."

She swatted his arm. "You would like him."

"I will like him if he does right by you."

"You would like him regardless," she insisted and snuggled into the corner of the settee, tucking her bare feet beneath her and hugging the white pillow she pulled from behind her back.

Dagon offered advice and reassurance. "You face your greatest challenge. One you have chosen yourself. You will do what is necessary and do it with pride and tenacity. Then you will not fail."

She smiled. "Such confidence in me."

"I have picked you up and brushed you off many times.

Your courage never wavered; that is what I admire and respect the most about you.''

''Because you possess the same sterling qualities.''

He laughed. ''We are much alike.''

Ali reached her hand out to him, and he grasped it tightly. ''You are the brother I never had and always wanted.''

''And you, dear heart, are the pesky little sister I had always prayed for and finally got.''

''I was never a pest,'' she protested with a laugh.

He raised a brow.

''Well, maybe just a little.''

Dagon brought her hand to his lips and kissed her gently. ''You must follow your heart even if it hurts.''

''I know, but this is one time I fear for the outcome.''

''Just be a pest and you are sure to win,'' he said, teasing her worry away.

She swatted at him again. ''It serves you right that Sebastian did a search on you.'' It was easier telling him when he was in a teasing mood; he was less likely to anger.

''I,'' he emphasized, thumbing his chest, ''unlike some, look before I leap.''

She pursed her lips and squinted her eyes, taking herself deep in thought and into his mind. ''You doctored your records.''

He laughed. ''And you, dear heart, have restored your powers tenfold. I am impressed, though unprepared. You shall not invade my thoughts again.''

She shrugged. ''I found what I needed, and besides, Sebastian knows you were only a ploy.''

''I could have told you that. My own research on the man indicated an above-average intelligence level. Though stubborn in nature.''

She sighed and asked for advice. ''How do I get past it?''

"Honesty," he answered. "Sebastian respects it and expects it. Don't play him for a fool. He isn't one and will not take lightly being treated as such."

"So what do I do? Turn him into a toad to demonstrate my powers and hope he doesn't croak?"

Dagon laughed heartily, and Ali couldn't help but join in the laughter.

He shook his head and attempted to control his humor. "Be yourself."

"In time," she said nervously.

He leaned closer to her and tapped her nose. "You don't have much of that, but you have something better."

"What's that?"

He smiled. "You have his love."

Twenty-one

Carol Smithers quietly entered Sebastian's private office after gently tapping on his door. He looked at her as she approached his desk and was amazed to see that something or someone had flustered the usually composed woman. In the near to six years she had worked for him, he had never seen her face flushed as it was now or her hands shake even when she clasped them together.

''Sir,'' she said, having to clear her voice since she croaked more than spoke the word. ''Sir, there is a gentleman to see you. He doesn't have an appointment, but he assures me you will want to talk with him.''

Sebastian furrowed his brow, now concerned for Ms. Smithers well being. No one, but no one got past her desk to him without an appointment. It was one of the qualities that endeared her to him. So who could have breached her defenses?

''His name is Dagon—''

Sebastian raised his hand. ''Say no more. Show him in.''

She turned to leave and did the most uncharacteristic thing he had ever seen her do. She patted her hair and adjusted her suit jacket before leaving his office.

Sebastian stood and walked around to the front of his desk. He always met an adversary head on.

Sebastian was impressed. He clearly understood what made Ms. Smithers react so oddly. The man was handsome enough to turn Medusa to stone. And he walked with an air of arrogant confidence that could part a crowd. He was every woman's dream and every man's nightmare.

"I thought it was time we met," Dagon said, his hands remaining casually at his sides.

Sebastian remained with his arms crossed over his chest. The battle line had been drawn. "If you feel it necessary."

"Very necessary," Dagon emphasized. "Alisande is an old and dear friend."

"Yes, she told me you two grew up together," Sebastian said, letting him know that Ali had freely discussed Dagon with him.

"Friends since childhood."

He nodded. "So I assumed. I suppose that is why she felt safe using you to get to me."

Dagon laughed, easing only slightly the tension between them. "Ali and I could never mate. She is much too impetuous, not to mention stubborn."

Sebastian smiled. "Her tenaciousness in certain matters can be appealing."

"She obviously loves you," Dagon said, waiting for his response.

Sebastian relaxed his arms and braced himself against the desk. He extended his hand to a nearby chair, but Dagon refused his offer of cordiality with a brief shake of his head.

"Are you here to ask me my intentions toward Ali?"

"I daresay you are already considering marriage, if I read the situation correctly."

Sebastian had no intention of denying his feelings or intent. "If by that you mean that I love Ali and have given marriage consideration, then you are correct."

Dagon grew irritated. "Is that all you have considered?"

"If you think I should ask your permission, think again,

pal. This isn't the Dark Ages, and Ali is a grown woman capable of making her own choices."

"That is debatable," Dagon said, frustrated.

Sebastian's own annoyance grew. "What exactly is it you came here for?"

"Simple," he said. "I believe mortals belong with mortals and witches with witches."

Sebastian threw his hands up in the air and shook his head. "Witches. I didn't know so many existed."

"There are many things you don't know, mortal." His tone bordered on confrontational.

Sebastian shot Dagon a warning look. "Then perhaps you should enlighten me."

"That would probably take a hundred years or more."

"You are treading dangerously close to me bodily throwing you out of here," Sebastian warned. "Unless of course you want to zap me with your magical powers."

Dagon would have liked nothing better, but he had Alisande to consider and the damn spell. "That would be a waste of my energy."

"I thought so," Sebastian said, not surprised that his suggestion was met with rejection.

Dagon fought to contain his temper, concentrating on his breathing and the reason he was here. "You have no idea what you have gotten yourself into."

With an abrupt laugh Sebastian shook his head. "I know I have fallen in love with a crazy woman who has just as many crazy relatives and friends."

Dagon carefully phrased his question, knowing full well the dangers of disrupting the spell. "You don't believe in witches?"

"Come on, pal," Sebastian said with a grin. "The Wiccan religion is one thing, but real honest to goodness witches? The kind that fly, float objects, and such?" He shook his head. "No such thing."

Dagon wanted to punch him in the face. Instead he had to rely on words as his weapons. "And I thought you were intelligent."

"I am; that's why I don't believe in witches."

"Then why remain with a woman who believes herself one?"

Sebastian answered with confidence. "Love does crazy things to a man, and besides, I'm sure I can eventually get her to see reason and stop this nonsense."

"You stupid fool," Dagon said angrily.

Sebastian straightened to his full height. "Watch it, pal. I don't take kindly to being called names."

Dagon threw his hands up in disgust and paced the floor in front of Sebastian. "What else do I call a man who does not understand the meaning of true love?"

"And you know the meaning? You have known true love?"

Dagon really, really wanted to punch him now.

Sebastian calmed his own temper and switched to good sound reasoning. "Look, I think it's great that Ali has a friend who cares so much for her, but I think you know as well as I do that she herself would tell you to mind your own business. The final decision will ultimately be hers and mine."

Dagon spoke more gently and from the heart. "I don't want to see her hurt."

Sebastian suddenly liked the man. It was obvious he cared deeply for Ali as a close brother would. "I can ease your mind where that is concerned. I would never hurt Ali. *Never.*"

Dagon looked deep into Sebastian's dark eyes. "No, I don't believe you honestly or *knowingly* would."

Sebastian held out his hand. "I would like us to be friends, since obviously you care so much for Ali and she for you."

Dagon didn't hesitate to accept his offer of friendship. Any man who would put his differences aside for the woman he loved was a man strong in courage and integrity. He shook his hand firmly.

Sebastian again extended an invitation for him to sit and this time Dagon accepted. Sebastian buzzed Ms. Smithers and requested coffee.

He shook his head when she left, marveling over how flushed and flustered she became around Dagon.

"Do you often affect women that way?" he asked with a hint of humor.

Dagon released a dramatic sigh. "A burden I must deal with."

Sebastian laughed and asked, "Was Ali a burden as a child?"

Dagon nodded, having just sipped his coffee. "She was impossible. A little stubborn hellion, who got herself into precarious situations almost on a daily basis."

"But you got her out?"

"More times than I can remember."

"You went to school together?" he asked, interested in discovering the truth about the woman he loved.

"Yes, and she drove our instructors crazy."

"That I could understand."

"It isn't easy to understand Alisande," Dagon corrected. "She is complex in nature and her passion runs deep."

"That I am fully aware of."

"She takes risks and chances she shouldn't."

Sebastian got the strangest and most overwhelming sensation that Dagon was attempting to tell him something. Something important. "I'll be there to help and protect her."

"Can you protect her from yourself?" he asked seriously.

"I told you I would never hurt her."

"Not intentionally."

"Not any way," Sebastian insisted.

"Then tell me this. Will you accept her being a witch?"

Sebastian shook his head, certain he heard rattling. "If thinking she is a witch makes her happy, then that's fine with me."

Dagon stood extending his hand. "I'm glad to hear that; just remember it when the time comes."

What time he meant Sebastian didn't know, but he would keep his warning in mind since it was delivered with such seriousness. He shook Dagon's hand and walked with him to the door.

"I'm glad we met and had this chance to talk," Dagon said.

"So am I, since I must admit our first introduction on the phone wasn't to my liking."

"She wasn't naked," Dagon said, sensing his need for confirmation. "Though that damn string bikini she wore barely covered her."

"That string bikini is history, except to my eyes," he said with a laugh.

"If ever you need anything, Sebastian, . . ." he said, leaving the rest unspoken, hoping he would understand.

"I won't hesitate to ask," Sebastian finished.

"Good, and I won't hesitate to help."

Sebastian sat at his desk clearing up the last few details of the day's work. Ali was meeting him at his house for supper, though she was picking something up, not cooking. He had learned quickly enough she was not talented in the kitchen but it did not disturb him. He enjoyed cooking and there was always takeout.

What did bother him was that he had not pushed the issue of her so-called magical powers since they had made love. If she was who she claimed to be, then her powers would be restored by now and she could pop right out of a room with the snap of her fingers, if he recalled her words correctly when they first met.

It wasn't so much that he was afraid she was actually a witch. He was concerned that when she attempted to demonstrate her special skill and failed, she would become upset. It was better that her powers lay dormant for a while, at least until their relationship was more secure and she could fully trust him enough to admit the truth. Until then he had no intentions of pushing the issue.

Ms. Smithers interrupted his thoughts when she announced over the intercom that Pierce Knowlin was there to see him.

Sebastian greeted him with a firm handshake. "Finished with your search?"

Pierce nodded, rubbing his shaved head, not a good sign. "I went in back doors, front doors, side doors, through trapdoors—you name a door, and I've been through it. I even created doors, and yet nobody answered. There is no information anywhere, no clue, no inkling as to who did such a thorough background search on you."

"I don't understand it," Sebastian said. "The incident this person discussed with me was known by few people, and still it was found out."

"I would suggest you look to the people who were there. That at least limits you to a few. Do you want to give me their names and I'll see what I can come up with?"

How do you tell someone about a fairy? Sebastian shook his head. "I think I'll work on the rest of it myself."

"No problem. If I can do anything to help . . ." Pierce offered.

"What about hallucinogenic drugs?" Sebastian asked, concerned with the answer he might get. "Find out anything on that?"

"Not a thing," Pierce said. "If any of the Wyrrd businesses are involved with such a project, it's tiptop secret. Though I must say that after researching them, it doesn't strike me as a project they would be interested in. The family interests seem more philanthropy-based."

Sebastian nodded, accepting his findings. Pierce was a good agent. You didn't get any better, and if he couldn't find anything . . .

Then did any such thing exist?

"How about that dated paper—have you gotten anywhere with it?" Sebastian asked, hoping for a small shred of possibility.

"Unfortunately no," Pierce admitted. "We can pinpoint that an Alisande Wyrrd was born somewhere around 1632 or '52, but after that we can't seem to trace her."

"Nothing?" Sebastian asked, finding it difficult to believe that she just disappeared. "No death record, letters, marriage certificate, documents?"

"No. There are a few references to other Wyrrds. There are a few copies of pages of family Bibles where births and deaths were recorded, but Alisande Wyrrd herself seemed to just vanish."

"No record of death?"

Pierce shook his head. "None we can find, but you must consider the time, Sebastian. Records weren't top priority back then; survival was."

"If you don't mind, I would like you to keep at it."

"Wouldn't think of stopping; this whole Wyrrd business has me fascinated. When you think you have something that connects one with the other, you wind up hitting a dead end. I must admit I have never run up against a search that presents so many twists and turns that take you nowhere."

"Crazy," Sebastian said, thinking out loud.

"It certainly is," Pierce agreed.

"Keep me abreast of any developments," Sebastian instructed, walking Pierce to the door.

"Will do," he said, and after a solid shake of hands Sebastian closed the door behind him.

He walked over to the row of windows and stared out at the quiet surroundings. Most people had already left for home and the capital was settling in for a peaceful summer night.

He would leave in a few minutes and join Ali at his place. They would share the evening meal together and make love, maybe twice. And still he would not mention a word about her being a witch.

Why?

Perhaps he was afraid of the answer after all.

Twenty-two

The Chinese food that Ali had set out on the table grew cold as they grew hot tumbling together naked on the floor of the gathering room.

Sebastian no sooner walked in the door and took one look at her in the sheer white ankle-length dress that seductively silhouetted her naked body and all was lost. In no time they were both rolling naked on the carpeted floor before the cold fireplace that ran the full length of the back wall.

She pinned him to the floor, stretching her body over his and delivering sweet, agonizingly slow kisses to every part of his body. When she finished her erotic perusal of his anatomy, she moved over him in an attempt to take further control of their lovemaking.

He surprised her and she squealed with delight when he grabbed her about the waist and in a flash, though with a gentle forcefulness, slipped her beneath him.

"My turn," he announced with a grin that warned her it was payback time.

She laughed and threw her hands out in feigned supplication.

He showed her no mercy. He started with his tongue; slow and wicked he stroked her intimately, enjoying her sweet passage and teaching her the meaning of complete surrender. And just when she was about to release the last vestige of sanity to him, he entered her.

He kneeled between her legs and tenderly stroked her thighs as he spread them farther apart and slipped his arms under her knees lifting her up to meet him.

His entrance was swift and furious, and that was how he took her. With an unbridled passion that fired both their senses.

Ali felt herself spin out of control with each determined thrust. She had never felt so alive, never felt so connected, and never so much in love.

She moaned, she cried, she pleaded, his name repeatedly falling from her lips, and he in turn responded. He touched, he taunted, he toppled them both over the edge into the realm of magic where they both spun like swirling tops out of control until colliding together in an climactic explosion.

He collapsed on top of her, trying in vain to ease his weight but failing miserably. His thunderous climax had completely depleted him, and he couldn't move a muscle.

She hugged him to her as if he weighed no more than a feather. She squeezed him, kissed him, and sighed her absolute delight in his ear.

Then she announced in all seriousness, ''I'm starving.''

He raised his head, shaking it, and laughed. ''You are adorably impossible.''

She gave him a quick kiss on the cheek and pushed at his chest. ''Thank you, but I really need nourishment.''

Her energy had been running extremely high especially since she hadn't really performed any major magical feats. Soon she would have no choice, but she didn't want him around to witness her powers. At least not until she was sure he believed and was sure he could handle the results of such knowledge.

He moved off her and stood, holding out his hand to her.

She took it and he yanked her up into his arms.

"Is that why you bought so much food?" he asked, with a nod of his head to the table in the kitchen where four different meals, barbecued ribs, and three different rices sat waiting.

She smiled, patted his chest, and pulled away in search of her dress. "I knew we would be famished after we made love."

She slipped the sheer dress over her head, popping her arms through the sleeveless holes and gathering her hair together to twist up and pin to the top of her head.

"You wore that tempting piece of nothing on purpose," he said, and reached for a pair of blue knit shorts that just so happened to be on the nearby chair.

She wagged a finger in his face as she rushed past him. "If you're accusing me of planning this little scene of seduction, you're absolutely right."

With that she grabbed for a rib and settled herself cross-legged in the chair.

He joined her, stealing a rib for himself and pouring them each iced tea from the pitcher on the table.

"You didn't plan on eating first," he accused.

She laughed gaily and licked at her sticky, tasty fingers. "Oh, I planned on eating."

He wagged *his* finger in her face this time. "You're incorrigible."

She playfully nipped at his finger. "Would you want me any other way?"

Sebastian didn't need to think, reason or debate. "Never."

He wanted her just the way she was. Sexy, fun-loving, intelligent, and utterly selfish in her pursuit of him. If that meant she was crazy, then perhaps it was time he tried a little insanity.

"Before I forget," she said, spooning a hefty portion of

chicken fried rice on her plate, "Aunt Sydney would like you to join us for lunch tomorrow. She wants you to meet Dagon. It is her way of apologizing for assisting me in trapping you."

"I would love to, though I have already met Dagon." He reached for the chicken fried rice.

She grabbed at him. "What do you mean, you met Dagon?"

He glanced down at her hand, grasping his wrist with more strength than he thought her capable of. She eased her hand off him and waited for him to respond.

Sebastian added several spoonfuls of rice to his plate and a heaping portion of Hunan chicken before giving her an answer.

"He stopped by my office today."

"Dagon?" she asked, prepared to do him harm when she got a hold of him.

"He cares deeply for you."

"He is a cherished and dear friend, as I explained to you."

Sebastian was honest in his opinion of him. "He's arrogant, but I like him."

She didn't hesitate in supplying her own opinion. "Probably because you two are so similar."

Sebastian halted the movement of his fork to his mouth. "You think I'm arrogant?"

Ali placed her hand over his and guided his fork to enter his mouth. "A nice sort of arrogance. The kind that is confident and in control of himself."

After finishing the mouthful of food, he replied, "Good way of putting it."

"Well, I couldn't very well say you two are both obstinate and demanding," she said with a cheerful smile.

"I am not," he protested with a grin that told her he thought otherwise.

"See," she said, poking him in the arm. "You know yourself. A rare quality in a man."

"I'm a rare man," he said with pride.

She leaned over and kissed him soundly. "I wouldn't have you otherwise."

He dropped his fork to his plate and shook his head, releasing a sigh. "You want me again? Can't get enough of me, can you? Always touching me. Always demanding."

Ali laughed. She loved this playful side of him. She placed her own fork down on her plate and ran a teasing hand up his leg to intimately slip over him. "I always want you."

Damn.

He had meant to tease, not titillate, though her stroking hand felt awfully good. He reached down and grabbed her wrist.

"First sustenance, then pleasure."

She sighed her regret. "I suppose you're right, and I am still hungry."

"Then eat," he ordered, pushing the containers toward her plate.

"Only if you promise me I can choose my own dessert," she said with a lascivious lick of her lips.

"You," he said with a poke to her pert nose, "are bad."

She sighed in disappointment. "And here I was looking forward to vanilla ice cream with a dash of whipped cream on top."

He was surprised at her response. "I think we can accommodate that request."

She slowly licked off the sweet-and-sour sauce that had dripped on her finger. She then leaned over and just as Sebastian took a forkful in his mouth she whispered, "I would like the ice cream intimately served on you with the dash of whipped cream on your . . ."

He almost chocked on his food, not to mention that he

sprang to full life at an alarming rate. When he was finally able to speak, he sent a threatening look directly at her.

She smiled. "Can you oblige that?"

His hand snapped out, grasped her by the neck and yanked her to him. "I can oblige anything you want, witch." And he kissed her until her toes curled.

Later that night, when they lay wrapped in each others arms after satisfying Ali's dessert request, Sebastian requested that she tell him of witches.

"You really want to know?" she asked, skeptical about his intentions.

"Yes, I do," he answered sincerely. "I have read some books, but I feel there is much that is unknown and misconstrued about their origin and their nature."

"You are perceptive."

He disagreed. "I am eager to learn and learn the truth, not what some scholar hypothesizes the truth to be, but fact."

"Sound reasoning."

"You got it," he said, nibbling at her neck with his lips.

She shivered as she always did when his lips played with her. It didn't matter where he touched, stroked, teased, she responded.

"What if sound reasoning doesn't make sense as you know it?"

"Reasoning is reasoning," he debated.

"Reasoning is only what you have been taught to believe as logical."

"Logic can be substantiated by fact," he argued.

"Fact as you have been programmed to accept it."

The conversation stimulated his senses, and he pulled himself up in bed, dragging her along with him to rest comfortably against the antique oak headboard.

"I am not programmed," he said, interested in clarifying and understanding what she attempted to relate to him. "I read, study, and reach an objective conclusion. I find critical thinking of the utmost necessity.''

''But still you choose the path of least resistance,'' she insisted, needing him to open his eyes to the impossible, the magical.

''I choose logic. I choose what my intelligence helps me to understand and believe.''

''And what can easily be explained.''

He nodded. ''All things hold explanations.''

''Even witches?''

He chose his words carefully and with knowledge he had recently acquired. ''I believe that witches existed, perhaps to some degree still do. But I believe that witches were people endowed with paranormal abilities in a time when fear and conformity were the guiding rule and anyone who stepped out of bounds suffered.''

He came so close to the truth that he frightened Alisande. ''Go on,'' she encouraged, impressed with his intelligence.

''They were persecuted for an ability they didn't understand but accepted because it was so much a part of them. And I believe that *they* believed their ability was a divine gift. Unfortunately those who were narrow-minded and ruled by the dictates of conventional society chose to label them as evil.''

Ali locked her fingers with his squeezing tightly. He would have protected her back then in those dark days when ignorance brought unnecessary suffering to the innocent even if it had meant his life. He was a man strong in his convictions and honor, and if it were possible she loved him even more now than she did a few moments before.

''But they survived,'' she said.

''Though they lost some of their autonomy along the way. It mixed with the present day illusion of witches, causing them to be viewed subjectively and often times with erroneous humor.''

''Leaving you to believe what?'' she asked cautiously.

He chose his words with great care, hoping to dispel her obvious concern. ''That witches exist to some extent in today's society.''

She rested her head on his bare chest, closing her eyes. He was being so considerate of her feelings and so dishonest with his own. He would believe in witches if she wished him to, but did he really believe? She would not have a true answer to that question until he saw the full results of her powers. And she wasn't quite ready for a demonstration. She wanted to enjoy him just awhile longer, linger in their love and passion, build memories, in case that was all she would have left of him.

He slipped his fingers beneath her chin and raised her face up to look in her eyes. ''You are my witch,'' he whispered.

''Forever and always?'' she asked, tears threatening her eyes.

''For all eternity and than some,'' he assured her and brushed a faint kiss over her lips.

''That's a long time,'' she warned.

''Not long enough,'' he answered firmly and stole a kiss that stole her breath, that in turn stole her heart.

And as they slid down along the bed to once again lose themselves in magical love, she wondered with a nagging worry what he would do when she demonstrated for him the full power of her heritage.

Twenty-three

Ali fidgeted in her chair while impatiently waiting for Sebastian and Dagon to arrive at the restaurant.

"Sit still or you will wrinkle yourself," Sydney scolded, patting her niece's arm.

Ali sighed and quieted her nervous movements.

"Your excess energy needs to be freed," her aunt said sympathetically. "A good cast or feat would serve you well and calm some of that energy that yearns to be unleashed. Is it on purpose that you have kept restraints on it?"

"In all honesty, I am not sure," she admitted. "Things are going wonderfully between Sebastian and me, and I suppose I don't wish to take the chance and ruin our blossoming relationship."

"He has accepted you being a witch, then?"

Admitting the truth to herself was difficult, speaking of it with her aunt was even more difficult. She had, after all, warned her of the consequences. "Not exactly."

Sydney passed no judgment nor comment; she simply waited for an explanation.

Ali fiddled with the silver spoon beside the fine china plate. With her powers restored, she and her aunt could converse entirely through their thoughts, and yet her aunt obviously wished to hear her openly, recognizing the problem at hand.

"You are forcing me to—"

"Look before you leap," her aunt finished.

Ali smiled and rested her nervous hands in her lap.

Sydney spoke, attempting to ease her niece's concern. "Unknowingly Sebastian has bought you time. I assume he has agreed to believe in your outrageous claim of being a witch to satisfy you. In so doing he has prevented the spell from going any further. But," her aunt warned softly, "once he learns of your true nature and fails to accept who you are, the spell must be fulfilled."

Ali sighed heavily, the weight of her problem suddenly burdensome. "I have thought of numerous ways in which to gently introduce him to my heritage, and yet none seem appropriate to my current situation."

Sydney spoke candidly. "There is no easy or simple way to demonstrate your powers to Sebastian. He is a man who would find good, solid reason for any modest feat you performed. Only a startling revelation would open his eyes to the truth."

"Or frighten him away."

"There is that possibility."

"A possibility I must eventually face," Ali conceded.

Sydney offered hope. "Do not underestimate your mortal. He loves you more strongly than you will ever know and love is the key that will seal this spell forever."

Ali remained silent seeing Dagon approach and her aunt reached beneath the table to Ali's lap to give her hand a reassuring squeeze.

"My two favorite women," Dagon said with a generous smile and kissed each one of them on the cheek.

"What's the problem?" Sydney immediately asked after he took a seat opposite Ali.

"Whatever makes you—"

"Don't insult me, Dagon. I know you too well and your concern is palpable," Sydney said sternly.

Dagon looked to Ali for assistance. "I agree. I can feel your discomfort."

Dagon mumbled beneath his breath and signaled the waiter. "A double Scotch."

Both women glared at him.

"I should have known you both would sense my troubled thoughts. Especially you, brat," he said to Ali. "With your powers returned, your energy is fine tuned."

"Stop changing the subject and tell us what ails you," Sydney instructed like a parent impatient with her child.

The waiter delivered the Scotch, and Dagon took a drink before answering. "I must make a trip to my estate in Scotland. There seems to be a problem with the staff."

Sydney looked at him oddly. "Your staff has been with you for ages. What possibly could be wrong?"

Dagon took another swallow. "A new staff member who had come highly recommended seems to be creating havoc."

"Havoc?" Ali repeated. "By highly recommended I assume you mean through our own kind? And if so, how could the person create havoc?"

"Through our own kind is right," he informed her, "but it appears that this person isn't as highly qualified as I was led to believe."

"Oh, the poor dear witch has limited powers," Sydney said with a sad shake of her head. Sydney reached her hand out and patted Dagon's arm. "You simply cannot fire her, my dear boy. It would be inappropriate."

Dagon looked incredulously at her. "I most certainly can. My whole staff—faithful staff might I add—is threatening to quit. Right there is grounds enough for discontinuing her employment."

Sydney shook her head. ''I am warning you. Do not fire her, you know not what you deal with.''

''I deal with a bumbling, inept witch who has no place in my home and—''

Sydney silenced him with a searing glare. ''Be careful, Dagon, this is more than you can handle.''

Dagon didn't take well to her reproachful warning. ''I think not. I will handle it efficiently and effectively upon my arrival.''

Sydney spotted Sebastian talking with the maître d' and leaned over to whisper to Dagon, ''Remember my advice.''

Sebastian walked up to the table and graciously placed a tender kiss on Sydney's cheek and a more familiar one on Ali's lips before taking the seat next to Ali.

''Good to see you again, Dagon,'' he said.

Dagon nodded, raising his glass in a salute. ''I'm impressed, Sebastian. You don't seem the least bit intimidated by the presence of three witches.''

Ali shot him a lethal look, and Sydney remained Sydney, in control and dignified.

''You mean in the presence of two mannered witches and one ill-tempered one,'' Sydney corrected.

It was Sebastian's turn to be impressed as he watched Dagon turn contrite and apologize.

''Forgive me,'' he said sincerely, ''there is no excuse for such abhorrent manners.''

''Bad morning?'' Sebastian asked in understanding.

Dagon smiled graciously. ''Extremely.''

The waiter appeared and took their orders.

Sydney started the conversation. ''I also must beg your forgiveness, Sebastian. My niece holds a soft spot in my heart, and there isn't anything I wouldn't do for her.''

''See what I must contend with?'' Dagon said teasingly.

Sebastian spoke with sincerity to Dagon. ''I envy you the special bond you share.''

"Our heritage allows for nothing less," Dagon said. "We protect each other out of necessity for survival, but we care because we are aware."

"Aware?" Sebastian asked, wondering if he was being drawn into the world of the insane or actually facing reality.

Sydney continued from there. "Life is awareness. Awareness of all, everything, and particularly yourself. With this knowledge comes great power and with that power responsibility."

"Responsibility?" He knew he sounded naive like a young schoolboy uncertain of his lessons, but then one didn't learn if one didn't question. And he wanted to know all. It was the only way he could completely understand and cope with their belief in witchcraft.

"Study the lesson, Sebastian," Sydney offered. "Then you will learn what you seek."

Sebastian's curiosity drove him on. "I thought witches cast spells, chanted, and held ceremonies. Yet here you tell me of awareness and responsibility, more mortal traits than witches."

Ali wasn't surprised at his genuine interest. His practical side urged him to search for the logical behind the illogical. And if anyone could initiate a neophyte to witchcraft, it was her aunt.

"Mortal traits?" she asked with a smile. "What makes you think they first belonged to mortals?"

Sebastian shook his head.

"Witches introduced many wonders to mortals. It was up to them to learn and grow." She shrugged. "Unfortunately their growth has been slow."

The food arrived, giving Sebastian time to pause and think. Sydney was obviously an intelligent woman, and yet she believed herself to be a witch. A six-hundred-year-old witch to be exact. How did he rationalize that? Did he join them in their insanity? Or allow them their fantasies? Not once had any of them offered to prove their so-called powers, and he had not requested a demonstration. Was that the simple answer to this whole strange situation? Request a show of powers?

"Have I challenged your mind, Sebastian?" Sydney asked, adding a sprinkle of pepper to the roasted baby potatoes that accompanied her poached salmon.

"Enough to learn more," he said.

Dagon remained skeptical and concerned. "You are willing to learn?"

Sebastian smiled at Ali and reached out to squeeze her hand. "I feel as Sydney does. Ali has more than a soft spot in my heart, she has my complete love, and there isn't anything I wouldn't do for her."

Ali smiled in return, though her heart ached. He thoughtfully did this for her out of love, a generous reason and a reasonable one. An unreasonable one would have been him believing, honestly believing her to be a witch. Unfortunately he found that difficult to do.

"Does that include believing in witches?" Dagon asked, voicing everyone's concern.

Sebastian spoke firmly and with a sense of his own beliefs. "Yes, it does and I respect your beliefs and practice in the craft. I have read extensively on the subject since meeting Ali, and I have come to realize just how many practicing witches exist today. It is an old religion that has seen a tremendous revival."

Dagon said nothing; neither did Sydney. They waited for Ali to speak.

"You accept me as a witch?" she asked him with trepidation.

Sebastian didn't want to hurt her, didn't want her placed in an awkward situation, didn't want to embarrass her.

"If it is a witch you believe to be, then it is a witch you are," he said.

"You believe because I believe?" she asked, her heart filled with pain, having hoped he would have *truly* believed.

"I believe in you, Ali."

She smiled as best she could, though the sorrow showed. She excused herself and retreated to the ladies' room to quell her tears.

Sebastian confronted the two as soon as Ali was out of sight. "I am a practical man. Sound reasoning is what makes sense to me. If you believe in witchcraft fine, but to contend to be hundreds of years old? Why? What good does it do but label you eccentrics?"

Sydney spoke softly and with a hint of disappointment in her persuasive voice. "We have worn many labels over the years, some far worse than others. We hope and often pray that mortals will eventually come to understand our ways, perhaps even accept them. Unfortunately we are always disappointed. I had thought you were different, capable of stepping beyond the ordinary, or to you the reasonable. Please, don't disappoint me."

Sebastian felt chastened like a child who had badly disappointed a favorite parent and whose apology would not be enough to make amends.

Ali returned to a silent table, and she began to chatter to fill the void, to ease her ache, to stop the pain. Dagon joined in, sensing her distress, and Sydney did the same.

Talk eventually turned to laughter and an awkward meal was soon transformed into a pleasant one.

Sebastian departed from them with a strong sense of camaraderie and an equally strong sense to take heed of Sydney's words.

It was late. Sebastian sat on his deck alone. He had had a late night meeting with prospective clients. He had hoped to see Ali, but she had a previous commitment with her aunt, so here he sat in solitude.

Where did their relationship go from here? He wanted a firm commitment. Marriage. Children. A lifetime together. Could he have that with Ali?

He certainly loved her enough, and he had no doubt of her love for him, so what now?

Did he demand she reject this crazy notion of being a witch? Did he accept her for who she was?

He stood and paced the deck. He had always found sound logic comforting. It was solid and could be counted on to solve any number of problems. But Ali defied logic, and because of this he found it hard defining who she was.

And no amount of research had solved his problem. Sound deductive reasoning didn't apply to Ali. She was different in every sense of the word, and in a strange way he was drawn to her individuality.

So why would he want her to change?

He shook his head. Perhaps he was the crazy one and she sane. All families had their strange quirks, so what if Ali's family believed themselves witches.

Six-hundred-year-old witches? His own rational mind argued with him.

He had driven himself crazy since meeting her. He could find no sound explanation for her undetected entrance into his office, except for fairy dust. Not an acceptable reason. He found no sensible answer for his vision of a fairy, namely Beatrice.

He peeked cautiously to his shoulder, shaking his head at his own ridiculous actions.

''Delusional might suffice,'' he told himself.

The only logical answer he had for anything that had occurred since Ali popped into his life was that he had fallen completely and madly in love with her.

And love certainly made no sense, so how did he expect to understand anything at all that was happening to him?

In some way his rationalizing the situation seemed to

make some cohesive sense, which pleased him and gave him purpose.

He would call Ali now. Right now, no matter the hour. He would tell her how very much he loved her. How he couldn't live without her. How he wanted her a part of his life always. He would propose to her and finally end this madness.

He marched into the house and grabbed for the phone.

Ali sat by the pool in her white nightgown. It was late, but she wasn't tired. All she could think about was Sebastian and where their relationship went from here.

He agreed to accept her as a witch, though only because she believed herself one. Did that really matter? He accepted her and that was all the spell called for, his acceptance.

He truly loved her, she had no doubt of that. So what was the problem? What was preventing them from sealing their love forever? Her powers? He loved her, and wasn't love acceptance? So there was nothing to stop them. Really nothing stood in their way except their stubborn pride. And why shouldn't their stubbornness interfere? He was practical. She was a witch. But he accepted her in his own sensible way, and she certainly accepted him.

So what were they waiting for? She should call him this very minute. She should tell him she must see him now. Right now. She would admit her complete, undying love for him, and if sound logic were to follow, the next step would be a proposal of marriage.

She smiled wide. That is what she would do. She would propose and end this crazy business once and for all.

She reached for the phone.

Twenty-four

Ali was waiting impatiently at the door for him. His arrival was imminent. They had talked briefly, both surprised when they picked up the phone to find that the other one waited on the opposite end. There had been no dial tone, no ring, just a connection.

A magical omen, Sebastian had suggested with a laugh, and her heart had soared with happiness. Now he was on his way over, insisting he had to speak with her and she insisting just as strongly that she must do the same.

His car headlights appeared down the long driveway, and Ali fluffed her long loose hair with her fingers and gently nibbled her lips to rush a dash of color to them.

She was so excited she tingled. The evening would end wonderfully, with them planning an immediate wedding.

His car no sooner came to a stop than he sprinted out and up the steps. His attire confirmed his eagerness for a speedy arrival. He wore dark trousers and a tan dress shirt, minus a tie and with the sleeves rolled up. He looked as if he had just arrived home from work and was ready to relax.

He took the steps two at a time, hurried over to her, grabbing her around the waist, and lifting her to meet his mouth.

His demanding kiss stole her senses. He tasted delicious,

warm, sweet, and appetizing. If she didn't focus on the matter at hand, they would soon be naked and furiously making love.

Awareness must have dawned on him as well, for he lowered her feet to the floor and reluctantly eased her away from him.

''Later,'' he said with promise. ''We need to talk.''

She took his hand and pressed her finger to her lips cautioning him to remain silent. All in the house were asleep, and she intended to keep it that way. She tugged him along, and he willingly followed her through the foyer, down the hall, and to the indoor pool area.

''This will give us privacy,'' she said, refusing to relinquish his hand. His long lean fingers felt strong and secure being locked solidly with hers.

''You have been on my mind all night,'' he said. ''I can't stop thinking about you. I don't want to stop thinking about you. I never knew love could feel like this.''

''How?'' she asked, wanting to hear how he defined love.

He slipped his hand from hers and turned away from her, raking his fingers through his dark hair. When he swerved back around, the expression on his face stole her breath.

He wore his emotions openly for her to see, the torment, the doubt that tore at him, and the love. The love so strong that it shone in the depths of his eyes clear down to his soul.

''I can't live without you, Ali.'' He shook his head. ''That's crazy. In reality I could, I would have no choice, but *I don't want to.* I don't want to wake without you beside me in the morning or drift off to sleep without you in my arms. I want to share laughter and tears. I want to hold you when you need comforting, tease you when you need to laugh, and love you every day for the rest of our lives. We belong together. One cannot exist without the other.

Your breath is mine, mine is yours. Your heart belongs to me and mine to you. Our souls are one and forever. I love you Ali and I want—''

''Marry me,'' she said, stealing his words.

He laughed and walked over to her, cupping her face in his hands and kissing her gently.

''Marry me,'' she said again and returned his kisses.

''I can't wait for our children to hear the story of how I proposed marriage to their mother.''

She poked him in the chest. ''You haven't accepted my offer yet.''

''Yes,'' he said, kissing her cheek. ''Yes,'' he repeated, kissing her eyes. ''Yes,'' he went on kissing her chin. ''Yes, I will marry you,'' he finished and planted a kiss on her lips that left no doubt how he felt about her.

Ali sighed, completely satisfied. It was done, all taken care of, finally finished. They would spend the rest of their lives together.

''I think we should marry immediately,'' she said, tugging his hand for him to follow her to the chaise lounge.

His firm grip on her hand stopped her from going far. ''If we sit on that, talk will be forgotten mighty fast.''

She eyed the chaise and eyed him up and down and nodded. ''You're right. We better stand and discuss the wedding plans.''

He smiled and shook his head. ''Don't ever change, Ali. I love you for who you are.''

Her heart soared. His love was strong for *her*. Who she was, not who he wanted her to be, but she herself. She had chosen an extraordinary man.

''Now about the wedding,'' he said. ''While I would love an immediate wedding, I also would love a wedding where I can show off my pride in my bride.''

She grinned with pleasure. ''Aunt Sydney and I could put a wonderful wedding celebration together in two to three months. How about October or November?"

"A perfect time," he agreed.

She grew excited at the prospect of planning the special event. "Of course we must be careful of the date so it doesn't interfere with the Autumn Equinox or All Hallows' Eve."

She continued, not noticing the odd look Sebastian sent her. "And we should marry before either festivity so you will at least be familiar with my family before the first seasonal celebration."

A warning bell went off in Sebastian's head. A tiny *ping,* reminding him that this issue needed addressing before they committed completely to each other, and there was only one way. One way to settle it once and for all.

He cleared his throat, and the attention-getting sound did exactly that. It caught her attention and jolted her senses.

He took a step away from her, and Ali sensed the fight within him. She couldn't bear to feel his distress and decided the moment was at hand. If they were to marry, then he had to be aware, had to believe.

"You want a display of my powers," she said softly.

He stared at her. "I should be accustomed to you reading my mind, but your skill takes some getting used to."

What would he do when he discovered just how much *skill* she actually possessed? Would he run? Would he believe? Or would he love her?

"I understand and it is best that you know what you are getting yourself into."

Her words didn't help to convince him. He feared that it would be he who would need to comfort her when her little tricks failed to work and then what? How would she feel? And where would it leave them?

"Let's get this over with," she said, suddenly feeling nervous. A reaction she had not experienced since she was young and directed to perform her first magical feat before her family. Of course it had been simple, but she had been merely a child and understandably nervous. Now she was an adult with controlled and precise powers that were hers to command. And still she found herself nervous but now for a vastly different reason.

"Anything in particular you would like me to do?" she asked, uncertain as to where to begin, especially since he was a nonbeliever and so damn practical. A small feat probably wouldn't convince him, yet a large feat might just frighten him away.

He found his nerves on edge, more for her than for him, and he wanted this over and done. He shrugged. "You choose."

She glanced around the pool area and noticed her empty teacup on the table beside the chaise. "I could float that teacup in the air."

He nodded.

She pointed her finger at the delicate china cup, and it slowly rose to steadily float over the glass-top table.

"Good," he said with a nod, realizing any first-rate magician could perform such a trick, and perhaps she was skilled in magic. She could, after all, read minds. Another magician's trick.

His thought hit her full force. *He didn't think it real.*

He actually thought she was using mortal magic. So annoyed with his doubting thoughts she forgot herself and swung her finger away from the cup. It crashed to the tabletop and splintered in pieces.

Sebastian remained silent.

Ali grew irritated. What did he think this was, fun and games? A show to entertain him?

"I'll turn that ceramic frog sitting amongst the plants by the end of the pool into a real one," she said sharply.

"Ali, that was enough. I don't need any more proof," he urged, not wanting her to suffer needless humiliation.

"Yes, you do." And with that she shot her finger directly at the frog. It took two hops and released a croak.

Sebastian nodded, common sense telling him the frog was probably real to begin with.

Ali glared at him wide-eyed. "What do you mean, it was probably a real frog to begin with?"

"Stop reading my mind," he ordered.

"Then open it and see clearly for the first time in your life."

"Fine," he said, raising his voice. "You are skilled in magic. In creating an illusion. You are a witch."

"I am a witch." Her temper soaring, she rubbed her hands together, creating a ball of white sparkling energy, then she tossed it up over her head and it burst, sprinkling down around her in twinkling lights.

"All right," he insisted. "You are skilled—"

"In what?" she demanded, her green eyes shining so brightly they looked to be on fire.

"Magic," he said firmly.

Ali was proud of who she was and her heritage. She would not have him equate her powerful skills to that of a mortal magician.

"You are familiar with how magicians levitate?" she asked, her hands spreading out in front of her as if demonstrating she possessed nothing and concealed nothing.

"I'm not certain exactly how it is done, but I know it is an illusion," he said, wondering what she intended to do.

"And you know that for the illusion to be successful everyone must work together to create it?"

"Of course," he agreed. "How could you levitate someone if they weren't part of the act?"

"A witch requires no such preparation," she said and cast her hands out in front of her, her fingers pointing directly at him.

Sebastian wasn't sure how she did it. He felt nothing,

barely realized he was being lifted. But she had him off the ground, his body rising slowly, and then to his surprise his whole body turned and he was brought to lay straight out on his back as if on a table, his eyes looking directly up at the ceiling fan over head.

She walked over to him, his floating body eye level with her chest. "Convinced?"

He took a deep breath. *Could it be a dream?*

"No, Sebastian, it isn't a dream. You are floating in thin air."

"There must me a reasonable—"

"Enough!" she shouted and with a finger pointed to the pool and asked, "A dip?"

He floated slowly toward the pool, his body turning and lowering just as slowly until he came to a stop dead center over the pool, his nose a mere inch away from touching the water.

His body remained stiff and unmovable whether by his choice or her command, he wasn't certain.

This wasn't happening. This couldn't be happening. It was impossible.

"Oh, but it is happening and it is possible," she assured him, standing at the edge of the pool.

He caught sight of her out of the corner of his eye. Her hands were spread out in a gesture that appeared to him to be his only means of actual support.

She couldn't possess such startling powers. It was simply impossible. He would find a reason for this. He would—

"No, Sebastian," she said calmly. "There is no sane, rational explanation for what is happening to you, except—"

"You're a witch," he finished.

"Do you believe now?"

He wouldn't look at her. He wouldn't answer. He didn't know how to respond. He shook his head.

"Then perhaps this will help you to decide," she said.

He quickly shut his eyes, thinking she intended to release him into the water below. He dropped suddenly and before he could catch his breath, he stopped just as suddenly.

He opened his eyes and they widened in shock. He was only inches from the bottom of the pool, and there was no water beneath him or around him. His body turned over once again, and there, rising up above, to the sides like majestic waterfalls, was the pool water split in half.

Before he could breathe, reason, or speak, his body began to move, drifting up and out of the pool. He was turned to a standing position and brought to rest soundly on his feet at the pool's edge. Then he watched in stunned silence as the water cascaded gently back into the pool.

Ali stood waiting for his reaction. She hadn't intended to take her powers to such extreme, but his skepticism irritated her. She had thought, had hoped that there was a hint of belief in him. At least if there was there would be a shred of hope to build on.

But was he too rooted in logic to comprehend true magic?

He released a slow, steady breath before turning to face her.

She held her head up with pride. Her green eyes shone brilliantly in a face so beautiful it could steal a man's breath away.

He wanted to speak. Wanted to say something, but all sensible thought eluded him. He couldn't understand. She was a real, honest to goodness *witch.*

Which meant she cast spells. Real spells. Not fun-and-game spells. Had she cast a spell on him to love her?

Eccentric.

Why couldn't she have just been eccentric? That he could have dealt with. But a witch?

A real witch?

He shook his head, looked at Ali, and without speaking a word he walked past her, out of the pool area, out through the house, out the front door, and, Ali feared, out of her life.

Twenty-five

Sebastian sat in his office, all appointments for the day canceled. He had thought of staying home, but the idea of spending the entire day alone in the house with just his irrational thoughts propelled him to come to work.

Once here he found himself unable to concentrate on anything but Alisande and last night's incident. He had directed Ms. Smithers to cancel all his activities for the day and not to disturb him. For anyone or for any reason. That meant he would take no calls from any member of the Wyrrd family or their friends.

Ms. Smithers acknowledged his instructions with a simple nod and a worried frown and had quietly closed the door behind her.

That had been early this morning. It was now almost two in the afternoon, and he hadn't budged from the leather chair behind his desk.

Last night was no dream, but it certainly felt like a nightmare. He had tried to understand and make at least an ounce of sense out of the strange and incomprehensible incident.

Impossible.

He shook his head, an action he had repeated frequently all day. How did one accept and cope with the probability of the person he loved being a witch? Especially when you, yourself, don't believe in witches? When your beliefs are rooted in the sound and the practical, how do you accept the illogical?

He hadn't slept all night, and after endless hours of pacing the floor and then twisting and turning in his bed, he gave up and went to his computer. He researched magic. Mortal magic. He had even managed to find a magician, a few degrees above amateur he claimed, who was on-line and who he had spoken with in great length.

There was absolutely no way that Ali could have rigged the demonstration, which meant her powers were genuine. She was a full-fledged *witch*?

No matter how many times he admitted that to himself, he still had difficulty accepting it. He assumed his background, based so solidly on sound reasoning and sensibility, refused to allow him to believe in anything beyond the acceptable and proven.

But Ali had certainly proven her abilities to him.

And with that proof came a startling realization. Had the spell she cast on him when they first met been the reason he had fallen so madly in love with her?

Was what he felt based on magic or true love?

He had thought of calling her, actually he ached to see her, to speak with her, to hold her, and yet he prevented himself from doing so. He had to determine what she had done to him. Until he sorted this whole mess out, he couldn't, nor would he, speak with her.

Sebastian pressed the intercom button. "Ms. Smithers, please come in here a moment."

The woman entered quietly prepared with pen and notebook in hand.

Sebastian stood. "I am going to take the rest of the day off and . . ." He paused a moment as if just deciding. "I will not be coming to work tomorrow. Please see to clearing my calendar."

Carol Smithers nodded, speechless. Sebastian Wainwright hadn't missed a day of work the whole time she had been in his employment.

"Sir," she said softly.

He waited for her to continue.

"Alisande Wyrrd has left numerous messages for you."

"Thank you" was all he said.

Ms. Smithers, familiar with a dismissal, nodded and left as quietly as she had entered.

He sighed and plopped back down in his chair. He was far from a coward. He had faced difficult, even life-threatening situations, but never, never had he faced a witch. A bona fide, spell-casting, object-floating witch.

"Damn, damn, damn," he muttered and stood and with determined strides walked out of his office and straight out of the building without a cordial word to anyone.

Ali walked in the woods that surrounded the Wyrrd estate. She always found solace and peace in nature. It was so simple and pure and the energy it offered freely was soothing to the soul.

What was she to do now? She had attempted to contact him all day, and he refused her phone calls. Ms. Smithers was gracious about it, explaining he was detained with an important matter, but Ali sensed the truth, and it hurt that he didn't want to speak with her.

She had literally scolded herself senseless last night. She should have never used her powers in such an outrageous fashion. She should have proceeded with caution; after all, Sebastian was a mere mortal. How could she expect him to react any differently than he did? She had shocked him senseless and expected what?

Acceptance?

She supposed it was the fact that he claimed to love her, and with love, at least to Ali, was acceptance. He would not believe who she was. He still assumed that she performed little magic tricks. She had allowed her emotions to rule and a witch knew better, but she had totally disregarded her own knowledge and had acted abominably.

His shock had been tangible. She had felt it as though his reaction were her own. And she knew before he took a step that he would walk away from her. When he had walked out the door and she had heard it shut, her first thought was that he was lost to her forever.

This morning with the sun shining brightly, the weather not so humid, and the promise of a new day, she felt a small sense of relief. Her unanswered phone calls soon turned her slim thread of hope to abject despair.

When her aunt and Dagon learned of the incident, they empathized with her and attempted to offer helpful suggestions. Her aunt, though, also warned her of the consequences. Time was now her enemy. If she was determined not to lose Sebastian, then she had no choice but to pursue him and fight for the survival of their love.

How did one fight for the survival of love when you had to fight the very person who claimed to love you?

Ali walked deeper into the woods. The large trees with their long abundant, draping branches shaded the fragile foliage and protected the flower blossoms from the summer heat.

Here was magic at its best.

She sat under the shade of an old oak tree, leaning back against the sturdy trunk and staring up at the brilliant green leaves that swayed softly in the gentle summer breeze.

Sunlight peeked its way through the branches and faintly kissed her face, the warm rays comforting.

The tears started then; she couldn't stop them and didn't want to. She bowed her head, closing her eyes to shield the tears and hide the pain.

''Now, don't go crying,'' the soft voice chastened.

The familiar voice brought a tentative smile to her face. "Beatrice."

"Look at me, Ali," the tiny fairy ordered.

Ali felt her small fingers tap delicately at her cheek, and she lifted her head and did as she was told.

Beatrice stood on her right shoulder, pushing at her drooping head wreath and fluttering her crooked wings. She wore a concerned smile and raised a wagging finger to Ali's face.

"Now, you can't go giving up."

Ali remained silent. She had learned over a century ago that you did not interrupt Beatrice when she preached her lessons.

"He's a stubborn one, that Sebastian Wainwright, but not unsalvageable. He wants to believe. He truly does," she insisted and leaned against Ali's cheek to wipe a tiny tear that trickled from her eye.

"You can't be expecting a man who has based his growth and knowledge on sound reasoning to easily accept that which to him is illogical."

Ali sighed. "True, but you see I rashly used a spell on him that I had full confidence would succeed."

"The magical love spell, of course," Beatrice said matter-of-factly. "What other spell could you use on such a powerful mortal?"

Ali's eyes rounded wide. "You don't think I was foolish?"

Beatrice laughed and waved her small arms joyously in the air. "Love is foolish, so what makes you think then that you won't act foolishly?"

"But I had only met him."

Beatrice tapped her cheek. "Listen up, Alisande. You listened to your heart and soul and they never lie. They told you true that when you met him he was for you and you for him. If you did not truly believe, you would have never cast the spell. You are far too intelligent and I am far too good of a teacher to have my student act impulsively. You acted foolishly, an acceptable behavior when you are in love.''

''Then why didn't he act foolishly?''

Beatrice laughed so hard her head wreath fell down to completely cover one eye. She pushed it up, holding it there for a moment while she regained her composure.

''You don't call talking to fairies in the woods foolish?''

''No, not at all,'' she said with a heavy sigh.

''Pay attention here, Alisande,'' Beatrice directed, tapping her cheek. ''We are talking about a mortal, not a witch.''

A faint smile surfaced on Ali's face. ''True.''

''And did he not roll around on the grass making love with you?''

That gave Ali pause. He had not hesitated in joining her, but he was mortal. ''He is a mortal man with mortal desires.''

''You mean he is a mortal man in love with a desirable witch, which in turn makes him act foolishly.''

Ali shook her head. ''I just don't know.''

''It's what you *do* know that counts,'' Beatrice urged. ''The only thing that matters is your love for him and his love for you. With love anything is possible.''

''Even between a witch and a mortal?'' she asked reluctantly.

''No, lovey,'' Beatrice said softly. ''Between a man and a woman.''

As usual, Beatrice made sense, but there was still the matter of him refusing to speak with her. ''He won't answer my phone calls.''

''Then go to him.''

''What if he won't let me in?''

"Pop in," Beatrice said with a smile and a snap of her tiny fingers.

"What if—"

Beatrice placed a finger to her lips to silence her. "*What if* are but little words. Will you allow two small words to determine your future?"

Ali's smile grew a little bolder. "You always taught that individuals determined their future."

"So what is in your future, Ali?"

"A battle," she answered with a laugh.

"And your weapon?" Beatrice asked, holding up a clasped hand as if she held an imaginary sword.

Ali's smile grew bright. "Love."

Sebastian sat in the gathering room watching twilight descend beyond the sliding-glass doors. He had poured himself a glass of wine more than an hour ago and had yet to touch it. He was too lost in his emotions to move.

He had changed to black knit shorts when he arrived home, had gotten the wine, and had deposited himself on the couch, where he had remained. He had ignored the ring of the phone, the buzz of the doorbell, and the beep on his computer that signaled he had mail, important mail. He wanted solitude.

He had no doubt Ali continued to call him. She may have even been one of the people at his door, but he wasn't in the mood to talk with anyone.

He was too busy wallowing in his own misery.

And soon, very soon, he would have to make a decision, though within the last hour he had given thought to picking up and taking off for a week or two. Time away and alone just might clear his head sufficiently enough for him to think rationally.

Like a mortal.

Well, he was a mortal and there wasn't a damn thing he

could do about it or even wanted to do about it. It was who he was, a mortal man full of mortal values, opinions, and logic.

Something a particular woman simply did not understand.

A witch.

"All right, a witch," he said to the empty room or himself or whoever invaded his thoughts. "A witch who with the flick of her finger could send me flying up in midair and probably clear across the room. How does a mortal man cope with that?"

Delicately.

"I'm not delicate!" he shouted and jumped off the sofa. "I am a man strong in physical strength and with enough courage and obstinacy to face the most difficult situations and emerge the victor or at least better off for having tried."

He held up his fingers and glared at them. "But I can't snap my fingers and move people around like chess pieces. So how does a mortal male handle a witch?"

With lots of love.

Sebastian knew that voice. He heard it clearly in his head. He shut his eyes for a moment, refusing to accept the obvious, but then his stubbornness took root, and he opened his eyes and turned his head. He stared at the sliding-glass doors.

Ali stood on the other side. She wore a dress of white silk that glided adoringly along every curve of her temptress body. Her blond hair looked windswept, and her full lips wore a faint blush that begged to be kissed to a rosy dew.

She waited for him to invite her in, for him to talk with her and make amends.

He couldn't bring himself to move. If he let her in, he would have a difficult if not impossible time keeping his hands off her. He missed her terribly. One day he had been without her, and he felt as if it had been years since they last kissed, touched, made magic.

He remained as he was, standing there staring at her.

She placed one hand flat against the glass door and smiled. A smile filled with more pain and sorrow than happiness.

He moved then, walked over to the door, and pressed his hand flat on the cool glass where her palm rested, and closed his eyes.

The glass turned warm and sent a tingle up his arm. And then he felt her softness, the smoothness of her flesh so real against his hand.

His eyes popped open and there she stood in front of him, their hands touching, their bodies close, their lips only inches away.

Twenty-six

Sebastian locked his fingers with hers, gave a soft squeeze, and lowered his mouth to gently brush her lips before he stepped away from her.

The jolt of despair that hit his midsection halted his retreat for a moment, and then he took several more steps, needing to distance himself from her and her heartful emotions.

The short space did little good; he continued to feel the heart-wrenching ache in his gut, and when he turned to face her, he wondered if the painful sensation was his own or theirs combined.

"I wanted to apologize," Ali said. "I allowed my pride to rule my senses. I should never have introduced you to my heritage in such an extreme and indelicate fashion."

Sebastian rubbed at the back of his neck. "I doubt any other way would have been sufficient enough to convince me. I can be stubborn."

She smiled and her eyes lingered longingly over his bare chest so rich in muscle structure and his arms so strong yet tender in their ability to comfort.

"I had to speak with you," she said. "I am sorry for the intrusion, but you seemed intent on ignoring me."

"I need time," Sebastian said with a sadness to his voice that frightened her.

"I can understand you needing time, but I need something as well."

"Which is?" he asked cautiously.

Doubt assaulted her, his doubt, not hers.

She immediately asked her question. "I need to know if you love me."

A knife to his heart would have caused him less pain. He wanted to reach out, grab her around the waist, and yank her to him. He wanted to feel her body plastered against his, he wanted her to feel his need for her and her need for him. He wanted to make magical love with her.

Then why did he hesitate?

He voiced his doubts before he had a chance to consider otherwise. "Witches cast spells."

"Yes, they do," she agreed and began to understand the doubt that drove him to keep his distance.

"You cast a spell on me."

"Yes, I did."

He asked the question that had tormented him since discovering her a bona fide witch. "Did you make me fall in love with you?"

Ali was treading on dangerous ground. There was only so much information she could provide him with regarding the spell and regarding the outcome.

She moved to take a step toward him, but his upheld hand warned her to stay put. She did and spoke softly and with confidence. "Let me tell you something about spells and then perhaps you will better be able to determine the answer for yourself."

"No straight answer?" he asked with regret.

"The answer will be as clear as you wish it to be."

Sebastian nodded and stood with his arms crossed like a warrior of old whose brute strength alone was his only shield.

Ali thought of her single weapon. True love. Would its

magic penetrate his staunch defenses and allow him to see the truth?

She began. ''Spells are cast for a number of reasons. Good reasons. A true witch can cast no spell that brings pain or sorrow or hinders another. A spell can never be forced, only cast and presented to the heavens.''

''And the results?''

''Magic.''

''How so?'' he asked.

''Magic is your belief.''

Sebastian shook his head, wondering if the now involuntary movement had become an affliction. ''What you're saying is that if I believe I love you, then I do?''

''A spell cannot change a person's beliefs.''

''But a spell can place a suggestion in a person's mind,'' he clarified.

''Yes.''

''And that suggestion can grow,'' he said, pacing the floor in front of her.

''A suggestion can only flourish if there is something to nourish it.''

''Like you?''

''Me?''

''Seducing me, chasing me, tormenting me with your outrageous nature,'' he insisted, stopping his pacing to glare at her with eyes that questioned and accused.

''You call that nourishment?'' she asked incredulously.

His rational mind warned him to slow down, consider what she said, but his thoughts were anything but sane at the moment. And he wanted answers, direct and simple answers. Not damn, stupid riddles.

''Did you cast a love spell?'' he insisted with a wag of his finger.

''Yes, I cast a love spell, but have you listened to anything I have—''

"Enough," he said, interrupting her. "You cast a spell that placed the suggestion of love in my mind, and then you chased after me to nourish that suggestion, and now you expect me to believe that I fell madly in love with you of my own free will. That my sleepless nights and dream-filled days, which you constantly invaded, did not help in securing my predilection for you."

"Have you listened to nothing I've said?"

"I have heard enough."

"You heard what you wanted to hear."

Sebastian threw his hands up into the air. "Yes, finally."

Ali immediately concealed her emotions, shutting herself completely off to him. He had erected a solid shield and was allowing nothing, absolutely nothing to penetrate it.

"Do you hurt, Sebastian?" she asked candidly.

"You're damn right I do," he all but shouted at her. "I hurt so badly I feel like punching someone or something. I rage with the pain this whole absurd incident has caused. And through it all I still want you."

He shook his head and laughed, a crazy laugh. "I still want you. Can you believe that? After learning that all this is nothing but a stupid spell, I still ache for you."

Ali ached as well. Ached for his misunderstanding and what his logical mind was doing to him, to them, to their future.

He grabbed her then like a man long in need and short on restraint. He held her up against him and took her mouth with a savage need that befitted a warrior.

The kiss was electric, sending sparks of passion surging through them both at an alarming rate.

"I want you so badly," he said, his mouth separating from hers only long enough to utter his desire.

"Why?" she whispered against his lips and kissed him long and hard.

"I don't know," he admitted, breathless, when she finally released him to answer.

His mouth went back to hers, and his hands slipped down over her backside, kneading her firm flesh and pressing her to him.

"You make me crazy," he said and slipped his hands up around her waist to guide her along with him toward the couch.

She realized his intentions. He needed to make love with her, wild, unbridled love. And as much as she longed for his intimate touch and the magic they made, she understood it was not possible. Not now. Not until he settled his issues. Maybe not ever again.

She kissed him softly. "I love you, Sebastian, forever and always."

He felt that stab to his gut again and closed his eyes.

"Ali," he whispered gently and opened his eyes.

She was gone.

He looked around the room, spinning round in his haste to catch a fleeting glimpse of her. She was nowhere.

Had she ever been there?

He dropped down on the couch. She toyed with him. Tormented him. Nourished his unquenchable need for her.

She was a witch.

He bolted off the sofa and into his bedroom, slipping out of his shorts as he entered the bathroom.

He needed a cold shower.

He stepped under the rushing spray and yelped when the cold pellets stung his hot skin. He immediately adjusted it to a more tolerable temperature and stood with the lukewarm water soaking him.

He had to gather his sane thoughts and focus on the logical, the here and now. He was driving himself to the brink of insanity, and that was an unacceptable behavior. He was acting foolishly, almost like a young school boy totally distraught with the idea of losing his true love.

True love.

"Hah," he said loudly. "How can you truly love a witch when she can cast a spell on you and force you to love her?"

Cast to the heavens.

What was she trying to tell him? If the spell is cast to the heavens, then is it fate that decides the outcome? And not the witch?

But a witch plants a suggestion, he argued with himself.

But a suggestion can only grow where there is fertile ground. Otherwise it would wither and die off.

Had Ali sensed this and cast a spell that would nourish them along until each decided?

He had certainly been attracted to her on first sight, but then she was beautiful. But he had been involved with beautiful women before. What made Ali different?

The way she was so familiar with him on sight. Her touch was sure and direct, her intentions clear. She presented no hidden agenda, she told him what she wanted and who she was, and she openly cast the spell.

It was almost as if they belonged to each other from that first moment. He had never even given thought to a brief affair with her. It was all or nothing.

And she certainly had not pushed the issue of a lifetime commitment. He had. She had talked of their mating and a glorious love affair, but it was he who wanted more.

He sighed, braced his hands on the wall, closed his eyes, bowed his head, and allowed the water to ease the growing tension in his neck.

He had to keep his eyes closed. The reminder of how she affected him was still much too obvious and needy. She had felt good in his arms, as if she had always belonged there.

Forever and always.

He lifted his face to the spray. A mistake. The pinlike jabs assaulted his lips and reminded him just how much he continued to ache for the taste of her.

They had made love in the shower a few times, and with a much needed smile he recalled the feel of her naked skin against his. His hands had ridden the curve of her slim waist down to the blond tangle of curls between her legs. She had giggled and wiggled her nicely rounded backside against him, and he had grown even harder.

She had encouraged him to touch her. *All over.*

And he had.

He closed his eyes once again and pictured her there against him. His hands reached out and touched her just as she had urged him to, just as he had wanted to and he moaned.

He moaned with the exquisite feel of her upon his hands.

Warm, wet, and wonderfully real.

Ali informed her aunt that she wasn't feeling well and intended to go straight to her room and remain there for the rest of the evening.

Sydney did not argue with her. She simply informed her that she would be there if she needed her.

Ali understood she could cry on her aunt's sturdy shoulder whenever she wished, but this evening she wanted to cry alone.

She took herself straight to the shower, the scent of Sebastian so heavy upon her that she could barely breathe without throbbing for him.

Tears joined the warm spray that glided down Ali's face. She had tried so hard to make him understand, to actually see reason. This time his logic had failed him. What was she to do? She had no idea and at the moment didn't want to think about it.

She wanted to empty her mind and relax. Tomorrow

would be time enough to reevaluate the situation and make plans, or simply realize that she had done all she could. The rest remained up to him.

She raised her arms up, stretching her body and wiggling her fingers to ease the tension.

She gasped and looked quickly around her. She had felt a hand on her breast, she was sure of it. She paused a moment and listened. Nothing. She closed her eyes and stepped under the shower. Her own unfulfilled desires were playing tricks on her.

She gasped again, this time feeling her breasts being cupped firmly and her nipples being toyed with, and then she knew.

She whimpered softly when she felt his body move up behind her. She had thought she had successfully shut herself off to him, but somehow he had penetrated her defenses and managed to connect with her.

Foolish.

She sighed, whimpered and laughed all at the same time. Only a powerful love could connect two people this way, and he didn't even realize it.

She could fight him, her power was strong enough, but she didn't want to. She surrendered to his touch and the pleasure he brought her.

Ali.

Her name sounded like an aching plea that spilled almost reluctantly from his lips, and she smiled as she raised her arms up to slip back and over his head and to place her face next to his.

Touch me, all over.

He did. His hands moved from her breasts slowly down her stomach, exploring her with the strokes of a talented artist who admired fine art. His fingers glided leisurely down between her legs.

Open for me.

She did. And welcomed his intimate intrusion with a moan that rushed over his cheeks to whisper across his lips.

You're mine.

Yes, I am. All yours, forever and always.

Not long enough.

She smiled at his predictable response. A response that always filled her heart with joy.

He stroked her with a forcefulness that demanded she respond, and she did with whimpers of desire, moans of pleasure, and a rhythm all her own.

I want you.

His breath was rapid and his passion rampant.

Then take me.

He did. He twisted her around in his arms, braced her against the wall, lifted her up by her backside for her legs to wrap tightly around him and entered her so swiftly she cried out his name.

All reason vanished and there remained only the two of them, locked in magic. They rode to a fast and furious climax breaking together in an explosion that only magical love could create.

"Ali," he whispered and looked directly into her eyes, being there at that moment with her. "I love you."

"I love you," she said. "Forever and always."

"Not long enough," he said softly and shook his head as he faded away.

The water turned cold and jolted Sebastian back to his senses. That is, if he had any senses left.

He steadied himself, pressing a firm hand flat on the shower wall while the water raced over him and helped return him to reality.

"Damn." She had felt so real, tasted so real, been so real?

Had she invaded his thoughts. But *he* had thought about

her. Had he invaded her thoughts? Was it possible?

He turned off the shower and quickly dried himself, wrapping the towel around his waist as he rushed still half wet to the phone.

The housekeeper put him on hold until Ali picked up the phone a few minutes later.

"Are you all right?" he asked. He told himself he didn't know why he called her, but he knew. He was aware.

Her voice shook and she spoke slowly and so softly Sebastian had to strain to hear.

"Yes, I think."

How did he respond?

"I didn't realize, Ali," he said in a way of an explanation.

"Now you do," she said. "Please. Please be aware of your thoughts."

"How, Ali?" he asked, stunned by what sensibility would argue was merely a dream.

"When you discover the answer, you will know the truth."

Sebastian remained silent and confused.

"And, Sebastian," she said tentatively.

"Yes?"

"Be foolish."

Twenty-seven

One day off of work was enough for Sebastian, especially when the only thing he accomplished was to sulk. He wanted to resume his life.

His life.

And that was the problem. What had happened to his life? Ali had turned his normal, logical world upside down. Now when he looked at people he wondered who they really were. Mortals or witches.

He had decided running away from this dilemma would do him no good, so he chose not to go away but to stay, and besides, working when something troubled him always managed to help him solve his problem.

His calendar was full, which he expected, having ignored his business for the last two days. Several appointments with new clients and a business lunch with a senator would keep his mind occupied for the whole day.

Tonight he would have a late supper out and go home and drop straight into bed. He would shower in the morning when his mind was clear of *Ali.*

Her voice constantly sounded like a soft whisper in his head. He had maintained solid control of his thoughts after the shower incident. He didn't need any more erotic astral projection, if that's what it was.

He had not only been stunned by the episode, he had been shocked to see that he had been in Ali's shower, not his. And while he attempted to convince himself she had the power to move him about, he still found it difficult to believe that she could have caused the interlude. He knew, sensed, understood that the seductive scene was entirely of his own doing.

He shook his head, certain now that he was permanently afflicted with the annoying reaction and headed out his office door.

"Remember you have a two o'clock and a three-thirty appointment," Ms. Smithers reminded him as he walked past her desk.

"Not a problem. Senator Millon is a busy man and isn't one to waste time."

Her familiar cough stopped him dead and he turned. "Is there a problem?"

Ms. Smithers wasn't one to waste time, either, especially delivering news he wouldn't welcome.

"Senator Millon will not be having lunch with you today. Sydney Wyrrd will."

His first, brief thought was not to meet with her, but that would be refusing to face your adversary. And while he felt Sydney Wyrrd could provide him with no further help, he was curious as to what she had to say to him.

"Thank you, Carol," he said sincerely. "I assume you were requested to keep this information from me?"

"Only if I felt comfortable in doing so," she answered.

He smiled his appreciation. "Thank you for your loyalty."

Sebastian took the elevator down, Craig Munro from research joined him on the tenth floor.

"Glad I caught you, Mr. Wainwright," he said and fumbled with the hefty pile of papers he held in his hands. "I am so pleased to be working on this Wyrrd matter. I can't begin to detail the extensiveness of the Wyrrd Foundation research and the significance of their findings. They are truly a pioneer in the field of development, any development, their interests are so wide and varied. And the craziest thing is that most of their findings have a fundamental basis in nature. It is incredible, simply incredible.''

Sebastian caught the flush of excitement that stained the young man's face. A flush that was inherent to researchers upon a fascinating discovery. ''How did you find this out? I only requested basic information on their research projects. Nothing intrusive.''

''I never intruded, sir,'' Craig clarified. ''I was running through one of their programs, attainable when requested through proper channels, when a Wyrrd employee popped in and asked if he could assist me. He was extremely cordial and more than helpful, providing me with information far beyond what I had hoped to find. I'm writing up a report for you now.'' He tapped at the stack of papers in his hand.

''I look forward to reading it,'' Sebastian said as the elevator arrived at the lobby level, and he briefly wondered who at the Wyrrd Foundation had given permission for Wainwright Security to receive the information.

Both men got off.

''You know what the strangest thing was?'' Craig said with a shake of his head. ''I still can't figure out how the guy from the Wyrrd Foundation knew my name. I signed on under the company password, and there was no way they could have known who I was, and yet this guy immediately upon greeting me used my full name. Not just a first name, but my full, given name. Crazy.''

Craig walked away still shaking his head.

Not if you are witches.

Sebastian kept tight rein on his head and walked out the door.

• • •

Sydney looked elegant in a silk pale blue suit, pearl knob earrings, and a three-strand pearl necklace. She appeared to be the perfect Washington lady, poised, educated, and well-bred.

No one would ever suspect she was a *witch*.

Sebastian, however, knew the truth. He walked over to where she sat waiting for him at a corner table that was discreetly tucked away from the usual chaotic lunch crowd.

She greeted him with a smile, and he graciously kissed her cheek before taking the seat beside her.

"You were so sure I would come?" he asked.

She looked surprised. "Of course, you are much too wise a man not to. And besides I assumed you live by a code that advises you to keep your opponent as close to you as you would a friend."

Sebastian couldn't help but smile. He liked Sydney. She was a remarkable woman. Witch or not.

"Now I know why all the men chase after you."

She laughed softly. "Why is that, my dear boy?"

"You bewitch them with your charm, grace, and intelligence."

"Only after years of practice and *sensible* knowledge," she added with a wink.

Sebastian laughed himself.

"Have I bewitched you, Sebastian?" she asked more seriously.

His answer was delayed by the waiter's presence, and as soon as orders were taken, Sydney looked to him for an answer.

"Your niece has more than demonstrated the powers of a witch."

"That doesn't answer my question," she said softly. "Have I bewitched you?"

He answered without hesitation. "I think you bewitch every man you meet, but in the mortal sense."

She smiled and nodded. "You are as intelligent as I believed."

"What do you want from me, Sydney?"

She reached out and patted his hand. "To let you know that I care."

"Not to help your niece snag me?"

She placed her hand over her heart and feigned a stricken look. "To think I would do such a thing."

He reached for his filled wineglass. "I think you would do anything for your niece."

"She is impetuous and stubborn. Often not looking before she leaps."

"That's an understatement," he said and gulped down a good portion of the wine.

"She reacts more with her heart than her wisdom."

That statement got Sebastian's attention, and he ignored the remainder of wine in his glass.

"Witches are really not a complicated breed," she continued. "They care deeply and wish harm to no one. They are aware of the consequences of their actions if they do not follow their heritage. Still there are a few who find boundaries impossible to accept. They take chances and go beyond, but then, I suppose mortals would refer to them as visionaries."

"You can't change her, you know," he said without thinking.

"I am well aware of that. She is who she is."

"A witch," he whispered and reached once again for his wineglass.

"This troubles you?"

"There are so many variables, and I am not sure what is real and what is not. I am attempting to understand but find it difficult. A witch has power. Powers far beyond the imaginable. How do I deal with the probabilities of those powers and what they represent?"

"You have not found the answer?" she asked sadly.

"I sometimes think it is close, and then I feel I can't grasp it at all." He shook his head and laughed. "And if I shake my head one more time, I think it will finally unscrew from my neck and fall off, then I will not have to concern myself with anything."

Sydney smiled and pushed randomly at her Caesar salad with her fork. "What do you plan to do?"

"Take time to make sense of it all," he said, ignoring his Cobb salad.

"Is there nothing I can do?" she asked, choosing her words carefully.

"This is something I must do on my own," he admitted with his usual stubbornness.

"And what is it you will do?"

He looked directly at her and answered, "Search for the truth." He laughed and added, "And be foolish."

Foolish.

Was he being foolish in dating another woman?

It was Friday night and he had a date. He was dressed in his black tuxedo and all ready to attend a charity ball. A least it wasn't a Wyrrd Foundation charity ball. And it was a last-minute decision.

James had called him yesterday and had begged him to help him out. His associate's date had canceled at the last minute and she couldn't find a replacement. Would he please fill in in a pinch?

He almost refused and then thought better of it. He hadn't been able to get Alisande off his mind all week. Not that she had pursued him; on the contrary, she had completely ignored him. No phone calls. No mind intrusions. No dreams.

Damn, how he missed those dreams.

He thought that if he could blank his mind he could rid

himself of any spell she had cast over him, and yet he found himself missing her more each day.

Was he being foolish in accepting this date? It meant nothing to him. He wasn't interested in the woman; it was a mere favor to a friend. And what in the hell did he think it would accomplish anyway?

"Damn," he muttered to himself, angry that he had agreed to the stupid evening after all and grabbed his keys off his dresser and headed out of the house.

The evening was half over, and Sebastian couldn't wait for it to end. Janelle, his date, was nice enough but—

Ordinary.

He almost laughed at his own thought. Ali had certainly spoiled him. Her audacious manner and temptress nature was something he hadn't realized was so important to him. They defined her, and they were definitions he had grown to admire and love.

He refused to shake his head in a crowd full of people, so he downed the remainder of his wine and went in search of another glass. Janelle had taken herself off with a group of her friends to talk business, and he was left to mingle and network, which he had no intentions of doing.

Downing more wine and keeping to himself sounded more appealing.

A sudden hush whispered across the filled room, the music slowed, the dancers stopped, table chatter softened, and Sebastian watched as all heads turned.

Sydney Wyrrd had entered on the arm of a retired admiral, silencing the usual gossiping tongues long enough for them to stare in awe at the woman who defied age. She was simply stunning in a black dress that spurned her advanced age and made her look twenty years younger.

He smiled at her outrageous and unexpected entrance and

turned to walk away, promising himself to pay his respects later in the evening.

He stopped short, his eyes resting on Alisande.

She stood only a few feet away from him, dressed in a purple gown that shocked the eyes and senses and was created strictly for seduction.

The sleeves were long, the bodice low, the waist curved and the remaining portion lethal. And her hair? A windswept creation that looked to be spawned from a night of ardent passion.

She was a vision of carnal temptation that could easily entice a saint to sin. But then he was no saint.

He made no move to approach her, and she made no move at all. He blinked his eyes a few times, thinking she might not actually be there but only a figment of his desires or the wine.

She whispered something, and he strained to hear her words. He shook his head, annoyed he was unable to catch even a faint sound.

She whispered again, her words riding on a gentle exhale of her breath.

He failed to catch them and grew even more irritated, yet still he did not move toward her.

She pressed three fingers to her lips and gently blew her message to him, then turned and slowly walked away.

His wide-eyed stare was glued to her erotically swaying backside and wasn't prepared for her words that were delivered with a punch to his lips.

The muscles in his face tightened, his dark eyes narrowed, and his nostrils flared. He dumped his near empty wineglass to the silver tray on a nearby stand so hard that the stem cracked.

He stormed after Ali with her words reverberating in his ears.

Prudent mortal.

Twenty-eight

Ali waited on the terrace for Sebastian. A smile tempted her moist lips, but she kept it at bay. It would do her no good to display such open confidence in her ability to challenge him successfully. He would assume it a witch's trick when it was simply mortal logic.

The thought brought a brief surface smile, which she quickly suppressed. Confidence was one thing, arrogance another. She might be able to make him follow her, but what then?

She couldn't make him love her. That was his choice and his choice alone. She could only try to make him see reason, an absurd idea since she had been trying desperately upon first meeting him to convince him otherwise.

Strange the tricks life played. Here she was a witch using logic to help a mortal understand magic.

This mortal just happened to be too stubborn for his own good, refusing not only to see the obvious but to admit it. And time was running out, if he did not request help soon or admit that he loved her of his own volition and with no help from the spell, then the spell would begin to weave its final magic and all would be lost.

Ali raised her face to the heavenly night sky and wished on the brightest twinkling star that—

His arm shot out past the side of her face, and he grasped at the dark sky. He brought his clasped hand back to hold just beneath Ali's wide eyes.

He whispered near her ear. "Make a wish."

Ali slowly released the breath that had caught so nervously in her throat. She brought her hand up to rest over his clasped one and gently directed it to rest against her breast over her heart.

His hand was warm, taut, and filled with the strength of his warring emotions. She closed her eyes and squeezed his clutched hand in hers.

Please. Please let him believe.

His hand opened slowly, and he pressed it firmly over the swell of her breasts that rose full from her dress. He eased her back against him, and his words sounded more like anguished pleas than mere whispers.

"You drive me to the brink of insanity time and time again, and still I want you."

"Then you have not been truthful with yourself," she said, relaxing her body back along his.

"Truth?" He laughed softly. "Does the word exist for you?"

"Have I been anything but truthful with you? Or is it that you have failed to see?"

"I am not blind."

"But you do not see."

"You talk in riddles like witches do."

"I speak the truth as witches cannot speak otherwise."

"Then tell me what is the truth?" he demanded, roughly turning her around to face him.

"I love you," Ali said without hesitation.

"And you are a witch," he added as if in someway it tainted her acknowledgment.

"I have never denied my heritage to you."

"And the spell—"

"Is yours to decide."

He stepped away from her, though his dark eyes remained fixed on her green ones. "So you say."

"I say nothing, the spell does."

"Repeat the spell for me," he ordered, his dark intent eyes challenging her.

"You wish it repeated to see if you can make sense of it," she said with an insolent smile that announced the acceptance of his dare.

He remained silent, unwilling to confirm her suspicions.

He folded his arms over his chest, and Ali couldn't help but wonder if the movement was instinctive or protective.

She gave her head a toss; dramatics were definitely called for—after all, mortals expected them and she didn't wish to disappoint Sebastian. She raised her hands to the night sky and spoke in a voice that soothed and lulled the listener.

"True love is often rare; forever love is always shared; mistaken love cannot be denied; make-believe love cannot hide; practical love makes two people whole; but magical love *touches* the soul."

Sebastian felt a shiver race over him and rolled his eyes to see if he caught any glimpse of gold dust floating down around him.

"Once a spell is cast, it cannot be cast again, Sebastian," Ali said, hoping to alleviate his concern.

"Why?"

"The strength of a spell is in its cast. Subsequent casts would serve little purpose. Either you believe when you cast it or you don't."

"You believed?"

"I wouldn't have cast the spell if I didn't. A spell is issued for a reason. A good, sound, proper reason."

"And making someone fall in love with you is a proper reason?" he asked with a brief shake of his head before stopping himself.

She smiled and sadly shook her head. "You have just answered your own question."

He stared at her in complete confusion.

She walked over to him and gently tapped her finger to his temple. "The spell is yours to recall and yours to understand if you so choose."

"I suppose that means within the spell lies the answer."

She ran her hand lovingly over his white dress shirt and sighed sensually.

Her intentionally silent, sexy invitation sent his testosterone level soaring, the results being evident when Ali brushed herself suggestively against him before she reluctantly stepped away.

"Could the answer be that simple, Sebastian?" she said with a teasing smile, finding it nearly impossible to control her own hormones when his were so obviously potent.

"Where you are concerned nothing is simple," he said, taking a deep breath and berating himself for his uncontrollable desire for her.

"Simple? Complicated? It is all how you perceive it."

"Crazy," he said, this time shaking his head on purpose.

"Who?" she asked, sending the question to him on a soft breath that reached his lips in a faint hush.

He stormed over to her, grabbing her by the arms with a determined strength that still possessed enough gentleness not to hurt her.

"You," he said, his mouth a bare inch from hers. "You tempt me, you torment me, you—"

"Love me," she finished and captured his lips in a breath-stealing kiss before he had a chance to think or respond.

He surrendered to the passion that raged through him and lost himself in the questionable love that surrounded them. Later was time enough to argue, to debate, to make decisions. There was time. Plenty of time.

Not enough.

He heard the soft warning in his head. Had it come from Ali, or from himself?

He felt the earth spin around him, felt their bodies lock tightly together, felt a rushing heat that almost consumed him, and then in a flash it ceased.

He stood alone, his head spinning, his lips aching, and his heart hurting.

''She really leaves an impact, doesn't she?'' the familiar voice said.

Sebastian took a moment to settle the strange sensations assaulting him before turning around and facing yet another witch, Dagon.

''She was here, then?'' he asked, feeling foolish, light-headed, and completely distraught but nonetheless needing to know for sure.

Dagon handed him a full glass of wine. ''Without a doubt.''

Sebastian downed a generous gulp.

''Ali possesses a nature that defies all logic,'' Dagon said, raising his own wineglass in a mock salute.

Sebastian raised his own glass. ''You can count on it.''

''A character trait that seldom appeals to a mortal.''

Sebastian shrugged. ''Appeal? Tempt is more like it.''

''Just like a witch,'' Dagon said.

Sebastian eyed the handsome man skeptically. He was obviously up to something, and since he had made his opinions of mortals clear, he was certain Dagon wasn't there to console him. ''What are you getting at?''

''Mortals don't trust witches. Your history has proved that.''

''I forget,'' Sebastian said with a dawning nod. ''You believe witches belong with witches and mortals with mortals.''

"Let's call it a balance of nature," he suggested seriously. "Mortals have never been able to cope with witches and their innate abilities. They either refuse to understand us or feel that anything more powerful than themselves is reason to label it evil and of course persecute."

"You are asking mortals to accept the illogical," Sebastian said in defense of his kind.

"To you," Dagon said, pointing an accusing finger at him, "it is illogical. To us it is natural."

Sebastian paused in his response to give his words thought. He had been taught to think one way. For all intents and purposes it was believed to be the acceptable way, and now?

He rubbed at the back of his neck.

"Witches belong with witches," Dagon reiterated.

Sebastian's own words surprised him. "What about love?"

"Love requires unconditional acceptance. Mortals fail to accept or love unconditionally," he said with disdain. "Let Alisande go."

His words penetrated Sebastian like a sharp-edged knife inflicting permanent damage. *Let Alisande go.*

Could he?

Could he walk away from her forever? Never hold her again? Never touch her again? Never make magic with her again?

Dagon walked up to Sebastian, the two adversaries standing face to face. "I will not see her hurt. I leave soon for Scotland, and before I go I will see that Alisande is at peace with this situation."

"A threat?" Sebastian asked with equal bravado.

"A promise," Dagon said with a smile that warned.

"I don't fear you," Sebastian said with an arrogant smirk that impressed and startled Dagon.

He grinned at Sebastian and slapped him on the back. "Then you truly are foolish."

Sebastian couldn't sleep. He had left the affair early, explaining to Janelle and James that he had an emergency. Which he did.

Leave or lose his mind.

He arrived home before eleven, and it was now almost midnight and sleep still eluded him. He sat up in his bed, the small bedside table lamp casting a soft glow to an otherwise dark, shadowy room.

His chattering thoughts had plagued him all night, and that damn magical love spell tumbled repeatedly in his head.

Research and examination of the facts always managed to help him in reaching a satisfactory conclusion. He reached in the nightstand drawer and withdrew a pad and pen.

He positioned himself comfortably in his bed and put pen to paper. He scribbled the spell out to examine, dissect, and hopefully understand it line for line.

He rested his pen next to the first verse, reciting the words out loud as if hearing them spoken would help their magical meaning penetrate his logical brain.

"True love is often rare."

How many times had he heard people talk of true love? Women sighed over it and men laughed at it while silently searching for it. True love was what movies were made of. A love that binds two people together forever and always.

Not long enough.

His own words haunted his thoughts.

He chased the stalking words away if only for the moment and moved to the next line.

"Forever love is always shared."

A love that lasts forever cannot exist unless it is shared by two willing people. Forever love exists deeply-rooted within each soul for eternity.

Not long enough.

He didn't bother to shake his head. The useless gesture wouldn't chase away the nagging words.

He read the third verse. "Mistaken love cannot be denied."

It is mistaken because it cannot be denied. The love is there between the souls whether they accept it or not since neither can truly deny their feelings. It will *forever* be a part of them no matter the outcome.

Not long enough.

He expected to hear them. The silent, persistent words were as much a part of the spell as the words he spoke.

Line four was next.

"Make-believe love cannot hide."

He smiled. No matter how much you wanted to make believe you loved a person, you couldn't. It was impossible to pretend to love. You either loved or you didn't and making believe couldn't change that. Love was *always*—

The familiar words interrupted his thoughts.

Not long enough.

He read verse five nodding his head. "Practical love makes two people whole."

Now here was the truth. Practical love filled the empty void. It was solid, reliable, something you could count on like the person being there in the morning when you woke up or wrapped in your arms at night or beside you when you needed to feel her warmth and security. This kind of love was durable and secured two people together *forever.*

Not long enough.

Soon those incessant words were going to be imprinted on his forehead. But did he need reminding? If they kept repeating so frequently in his head, maybe he did.

His eyes scanned the last line and he softly recited the verse. "But magical love *touches* the soul."

He dropped his head back against the headboard, ignoring the whack he took to his skull.

He couldn't deny what he felt for Ali was magic. And as far as touching the soul? He was certain they had accomplished that monumental feat every time they made love. Made magic? But was magic real and did it endure as favorably as the other loves?

And most of all what was the spell trying to tell him? What did it all mean?

Was this the love she was after and wanted from him?

Magical love?

And what about all these other loves? How did they differ from the last verse?

If the answer resided in the spell, it certainly hid itself well. A troublesome thought since he had broken many a complex code. So why was he having a problem with this?

Could it be that simple?

Her words offered a clue. Was he searching so hard he couldn't see the obvious?

What exactly had she made him feel when she cast the spell?

He recalled feeling a warm, strange sensation spreading in his chest. Not at all uncomfortable, rather soothing, even a bit titillating. What had she done to him? What had she made him or *forced* him to feel? Love?

He sprang straight up in bed, shaking his head and talking out loud to himself. "Could she have allowed me to feel a faint stirring of her heartfelt emotions for me? Had she given freely of her love for me to sample? Was the sensation I felt the love that was stirring and blossoming in her heart?"

He grew more excited and jumped out of bed, pacing the

floor naked. Did the spell contain all the ingredients that when mixed together created the last component and the most important, magical love?

He was finally getting somewhere. If he probed deeper, he would better understand and just possibly get somewhere in sorting out his troubled thoughts. He pounced on the bed, grabbing for the pen and pad.

The clock struck midnight

He shook his head. What had he planned to write? The thought was right there in his head, but he couldn't seem to grasp it. It was as if someone permanently erased it from his memory.

"What was it?" he mumbled angrily, tapping at his temple, trying to jar his thoughts.

"I can't forget. I can't," he warned himself, the very thought frightening.

The words drifted like a fearful omen in his head.

Not enough time.

Twenty-nine

"You take care, my dear boy," Sydney ordered like a concerned parent, walking arm and arm with Dagon toward the atrium.

"You must come visit," Dagon said and stopped just outside the etched-glass atrium door. "I have a strange feeling I may require your—"

"Help?" Sydney asked with a smile.

"Expertise," he said firmly. "I am quite capable of taking care of myself."

Sydney cast a worried glance inside the atrium to Ali, who sat on the wicker settee looking lost and troubled by her thoughts. "Sometimes we all need a little help."

Dagon cast a worrisome glance through the door. "I wish it wasn't necessary for me to leave right now. I thought I could help her through this, fix it, make it all better for her like I did when we were young."

Sydney patted his arm. "You aren't young anymore. She must face the consequences of her actions."

Dagon stepped away from Sydney and paced the area beside the door. "All that mortal needs to do is admit that his love for her is real and not caused by a witch's spell. What is stopping the fool?"

Before Sydney could respond, Dagon continued. "And

if he had enough sense to ask you or me for help, then we could tell him exactly what was needed without worry of the consequences of the blasted spell.''

Sydney smiled and approached Dagon. ''Calm down. There is no more you can do.''

''I feel I have failed her,'' he admitted reluctantly.

''Never,'' Sydney chastised with a gentle understanding. ''Ali's choice was made when the spell was cast. You must accept as she must accept the outcome.''

''Which is?'' Dagon asked cautiously.

''As it should be,'' Sydney said and kissed him on the cheek. ''I will leave you to say your goodbye.'' She gave a loving pat to his arm and walked away.

''Sydney,'' he called to her and she turned. ''I was thinking of stopping by Wainwright Security to say farewell. Do you think it wise?''

She smiled. ''I think you have already made your decision and the die has been cast.''

He waited until she was a safe distance away and mumbled, ''Damn.''

He heard her reprimand in his head. *Watch your manners, dear boy, and give my regards to Sebastian.*

It was all the encouragement he needed. He walked into the atrium feeling much relieved.

Ali jumped off the settee and ran to Dagon, and as usual he caught her in his arms in a comforting and secure hug.

''I wish you didn't have to leave so soon,'' she said, fighting the threatening tears and the feeling of loneliness she always experienced with his partings.

''You will come visit, I insist,'' he ordered her like a brother would a special sister. Her body trembled and he hugged her close to him, walking her to the settee, where he sat down beside her.

''I really messed things up this time,'' she confessed, the

tears starting to run slowly down her cheeks. "*You* couldn't even get me out of this one."

That cut him to the quick. He pried her gently away from him, held her firmly by the shoulders, and gave her a brief shake. "Ye of little faith."

Her wet eyes rounded and looked to him with such hope that he almost cried himself. Almost, not quite. A male witch simply did not shed tears.

She shrugged and collapsed back in the corner of the chair. "I'm being my usual selfish self."

"Wait, I want a witness to this admission," he said seriously but with a smile.

She waved a dismissive hand at him. "You have done all you can and I appreciate your help. I was foolish—"

"A normal affliction for you."

A weak smile joined the tears that slipped without regard down her face. "And one that has cost me dearly."

"Are you sure about your love for this mortal?"

"Without a doubt," she answered. "I want to spend the rest of my life making magic with him. I want to have his babies and share the pleasures and pains of watching them grow, and I want to grow old in his arms and when our time comes I want to face eternity together."

"That's a long time."

"Not long enough," she said. Her bottom lip quivered in a concentrated effort to fight back the burst of tears that gushed forth.

Dagon pulled her back into his arms. "I will do all I can, dear heart." He lifted her trembling chin. "If by some insane magic I can manage to right this crazy spell, you are to understand that from this day forward this mortal of yours will be your protector, and you, dear heart," he said with a wicked grin, "will owe me big time."

She sighed heavily. "If only you could do something, I would forever be in your debt."

He kissed her cheek. ''The challenge is too great for me to turn down.''

She looked at him with a mixture of hope and sorrow.

He kissed her once more and stood. ''I leave for Scotland this evening.'' He walked in his usual arrogant stride to the door and turned. ''I assume tonight you will cast a prayer to the heavens for help?''

She nodded. ''It is the only hope I have left.''

''Ye of little faith,'' he said once more, sent her a wink, and disappeared.

Ali didn't know what he was up to, and she knew how firmly his hands were tied in this matter, but knowing Dagon he would make an effort. And knowing Sebastian and his mortal nature, she wouldn't be surprised if they came to blows.

But then, maybe, just maybe Dagon might be able to conjure up a small amount of crazy magic that might help. Or maybe he would use mortal tactics against a mortal man.

The office staff had gone home around six, almost an hour ago, and yet Sebastian remained in his office alone. All day he had given thought to Ali and the spell, and all day his thoughts eluded him like haunting ghosts in his mind. They were there floating around, but he couldn't quite visualize them.

Frustration had set in by midafternoon and he had become so grouchy that Ms. Smithers threatened to quit. He had instantly taken control of his emotions, and now they lay warring within him.

Which meant he was none too happy when Dagon materialized in the middle of his office.

''What the hell do you want?'' he asked. ''And I prefer uninvited visitors to use the door.''

''A pleasant greeting to someone who has come to bid you goodbye,'' Dagon said and walked over to the chair in front of the large desk that Sebastian sat behind.

"A postcard would have sufficed," Sebastian said caustically.

"My, my, we are in a snit," Dagon responded with equal grace and candor.

Sebastian stood, sending his chair sprawling out behind him, and he slammed his hands flat down on his desk. "Look, I'm in no mood to deal pleasantly with a witch."

"Frustrated, are you?" Dagon asked and walked in front of the chair he stood behind and took a seat as if unconcerned with Sebastian's plight.

Sebastian fought to maintain his control. "Say your goodbye and get out."

Dagon wagged a warning finger at him. "You don't want to go up against me."

Sebastian stood straight, fists clenched at his sides. "No, I wouldn't want to do that, after all you are a witch and have those super-duper powers. Heaven forbid you fight me on my own level since you just might lose."

That brought Dagon out of his chair. "I don't think so, but if you wish to test your erroneous theory, by all means I will oblige you."

Sebastian was about to slip out of his jacket when he realized what he was doing. He was ready and willing to throw fists he was so distraught. He shook his head and rubbed at the back of his neck.

"She makes me crazy."

"Are you sure it's Ali who is driving you crazy?" Dagon challenged.

Sebastian looked at him as if he had grown two heads. "Don't talk in riddles. I hate riddles."

Dagon smiled, actually feeling sorry for the poor lovestruck mortal. "I'm only suggesting that perhaps you're driving yourself crazy."

"Oh, Ali has nothing to do with it? She just enters my

life, turns it upside down, and then expects me to—''

Sebastian looked strangely at Dagon. ''Damn, I forgot what I was going to say.''

Dagon looked startled.

''What's wrong?'' Sebastian asked, not caring for that concerned gleam in his eyes.

''Nothing,'' Dagon said much too quickly to Sebastian's perceptive ear.

''What aren't you telling me?'' Sebastian demanded, his frustration rushing to a new all-time high.

Dagon hesitated, not knowing how to proceed, his assistance much too limited by the boundaries of the spell.

''You're keeping something from me,'' Sebastian insisted with a look that warned of dire consequences.

Dagon shook his head.

Sebastian collapsed in his chair, shaking his head. ''I'm crazy, completely and absolutely crazy. That happens when you fall in love with a witch who has—''

''Forgotten again?'' Dagon asked.

Sebastian nodded this time, the seldom-used motion causing an ache in his neck.

''I love Ali so damn much it hurts.''

''Guess you would do anything for her,'' Dagon said, realizing mortal tactics were called for here.

''Anything in my meager powers,'' he agreed.

Dagon rubbed his chin and leaned forward toward the desk. ''She confuses me sometimes.''

Sebastian laughed. ''Only sometimes?''

''Well, I was thinking that if she confused me and I know her so well, what happens when I meet a woman and fall in love?''

''You lose your mind,'' Sebastian said with a weighty sigh.

Dagon smiled, though he wanted to laugh. ''Seriously, it concerns me. How do I know I'm in love? How do I know she is the right one? How do I know it's for real? It's a frightening thought.''

''Tell me about it,'' Sebastian agreed. ''You think that falling in love will be simple. You meet a woman, talk, get to know each other, fall in love, marry, have babies, fight, make up, have more babies.''

''Is that the way it goes?''

''Supposed to go unless you meet a crazy witch who seduces you at every turn and promises nights of magical love, which—'' Sebastian said, pointing a finger at Dagon. ''She delivers and in turn drives you completely senseless.''

''This really worries me,'' Dagon said.

''Why should you worry? You're a witch who wants a witch and who will understand a witch.''

''But what,'' Dagon said, holding up a questioning finger, ''if I fall in love with a mortal woman?''

Sebastian dismissed his worry with the wave of a hand. ''Just cast a spell.''

''No good,'' he said with a shake of his head. ''Spells can't force people to love. I need mortal help with a dilemma like this.''

His words sank into Sebastian's head, and he stared at Dagon.

''Will you *help* me?'' Dagon asked with fingers crossed. A mortal superstition, but one that might work.

Sebastian hesitated for a brief second, shutting his eyes and then opening them with renewed strength. ''Only if you help me.''

''Damn, I thought you would never ask,'' Dagon said, jumping out of his seat.

''What?'' Sebastian asked confused.

''Now I can finally answer all your questions, and we can get this mess straightened out once and for all—''

His sudden pause concerned Sebastian. "A problem? I thought we finally had a solution."

"Let's get through the explanation, and then we can see if there's a problem."

Sebastian nodded and it felt good, so did the sudden flood of relief that rushed through him.

"Let's start at the beginning," Dagon suggested.

"Where Ali strolled into my office without anyone seeing her?"

"Right," Dagon said. "She used fairy dust. She never played fair even as a kid."

Sebastian smiled. "She still doesn't."

Dagon grinned. "We'll fix that."

"Go on," Sebastian urged, the thought of getting even while settling this absurd dilemma sounding awfully good.

"The spell she cast was the strongest of love spells and rarely used. It allows the witch who casts it to let the recipient feel her love. Mind you, she hadn't planned on using it at first, but when she saw you—"

"She knew she loved me," Sebastian finished with a self-satisfied smirk.

"She never did look before she leaped."

"I'm glad she didn't. I think I secretly always wished for magical love but was too sensible to believe it existed. Ali taught me otherwise."

Dagon laughed. "No wonder you fell so hard for her. You were predisposed to the idea. All that was necessary was for it to be the right person."

Sebastian grinned broadly. "And she was."

"But," Dagon cautioned, "it was necessary for you to love her unconditionally."

He slammed his fist on the desk. "I was stupid. I thought the spell—" He shook his head, forgetting what he was about to say.

"That's the problem," Dagon warned. "The spell has a safety device, so to speak."

"Safety?" Sebastian asked.

"The safety device can be altered if the person openly admits to a witch he wants help. If not, then the person cast upon, being you, doesn't accept the caster's, being Ali, love unconditionally, then within a particular time frame the one cast upon, you, loses forever the memory of—"

"No!" Sebastian shouted, instantly realizing what Dagon was about to tell him. "I could never forget Ali, never. She is part of me. I couldn't live without her. I don't want to live without her."

He rushed around the desk, Dagon standing up in defense. Sebastian reached out and grabbed him by his suit jacket. "I'm a foolish mortal who needs help. Give me help, Dagon, or I swear I'll beat the hell out of you."

Dagon couldn't help but laugh.

Sebastian didn't find his humor funny. He shook him. "Help me, damn it, help me!"

Dagon finally controlled his laughter. "I'm going to help you, all right, and my dear Ali is going to owe me big time for the rest of her life."

"We'll name our first son after you," Sebastian offered hastily.

"She's not getting off that easily, and besides, you haven't heard the rest of what you must do if you want this union to be permanent."

Sebastian released him and stepped back. "Tell me. Whatever it is, I'll do it."

Dagon brushed at the few wrinkles in his suit jacket. "I think you just might be up to this particular challenge after all."

"As long as it unites me with Ali—"

"Forever and always?" Dagon asked.

Sebastian smiled. "Not long enough."

Dagon nodded and slipped his arm around Sebastian's shoulder. "Then my friend, I don't think that the problem I spoke of earlier is going to be a problem at all."

Sebastian was ready for anything. "I place myself in your competent hands."

"I like you, Sebastian, even though you are a mortal, and I, my friend, am going to teach you how to cast a special spell."

Thirty

Ali stood on the terrace in her pure white ceremonial robe. It was almost midnight, the beginning of a new day. A new day to Ali always brought with it the promise of hope. And the stars in the heavens above knew she needed a large dose of it.

The warm summer breeze kissed her face and she smiled. It was a stunning night to cast a prayer to the Mother Sky. The temperate breeze ruffled the leaves on the trees, producing a soothing melody. The night creatures joined in with their own magical sounds, and if one knew how to listen, they would hear the beauty of nature's symphony.

''A perfect night.''

Ali turned and greeted her aunt with a smile.

''I wanted to speak with you,'' Sydney said, walking up to her niece and hooking her arm in hers.

Ali moved along with her aunt as she stepped from the terrace onto the thick carpet of moist grass. Neither of them wore shoes. It was a night to feel the energy of the earth, to call on its power and renew and give thanks.

Sydney wore a silk pale blue caftan that gave her body freedom of movement and freedom to feel nature's wonders. They walked slowly toward the trees that led to the woods beyond. They were like sisters, mother and daughter, niece and aunt, lifelong friends, women sharing a special female bond.

Sydney spoke and Ali listened, for she knew no wiser woman, nor admired one as much as her aunt.

"I remember the night you were born. Stubborn you were, giving your mother the hardest of times, and I always felt it was because you wanted to be born on a particular day, as if you sensed that that day held special magic just for you. I watched you grow in courage and strength. You amazed me and made me so very proud of the remarkable woman you have become."

"I wouldn't have become half the woman I am without your love and guidance."

"Perhaps," Sydney said a with gentle nod, "but regardless you have grown into a woman I much admire and respect."

Sydney's words touched Ali deeply. To know her aunt thought so highly of her filled her with immense satisfaction and gratitude.

Sydney stopped not far from the line of trees that marked the entrance to the woods. She took Ali's hands in hers, squeezing them in a loving embrace and looked with gentle concern into her eyes.

"You possess far greater strength and courage than I could ever—"

Ali immediately attempted to differ, but her aunt refused to hear otherwise.

"Listen to me, Ali, for I have a story to tell you."

Ali remained silent, eager to hear her aunt's words, for they never failed to offer wisdom.

Her story unfolded in her soft exotic voice and kept Ali spellbound with each word.

"You once asked me if I ever truly loved, and I told you that my experience was better left to memories. But memories have a way of haunting and reminding one that decisions should sometimes be foolish.

"I was young, barely one hundred years old." She paused, her eyes misting. "*He* was the head of a clan, strong, brave, and proud. We loved with a carefree abandonment and at times wildly. He was everything I dreamed of and more. His strength was that of ten men, and yet when he held me it was with a gentle love that astonished me. He had the most beautiful green eyes, handsome features even with a scar that marred his left cheek and a mighty laugh that shook the treetops."

She paused again, took a reassuring breath, and proceeded. "He knew I was a witch and actually admired my heritage, which in turn made me proud. He wanted to marry me, actually insisted upon it, but I—"

Sydney choked on her words and fought the tears that refused to stay locked away. "I feared the very thing you are going through. He warned me most adamantly never to cast a spell on him. He said it wasn't necessary, that he loved me enough and no spell could make him love me more. The magical love spell was the one that would have granted us what I wanted most with him, eternity together."

Ali wiped at her own tears, feeling her aunt's regret.

"I have told myself many times over the years that I should have been foolish and simply leaped before I looked. I never loved another man the way I loved Duncan and I never will. And I will forever regret not taking the chance."

Sydney took another reaffirming breath. "That is why I so admire your extraordinary courage and persistence. No matter the consequences, you took that leap of faith in the name of love. And seldom does one have the bravery to tempt fate. You are truly a gallant woman."

With tears running down her pale cheeks, Sydney hugged her niece tightly to her and with a whispery sob said, "All my love, all my hope, and all my prayers go with you tonight.''

Ali embraced her aunt and found it difficult to let go. Being so much in love, she could fully understand the pain and anguish her aunt had suffered and still did. And with tomorrow's dawn she just might face the same sorrowful consequences.

Sydney released her, stepping back, ''Go. Time draws near for a good cast and good fortune.''

''I am frightened,'' she admitted.

Sydney stood straight and proud and offered prudent advice. ''Dispel your fear, my child, it will only hamper your skill and it can only exist if you give it life.''

Ali smiled, pressed her hand to her chest, and drew her tightly clasped hand away to place it in Sydney's outstretched hand. ''You will dispose of my fear?''

''With pleasure,'' she said, cupping her hands over Ali's and drawing away from her the one emotion that impedes even the strongest of men.

Ali turned and walked toward the woods, her aunt's soft voice whispering in her head.

My blessings go with you.

Ali made her way through the dark woods without fear. Her steps were firm and steady. She required no map or light to guide her way. She knew the path. The sacred place was a special part of her heritage, and she would always find her way in the dark without a problem.

It was a place her mother and aunt had often brought her to. A sacred place for witches. It sat deep in the center of the woods, protected and cared for by the trees, the foliage, the animals, and the fairies.

It was the heart of nature. It teemed with life, giving and receiving. Round and round. No beginning and no end. Constant and forever. It was the sacred well of eternity.

And a witch only cast or offered a prayer from the hallowed ground when absolutely necessary.

She had joined her mother and aunt there for lessons. And was taught the importance of a witch's heritage and knowledge. Few casts were made there and those that were were solitary casts.

One witch standing alone, asking for help from the great Mother Sky. And if two stood there?

Then eternity would be theirs.

She entered a small clearing and stood silent, head bowed, paying her respects.

The area formed a complete, perfect circle, not very large in size, and the tall surrounding trees stood guard like Roman centurions. The night sky capped the secluded domain, and a multitude of stars twinkled in homage to the full moon.

It was almost midnight. The blending of one day into the next. A continuation of the cycle. Over and over. As with life.

Ali descended to her knees and silently gave thanks for all she had and all life gave. She closed her eyes and placed her hands palms down on the ground beside her, relishing the energy in every blade.

This was her heritage. Part of who she was and always would be. She cared deeply for all around her and loved just as deeply.

And that love is what brought her here tonight to this sacred place. She would take one last chance and cast a powerful prayer to the Mother Sky and ask for her help.

What help she sent was entirely her choice. Her decision was accepted without question, since her choice always proved wise.

Ali understood that her spell could not be changed by what she did here tonight. The spell had to be adhered to, but she could request that Sebastian be given guidance, that he believe.

Believe in what?

She smiled at her warning thought. She had to make certain she handled this correctly, that what she requested didn't alter the spell.

So what exactly did Sebastian need to believe in?

Sebastian needed to believe in magical love and that it came from the heart and no witch no matter how powerful could force a mortal to love. Only the heart had that power.

He had to believe not in her love but his own and that he gave of it freely and willingly with no help or hindrance from another party.

She delayed the casting, giving thought to the exact words and emotions she wished to present. Soon, though, time would run out, and she would be faced with her task.

Her thoughts drifted to Sebastian and she smiled. He was the man of her dreams. Her eyes ached at the sight of him. Whether he was clothed or naked didn't matter: he appealed to her every time she laid eyes on him.

He was even appealing when he frowned or crossed his arms over his chest and took that warrior stance of his. And then there was the way he loved.

She sighed and the aching sound echoed through the trees.

It wasn't only the way he *made* love, it was the way he *loved*. It didn't matter if he simply held her in his arms with her head rested on his chest or if he slipped naked over her and into her in one swift motion. She could feel his love, strong and palpable racing through him, hot and urgent and necessary, so very necessary to the nourishment of their souls.

"And he can cook," she said with a laugh. What more could a woman want?

Her own thoughts cautioned her.

He could want a mortal woman.

Ali shook her head. A mortal woman would bore him to tears. He could never cope with female mortal flaws. He needed the excitement, the pleasure, the foolishness and the love only she, a witch, could give him.

She had to remember, though, that he was a man steeped in logic. While part of him wanted to romp carefree naked in the grass and surrender to the erotic tunes of her toe bell, another part of him reminded him of his mortal beliefs and common sense.

Common had no business being attached to sense. They were too opposite to mix well, at least in her world.

She sighed; she was stalling the inevitable. Her cast must be made at midnight. The time when two separate days are one. The continuous cycle, everlasting, eternal.

A warm breeze rushed through the clearing and over her. She could almost hear it whisper, *it's time*.

Ali stood straight and proud. Her shoulders were drawn back, her chin held in a defiant tilt displaying her confidence and strength.

Her hands shook as they reached to unfasten her robe, their slight tremble the only indication of her nervousness.

She released the four ties on her robe and slowly slipped the soft garment off her naked body. She closed her eyes a moment, feeling the tepid summer breeze caress her body. It filled her, wrapped around her, embraced her like a mother welcoming a lost child home to her arms.

Her eyes drifted open, and she took one last invigorating breath, drinking from nature's cup, nourishing herself, and stepped into the circle.

Her body felt fluid with each step she took, and when she reached the center she felt as if she were at the center of her own being. She heard the steady rhythm of her heart, felt life's blood rushing through her, sensed the pleasure of her flesh to the touch of the soft wind. This was the center and power of life.

Her determination returned in a flash, racing over and through her, and her confidence took flight and with it her courage.

She tossed her head up, smiled wide, and stretched her arms out, extending her hands in supplication to the Mother Sky, her prayer ready on her lips.

Thirty-one

"I told you not to go that way, but you wouldn't listen," Beatrice scolded, her wings fluttering as she stood suspended in the air next to Sebastian's head.

He rubbed his bruised knee, sitting on the thick fallen log he had tripped over. "I thought it was the right way. I don't want to be late."

Beatrice landed on his shoulder, her tiny hands planted on her round hips. "Not much confidence it is you're having in me."

Sebastian detected a hint of annoyance in her soft voice and explained. "It isn't you. It's me. I've bungled this whole thing from the start. And I have never in all my years made such a mess of something so simple."

"You are a mortal. What did you expect?" She flew down from her perch to land on his thigh. She made her way carefully to his knee and gently patted and blew a soft breath on the bruised area with her delicate tiny hands.

Sebastian released a frustrated sigh. "You make being mortal sound like an affliction."

"With proper attention ailments can be made better," she said and pointed to his knee. "Give it a try."

Sebastian didn't for once doubt her talent, after all she was a fairy.

He cautiously bent his knee and smiled. "Not an ounce of pain. Let's get going."

Before he could move, Beatrice's crooked wings were fluttering in front of his face.

"Whoa, me boy," she cautioned. "You keep yourself parked on that log a minute."

"But time—"

"We have some of right now. I won't let you be late. I want this union as badly as you do. Maybe then Alisande will mend her stubborn ways."

"She'll mend them all right," he said firmly. "Even if I have to take away her broomstick."

Beatrice shook her head, her flower wreath almost tumbling off her head. With a push she righted it. "And if it were brooms witches used, do you think she would surrender it so easily?"

Sebastian grinned and spoke with male confidence. "I know exactly how to make her surrender."

Beatrice blushed pink. "And does this male pride extend to you knowing how to cast this spell?"

Sebastian finally stood, impatient to be off. "Dagon was quite descriptive in his explanation. I don't think I'll have a problem."

Beatrice resumed her comfortable perch on his shoulder. "Take the path to the right. Then why did he summon me?"

"He obviously, and rightly so, lacked confidence in my ability to find my way in unfamiliar woods at night."

"Maybe," she said reluctantly and warned. "Watch out for that stump ahead."

He detoured around the barely visible thing in the dark, wondering how she ever saw it. "You don't sound too sure."

"I want to make certain all goes as it should."

"My sentiments exactly," Sebastian agreed, paying close heed to her instructions.

While the woods were dark, his eyes had managed to adjust to the darkness, and strangely enough the area surrounding him appeared visibly clear enough to his eyes to follow Beatrice's instruction with only a minimum of difficulty. Of course he had to ignore the need inside him that urged him to race ahead and get there. Get to Ali, tell her he loved her. *He* loved her because *he* wanted to. He loved her freely and without coercion on her part. He plain and simply—well, maybe not simply, nothing with Ali was simple—but he loved her and that was that.

"Don't you go and be getting your dander up with her," Beatrice warned.

He couldn't shake his head; she had gotten up and was now leaning against his cheek next to his ear. He didn't want to suddenly dislodge her. So he answered without the usual shake of his head.

"Not on your life. Not with her powers."

His statement brought him to an abrupt halt, causing Beatrice to grab on to his shirt collar to prevent herself from tumbling down his chest.

"Her powers do concern me," he admitted. "I had always thought I would be physically stronger than my wife."

"You are," Beatrice assured him, righting her head wreath after pulling herself up from the end of his collar, where she had slid down to.

"My physical powers cannot compare to the strength of her magical powers," he said, and this time he shook his head. "And let me tell you that when she gets her dander up, watch out. She could easily zap me to the next century."

Beatrice flew off his sturdy shoulder to flutter with a

wagging finger in front of his face. "Worry not, you have the power to stop her."

He laughed. "She walked through my closed sliding-glass doors, and I couldn't stop her."

"You didn't want to," Beatrice said. "Now move, time is wearing short."

Sebastian didn't argue, he started walking, her directions clear in his ear, since she returned once again to perch on his shoulder.

"Do all witches, fairies, and the magical so to speak talk in riddles instead of directly?"

"Watch the low branch," she warned and he ducked. "Mortals simply refuse to listen."

"I heard you clearly enough," he insisted, shoving leafy branches out of his way.

"If you heard me clearly," Beatrice pointed out with a tap of her tiny finger to his cheek. "You wouldn't have asked about riddles."

"Witches, fairies, goblins, and ghouls—whatever have I gotten myself into?" he said with a laugh.

"Certainly not goblins and ghouls. They're a messy lot." She tapped his cheek again. "Now pay attention. It gets a little confusing up ahead."

Sebastian turned quiet, listening to her soft voice guide him, and he was amazed how easily he responded to her every direction. But then he wanted to.

He wanted so badly to stand in front of Alisande, grab her to him, and tell her how very much he loved her and always would. He wanted to tell her that he wouldn't change a thing about her. He had fallen in love with her because of who she was and who she would always be.

She could sprinkle fairy dust, cast her spells, tease him, torment him, romp in the grass naked, with him of course, drive him crazy with her toe bell, and float him in the air, but there was one thing he refused to allow her to do.

He smiled. "I won't let her cook."

Beatrice giggled, and the tiny chime sound reverberated in the quiet woods. "Heavens, no. No one allows Alisande to cook."

"I wish someone had told me that, though. . . ." His thoughts drifted to her in his kitchen in her yellow bikini. Maybe he would give her lessons, if she agreed to his choice of attire.

His chest filled with immense pleasure. They had so much to look forward to. A whole lifetime together, and he planned on filling it with a lot of living. And children, they would have at least four children and a couple of dogs, maybe a few cats, and plenty of fairies in the woods.

When had life changed so suddenly?

When Ali walked into his life and taught him the true meaning of magical love. You didn't need to be a witch to understand. You simply had to look with open eyes and see past the surface to within. There is where you find the magic.

Hadn't Ali told him it was simple? Hadn't she warned him about being blind? How amazing to be able to see and yet be so blind.

Now that he could see clearly and was aware, he wanted to look at everything. He wanted to embrace life and actually see and feel it for the first time. And he would do that with Ali.

He grew anxious with each step he took. And the spell Dagon forced him to learn repeatedly echoed in his head. He must get the words right. Dagon warned him that each word must be spoken from the heart and with love and cast to the Mother Sky at midnight.

His spell would secure the blessings of the magical love spell and forever seal their union. He could do it. He was sure he could. Dagon had told him not worry, that everything would turn out just fine.

But just to make certain Dagon had suggested they enlist the aid of Beatrice. Sebastian was all for the tiny fairy's assistance. After all, if she had helped him find his way out of the woods once, she could certainly help him find his way in.

And once there?

He knew what to do. Dagon had coached him relentlessly for hours until he had felt as if he'd had a crash course in spell casting and had passed with an A plus.

"We're getting close," Beatrice whispered in his ear. "Slow down."

Sebastian obeyed without question.

"The sacred circle is up ahead. Walk softly and with reverence, this is a special place."

Sebastian once again obeyed without question, feeling the change in the gentle breeze that brushed his face and wrapped strangely, almost intimately around him. He almost wanted to sigh.

Beatrice continued to whisper directions in his ear, bringing him to a stop near a bush whose foliage appeared to tremble in excitement.

"Ali is just beyond," Beatrice said. "Look and see."

Sebastian was about to gently part the leaves when the bush separated its branches of its own accord. Shaking his head, he peered through the opening.

His breath caught.

Ali stood naked, ready to step into a small circle of grass. The moonlight was a soft beacon on her pale skin, and in its cascading light thousands of tiny sparkles rained down from the heavens to wash over her.

She was a sight to behold, an ethereal beauty born of magic and steeped in tradition as ancient as time.

His chest swelled with pride for who she was, who she would always be, and for who she was about to become—his wife.

''Hurry,'' Beatrice urged, ''time draws near.''

''I'm ready,'' Sebastian said anxiously. ''I know the spell and how to cast it.''

Beatrice's crooked wing sometimes made her appear to be flying lopsided, so Sebastian titled his head to get a better look at the strange stare she fixed on him.

''What's wrong?'' he asked.

''Didn't Dagon tell you what to do?'' she asked skeptically.

Sebastian nodded. ''He told me I should approach Ali from behind, extend my arms up along hers, join her hands with mine, and cast the spell.''

''That's it?'' Beatrice asked, her tiny hands going to her waist and her eyes gleaming with annoyance.

''What didn't he tell me?'' Sebastian asked, realizing there was more to this spell than Dagon had led him to believe.

''That boy is in for a tongue lashing to be sure,'' she said with a sharp wag of her finger.

''Whatever it is I can do it,'' he said with determination.

Beatrice laughed softly. ''That you can, my boy.''

He prepared himself. No matter what she told him, he would do it. Whatever the instructions he would grin and bear it and follow through. He wasn't too proud. This was for love. For Ali. For their future.

''Get naked,'' she ordered.

''What?''

''Shhh,'' she scolded and spoke softly. ''You see that Ali is naked.''

He nodded.

''Any spell cast from the sacred circle must be cast by the person completely naked. It is part of the ritual. You enter life bare and you enter the circle of life bare. You have nothing to hide, you present yourself to the Mother Sky free and willingly.''

"No problem," he said with a smile. "That I can do."

"And did Dagon bother to inform you how to seal your cast?" she asked.

Sebastian continued to unbutton his shirt, pulling the tail ends out of his pants. "Wait until I get my hands on him."

Beatrice smiled. "He has confidence in you. You will know what to do."

Sebastian panicked. "Now is not the time for riddles. Tell me."

"I cannot," she said with a smile. "This you must know on your own."

"What if I don't?" he asked, yanking his shoes and socks off and tossing them to the side to join his shirt.

She flew right to his cheek and gave it a comforting pat. "You will know."

Sebastian wanted to argue, to insist that she tell him, but he realized it would do no good. And he also realized he trusted Beatrice. If she believed that strongly in his ability to know, then he had to believe in himself.

His hands went to his belt.

"It's time for me to go, me boy," she said with a wink.

"You could turn around," he said teasingly.

"No, I really must go," she said with regret. "I have done all I can."

Sebastian was suddenly overcome with a feeling of loss. He didn't want to lose her. He just discovered the reality of fairies, and he didn't want to let her go. Especially since she had given him so much. She had given him the gift of hope and the ability to believe in the unbelievable. She had helped him to open his eyes and see clearly, and she had taught him that love comes in many sizes, even the tiniest.

"I will miss you," he said, feeling a choking lump wedge in his throat.

Beatrice attempted to reassure him. "We'll see each other again, me boy."

He nodded and spoke after clearing his throat. "You mean a lot to me."

"And you to me," she said and flew up to place a kiss on his cheek. "Remember—follow your heart; it never lies to you."

He nodded and watched her fly up in the night sky waving frantically while righting her lopsided head wreath.

He took a deep, reassuring breath and unzipped his pants. He was on his own now. He had been given all the help that was possible. The rest was up to him.

He tossed the last of his clothes to the pile near the tree stump and stood still for a moment, taking another deep reassuring breath.

He felt it then. Call it courage, determination, confidence, it didn't matter, it rushed over him like a tidal wave, washing over every inch of his being.

And then a calmness settled over him, wrapping around him like the warm summer breeze, catching him up and filling him with love. He felt as if he had come home for the first time in a very long time. He was returning, returning to life, stepping once again into its everlasting cycle of birth and renewal.

He approached the bush, and instead of reaching out to part the leaves, he silently requested to be admitted to the sacred place. The branches moved aside and bid him entrance.

He stepped through and stared at Ali, her back to him as she extended her hands up to the Mother Sky.

Quietly and with firm and steady footsteps he approached her. The breeze picked up and whipped softly around him, welcoming him with an urgent embrace. The energy of the earth rushed up his legs with every step he took, his pulse quickened, and his heart beat wildly.

Life.

It filled him to the brim and urged him on. For with life

came love, and he was anxious to claim and proclaim his love for Ali.

He took two more steady steps and entered the sacred circle.

Thirty-two

Ali felt him enter the circle; his strong presence swirled around her, sweeping up her energy and connecting it instantly with his.

She gasped at the strength of his love and passion for her. The power of it raced over her like a ripple that grew in force and spread out, forever expanding. His love was endless. His passion potent.

She cried out and her legs turned weak. He was there, his arms beneath hers, his strength holding her, his love cradling her, and his naked body supporting her.

"It is my turn to cast a spell," he whispered in her ear and lifted up her arms along with his to the heavens.

Her body trembled against his as she followed his direction, and he pressed more intimately against her reassuring her with the potency of his love.

She surrendered willingly to him, aware that he had shed all to enter this circle. He stripped himself bare for her, allowing her entrance to his very soul. Only someone who believed in magical love would dare risk so much.

Ali wanted to cry out her happiness. She wanted to turn around in his arms and kiss him senseless and shout her joy and love to the heavens, but they were in the sacred circle and a prayer or spell must be cast.

And never, never had she heard of a mortal entering the sacred circle. Was he aware of his actions? Did he fully understand the consequences? Or had he leaped without looking?

She smiled and rubbed her cheek against his. "Let me hear your spell, mortal."

"You know it, I dare you to join me," he said.

She shivered. Was he crazy? Did he know what he asked? Did he love her that much? *Forever and always.*

"Not long enough," he whispered.

She turned her face to him, wanting to make sure he understood.

"Shhh, it's time," he murmured and kissed her lips.

He had stolen her breath with his gentle kiss and his fervent words, and she could do nothing but turn her face up to the heavens, lock her fingers with his, and join him.

They recited the spell together.

"Mother of the earth and sky; hear me ask, hear me cry; your son and daughter wish to seal a love so great; please open up your portal gates; grant us an everlasting love; only you can send from the heavens above; and when our lips and bodies meet; let our love for eternity keep."

Sebastian didn't require a witch's knowledge to know how to seal the spell. The wisdom was as old as time and as natural.

He slowly stroked his hands down Ali's arms, over her full breasts and along her slim waist. He then gently turned her around to face him.

When she moved to speak, he silenced her with a finger to her lips. "Shhh, this part requires action not words."

She smiled that wickedly sensuous smile of hers and pressed against him.

He shook his head, a reaction that was now so much a part of him he didn't give it a second thought and smiled his own sinful smile. She was audaciously sexy, potently beautiful, and she was finally *his*.

He yanked her up against him and settled his dark eyes on her face. He wanted to watch her react to his touch, he wanted to feel what she felt, he wanted to unite with her and make magical love like they had never done before.

He ran a slow stroking hand over her breast, gently squeezing, caressing, and then torturing her soft nipple until it turned hard and sensitive beneath his fingers.

He watched and listened as her smile gave way to a low moan of pleasure, and his own smile grew more powerful.

He brought his lips to hers as her moan faded, and he kissed her tenderly at first, introducing himself as if this was his first time with her. Then after properly acquainting himself, his kiss turned urgent, and he demanded she respond in kind, and she did.

She kissed him with the need and desire of long-lost lovers reunited. She clung to him, fearful of letting him go, afraid if she did he would once again be lost to her.

Sebastian felt her worry, felt the hot burning need that ran through her for him, and felt her love so strong and tangible that it made his own deep-rooted love and passion rage near out of control.

He ended the kiss to regain his breath and rein in his rampant emotions. And while he took command of himself, he also took command of the situation, and with gentle arms and a warrior's strength and fortitude he lowered her to the thick carpet of grass.

He stood for a brief moment over her, looking down, drinking in her beauty, her love, her passion. She was his, now and always. They were one forever joined, two souls reunited.

She reached out to him, inviting him into her arms, into her body, into her soul.

His emotions soared so potently they briefly robbed him

of his breath and sanity, for at that moment he truly understood and felt the power and significance of magical love.

He dropped his head back and stared with wide eyes at the Mother Sky, gasped a deep breath, and sent a silent prayer of thanks to the heavens. Then he looked back down at Ali and all she so freely offered him and joined her.

"This will be our night to remember," he whispered in her ear. "Forever and always."

She laughed softly. "Not long enough."

He nipped at her ear. "All night, until the sun rises, we will stay in this circle and make magic."

"Promises, promises," she teased.

He leaned up and over her. "I promise to start at the top," he said, running a finger over her lips, "and deliberately work my way down slowly." His finger ran down her body to teasingly stroke between her legs.

She squirmed in pleasure before raising her hand to lovingly touch his face. "Promise me one other thing."

Sebastian bent down and invaded her mouth with a kiss like a warrior of old, stealing her breath and her voice. He then captured her face in his hands and looked directly into her wide, stunned eyes and told her what he knew instinctively she wished to hear and what he wished to openly and proudly admit.

"I will love you forever and always, throughout eternity and beyond time, past all boundaries and beliefs, eternally you are mine."

Ali gasped at his stunning acknowledgment, sighed over his loving declaration, and cried out her own, "Oh, Sebastian, I love you so very much."

His grin was playful, his touch loving. "My sweet witch, when I finish with you, you are going to love me even more."

"Promises, promises," she said with a generous smile

and shivered when his head descended down to her breast and her nipple disappeared into his mouth.

Sebastian had proved to be an exceptional lover; at least Ali believed him to be. He was now proving he was beyond exceptional. He was simply magnificent.

No, he was magical.

His touch enticed, enthralled, and encouraged her to surrender completely to his consummate skills and to his own overwhelming love for her.

He touched, he teased, he tormented, with his fingers, his lips, his tongue causing her immense pleasures. And as he worked his way with deliberate slowness down her stomach with kisses and intimate touches, she shivered with anticipation.

Ali not only relished the exquisiteness of his physical love, but she basked in the feeling of his emotional love. His touch was not only limited to pure physical pleasure, it was complimented by the intensity of his impassioned emotions.

To feel your own love is grand but to feel your partner's love is simply breathtaking and Sebastian freely gave her this.

She felt the restraint he held on his desires, raging powerfully within him, and yet he kept them in control, giving to her, loving her slowly and methodically so she would enjoy.

She gasped wistfully as his mouth intimately claimed her and all reality was lost.

He, this time, taught her the true meaning of magical love. He whisked her away to a place where pure passion reigned. Where reality was not even a memory, where time stood still, and where lustful love hit a fever pitch.

Nothing existed but the two of them and their need, their overwhelming need to unite, copulate, climax. To come together as one.

His name spilled in an anguished cry from her lips. She could take no more. She needed him inside her, filling her with himself, with his strength, with his love.

She cried out to him again, and he came to her, his body moving over her, his mouth finding hers.

"I love you," he said harshly against her mouth as he bruised her lips with rough kisses.

She fed on his hunger, eager for his taste and eager for him. "Please, Sebastian," she whispered. "Please."

Her soft pleas fueled his already primitive need, and he moved to enter her.

Ali never imagined that a forceful thrust could be delivered with such a gentle pleasure. But he managed to enter her like a warrior, who conquered with determination and tender caring.

His loving possession of her brought tears to her eyes, and he gripped her hands with his to stretch them up and over her head, and as he moved with powerful strides within her, he urged her to join him.

"Make magic with me, Ali."

And she did.

Their movements became one, each understanding, accepting, loving the other.

Ali's eyes fluttered open and closed, and as their rhythm intensified, escalated out of control, her eyes caught sight of a falling star, burning brightly as it fell toward earth.

And as the star burst, so did they in an explosion of complete and total magical surrender. They were finally one.

A cool, comforting air rushed down from the heavens and wrapped around the lovers who had yet to regain control of their emotions.

Their hands remained firmly clasped together, neither attempting to release the other. This time this uniting or reuniting had been too long in coming to fruition and neither wanted to surrender the eloquent moment.

They lay enjoying, relishing, and refusing to relinquish each other. They were whole and they liked the feeling of completeness. It not only satisfied the body, it nourished the soul.

Nature's creatures provided them with a soothing symphony that no mortal music could compare to, and the brilliant stars in the night sky twinkled more brightly and frequently offering them a canopy of beauty to gaze upon.

Magic surrounded them, love embraced them, and the Mother Sky smiled down upon them.

Sebastian made the first move, gently easing himself off her to her disappointment, which she was certain to register with a distressful sigh.

He stretched out beside her. "The night isn't over."

She moved next to him, resting her head on his chest, and placing her leg intimately against him.

He slipped his arm around her and patted her backside. "After tonight your backside may just be permanently tinged green."

She laughed. "Promises, promises."

"There is a promise I want you to make me," he said, and the seriousness of his tone caused her to look up at him.

"Anything," she said without hesitation.

He playfully slapped her backside. "Find out the promise before you agree to the promise."

"I trust you completely," she said. "You would ask nothing of me that I was not capable of giving."

He looked at her with such intense love, she almost cried. "You never cease to amaze me. You love without thought of conditions."

"True love—"

Before she could finish he did. "Magical love."

"You finally understand," she said with a pleased smile.

"It took me long enough." He stopped her before she could respond. "Don't tell me I'm only mortal."

She giggled. "You truly do understand."

He shook his head. "This spell thing can get a bit confusing, but if I study and research—"

He stopped himself when he felt her body shake with restrained laughter. "Am I being too reasonable again?"

She kissed him on the chin. "Reason all you want; in time you will need only magic."

He gave thought to her statement and was about to ask what she meant when he realized they had become distracted from the original question.

"The promise," he said.

She sat up, sitting cross-legged beside him, anxious to hear what he had to say.

Her hair raged wildly around her face and shoulders. Blades of grass poked out from between the blond strands, and her lips, curled in a beautiful smile, were red and puffy from his ardent kisses. She was a picture of seduction.

And he had a hard time—he stopped his thoughts. If he continued to focus on her, he would lose all rational thought and—

He looked at her again. Her nipples were hard, that word insisted on popping up in his thoughts. But her nipples *were* hard and rosy and probably sensitive from his insatiable desire to feast on them.

And then there was the way she sat crossed-legged, offering a faint intimate peek of—

"Damn," he muttered and sprang up, grabbing her about the waist and dragging her across his lap to rest intimately upon him.

"I want you again," he said, burying his face in the sweet earthy scent of her wild hair.

He hadn't noticed her breathing was rapid. "I want you, too."

He looked surprised. "Not too soon for you?"

"Not soon enough." She laughed.

He attempted to move her off him.

She stopped him. "I want to be on top this time."

He grabbed her face in his hands and planted a lustful kiss on her lips while his tongue wickedly attacked hers. When he was finished, he said, "With pleasure."

Ali pushed him back and proceeded to have her way with him.

She teased and tormented him into a frenzy, thoroughly enjoying herself while learning about her own power of control. She wanted him as badly as he did her, but she also wanted to give him the same insane pleasure that he had given her.

When Sebastian reached the point of no return, he grabbed her and begged her to finish him off.

She laughed and did exactly as he asked, basking in the power she held over him, shared with him, experienced with him. She watched him climax, his eyes shutting tight, his powerful moans reverberating out into the night, and she felt him buck and push and press against her as he emptied every last ounce of his strength into her.

Only then did she release her own need and as powerfully as he did, his muscled arms holding her tight, guiding her and helping her to share in the beauty of their fulfilling climaxes.

Exhausted they once again stretched out in the sacred circle.

When rational thought finally returned and his breathing normalized, Sebastian once again recalled the promise he wished to speak to her about.

"Did your wish ever come true?" she asked, delaying his query.

He turned on his side, bracing his elbow on the ground and resting his head in his hand. "Did yours?"

She nodded, moving into the same position as he so they faced opposite each other.

"Mine did, too," he admitted. "I finally believe."

She smiled. "I wished the same for you. To believe."

"I believe, I believe, I believe," he sang out.

"What do you believe?" she asked softly.

"That you love me with your whole heart and that I love you with my whole heart and that no spell caused me to feel this way. I fell in love with you of my own free will. Of course, you being an audacious seductress helped."

She playfully slapped him in the arm. "I was attracted to you. I couldn't help myself. You tempted me."

"I tempted you?" He laughed joyfully. "Think back, sweetheart, who was defending himself against a seductress?"

"Without much success," she teased.

"What can I say, you're too skilled. I had no choice but to surrender. And I suggest you keep practicing your skills on me so we keep you in tiptop shape."

"Tiptop shape for whom?" she asked, as if she had no idea.

"Me," he said, thumping his chest and suddenly recalled the promise. "Remember that—"

He stopped short. Ali was running her leg along his and her tiny toe bell was ringing an erotic chime.

"Not fair," he complained, suddenly struck by the potency of their own exotic scents that drifted like an aphrodisiac in the warm night air. And affected him just as potently.

"Keep that up and you know what will happen," he warned.

"Promises, promises," she said softly.

Promises, damn, but he had to get to that promise soon, he had to, but right now . . .

He reached out and gently pulled her to him. "This time I'm on top."

She smiled. "We'll see."

It was almost dawn, the sun near to breaking in the distance. Ali and Sebastian lay in the sacred circle, wrapped in each other's arms, feeling replete and depleted.

They had loved the night away. Time and time again finding themselves drawn to each other. Their need seemed never ending, a constant that was always there and always would be.

Forever and always.

Eternally.

Ali yawned. "Come to the house with me and we'll have breakfast. I'm starving."

He hesitantly asked, "Are you cooking?"

She gently punched him in the stomach. "Don't love me enough to eat my cooking?"

"You're asking a lot there, sweetheart."

She looked up at him with wide eyes. "I only ask for your love."

"You've got that," he said and once again recalled the promise. This time he refused to be distracted. "About that promise?"

She nodded and sighed. "I promise I won't cook."

He caught her chin in his hand and turned her face to look directly at him. "Cook as much as you want, I'll keep the medicine chest stocked with relief aids."

She smiled, her love for him radiant in her green eyes.

"The promise I want from you has nothing to do with cooking." He stood, reaching down to help her up.

Ali stood, anxiously waiting for him to continue.

He took her hands in his, brought them to his lips, and

kissed them lightly. He brushed several wild strands of her honey-blond hair off her face, gently kissed her lips, and said, "I love you, Alisande Wyrrd. I love you for who you are and who you will always be. And I want you to *promise* me to be my wife forever and always."

She cried out in joy and threw her arms around his neck and before planting a big, mushy acceptance kiss on his lips, she said, "Not long enough, mortal."

Epilogue

THREE MONTHS LATER

Ali was excited. It was her wedding night, a time for making memories and magic. She had prepared her large brass bed herself, decorating the wide headboard and footboard with fresh white flowers of all varieties and sizes and green ferns sprinkled with fairy dust so as to give the illusion of being surrounded by the woods.

The memory of their night in the sacred circle still brought a sigh of pleasure to her lips and probably always would. She wanted to once again connect with nature and recreate the peaceful tranquility of that evening.

She had made the bed with fresh white sheets. The numerous pillows were trimmed with delicate Irish lace. And of course she had filled the room with white candles of all shapes and sizes. The hundreds of flickering candles reminded her of the stars that twinkled so brightly in the night sky and had bathed Sebastian and her in their beauty.

She was pleased. She had recreated the best qualities of nature for their night of love.

And for herself? She smiled, looking herself over in the closet door mirror.

"Natural. Sebastian's favorite," she said and ran her hand down her naked hip and over her flat stomach. Soon his hands would be on her, caressing her intimately, exciting her with his familiar touch and becoming one with her. And together they would love the night away again and again. She sighed and shivered in anticipation.

She heard her husband approach from the next room and hurried into bed, pulling the lace-edged cover sheet up to her waist and striking a seductive pose against the pillows.

She smiled with delight. It had been such a glorious day: the wedding was perfect, her relatives graciously accepted Sebastian into the family, wonderful food was enjoyed, an abundance of dance and song filled the air, and a generosity of spirit and camaraderie was shared that she would long remember with love and gratitude.

And now there was tonight. Their first time together as husband and wife. More memories to make, a future to plan, and a lifetime to share.

The door opened and her husband walked in, naked and superbly male. He looked so deliciously sinful that she had to stop herself from jumping out of bed and jumping him. She didn't think she would ever tire of wanting him. Her passion for him seemed insatiable and her actions at times incorrigible. But then he never denied her, and he often tempted and teased her, his own desire equal to hers.

And now he truly belonged to her. With the exchange of their vows today he legally became hers. She had a husband.

My husband.

She liked the sound of it in her head and on her lips.

"My husband," she said and summoned him seductively with the crook of her finger. Just a little energy to the tip, and she could have him in bed beside her in no time, but he had warned her about using her powers on him.

He stood where he was near the end of the bed and raised a stern brow. ''Don't even think about it.''

''Don't you want to be here next to me in bed?'' she asked coyly, patting the empty spot beside her.

His smile warmed and his look was lethally sensual. ''That I do, but of my own accord, under my own steam, walking on my own two feet. Not floating through the air.''

''Then join me,'' she invited with an alluring softness and slowly peeled back the sheet to reveal—

''I almost forgot,'' she said suddenly and yanked the sheet back over herself, to Sebastian's disappointment.

''Forgot what?'' he asked, grabbing a tight rein on his rampaging male hormones.

''In that wood cabinet in the corner,'' she said, pointing to an old scarred piece of highly polished furniture, ''is an old book, the Wyrrd family record book. Please bring it to me, but be careful—it has grown worn with age.''

Sebastian did as she asked, cradling the weighty book with care in his strong hand and gently skimming through the faded pages. He suddenly stopped dead in his tracks only inches from the foot of the bed. His eyes were transfixed on the page, and he studied it as if reading it over and over again and still not believing what he saw.

''Is this birth date of yours correct?''

She nodded with a smile.

Sebastian read the date. ''December 21, 1652.''

''I guess I'm a little older than you expected,'' she said teasingly.

He joined her on the bed, handing the book to her. ''Give or take a few years, though I must admit you have maintained your age well.''

He kissed her then and not a simple kiss. A kiss that announced he was ready, willing, and impatient.

He watched as she carefully entered their names and their wedding date, glancing at other recorded dates on the page.

Dates to him that were mere history he had read about. But Ali had actually lived through them.

"What is the relative life span of a witch?" he asked, his mind suddenly scrambling in thought.

She heard the concern in his voice as she placed the family record book down on the night table beside the bed. She shrugged as she turned back to face him. "I'm not sure, quite old, I would say."

She reached out for him, and he took her hand, moving to meet her in the middle of the bed.

She ran a slow, teasing finger along his lips. "There is no need for you to worry. We will share a long life together."

He kissed and playfully nipped at her finger. "Need I remind you that I am but a mere mortal with a mere mortal's life span? Which at one time I thought was long enough, and now I see I haven't even begun to live compared to you. Nor do I cherish the thought of dying old in your beautiful arms."

Ali laughed softly.

"This isn't funny," he said, hurt and surprised by her insensitivity.

Ali bit at her lower lip as if attempting to hold back her words.

"What's going on?" he demanded, realizing she would never intentionally hurt him. "I can feel you're hiding something."

"Very good," she praised. "See how attuned you are to me."

"Forget it, Ali, we're not changing the subject even if you sing my praises to the rooftop."

Her hand moved to slip beneath the sheet, and he grabbed it before she could get intimate. "Oh, no, sweetheart, you're telling me what's going on first, and then you can play with me all you want."

She smiled and brought his hand out from under the sheet along with hers. She fiddled with his long fingers as if to distract herself from her task.

"I was going to tell you later, but I suppose now is a good time."

"Now is a perfect time," he said and grabbed her hand to still her delaying actions.

She looked him square in the eyes. "Dagon wasn't completely honest with you about the spell."

He was about to voice his anger when she quieted him with a soft kiss. "Let me finish."

He nodded knowing whatever the problem the deed was done and he would find a way to deal with it and Dagon. Ali was his wife and that would not change. Anything else wasn't important and could be managed.

Ali continued. "Dagon must have assumed you were looking for a lifetime commitment with me."

"He assumed correctly," he assured her, giving credit to Dagon for fully comprehending how he felt about Ali.

"Not your lifetime, *mine*."

He stared at her strangely, understanding dawning slowly but confused nevertheless.

"Dagon gave you a spell that would bind us together as one for eternity."

An odd sensation ran through Sebastian and tiny warning bells rang in his head, putting him on full alert.

Ali proceeded, knowing a clear explanation was essential. "When you stepped into the sacred circle, you were accepting without condition my way of life, and when you requested the portal gates to open to bless our union for eternity—"

She paused, placed her hand to his cheek, and kissed him softly before saying, "You were requesting to become part of my way of life forever and as soon as our bodies joined as one, you became a witch."

It took several moments for her words to fully sink in. He shook his head a couple of times—at least he thought he did. He wasn't certain. He wasn't even certain of her words or what they meant. He wasn't even certain who he was anymore, or who he had become.

"Are you all right, Sebastian?" she asked anxiously, tapping his pale cheek with her hand.

He asked what sounded like a foolish question to him. "You're telling me that I am a witch?"

She nodded, attempting to hide the smile that threatened to erupt into a laugh. He looked so adorably confused.

"A full-fledged, card-carrying, broom-flying witch?"

She patiently explained, "We don't have cards designating us as witches, and we don't fly on brooms."

"But you can go through sliding-glass doors and float people and objects around, right?" he said with a sudden excitement.

"Yes, we can—but," she warned like a teacher talking to a new student, "it takes practice."

A wide grin grew on his face. "I'll be able to do that? After practice of course."

"Yes, you will be able to do all that, after *much* practice."

He reached out and grabbed her around the waist, pulling her over to rest on top of him. "Will I be able to float you around with the crook of a finger?"

"Not for some time," she said with another more intent warning look. "That takes practice, and I'm not going to wind up with a sore rump while you're attempting to perfect your newfound skills."

"Can we float in the air together?" he teased with a nibbling kiss to her neck.

She whispered in his ear exactly what they could do while floating in the air together—after practice, of course.

''I want to practice right away, right now, this instant,'' he demanded with a wicked smile.

''It's our wedding night.''

''What a better night to learn magic,'' he said and claimed her lips with a hungry kiss.

''You would have to listen to my every command,'' she said a bit breathless from his ardent capture.

He ran the tip of his tongue slowly up her neck, over her chin, and faintly across her mouth before he made his way between her lips and challenged her to mate with him.

She did and was once again left breathless.

''I will follow your every instruction. I will make certain to please and satisfy you in every way possible. I will be a most apt student.''

Ali tested him. ''No matter what it is I ask of you?''

''No matter what it is, I will do it. What is it you want me to do, Ali?'' he whispered in her ear.

''Follow my every instruction,'' she said, placing her lips to his.

He followed, pressing his lips to hers. ''As you say, dear wife.''

She brushed her lips across his once more and said, ''Point your finger to the ceiling, Sebastian.''

He did without question.

''Repeat after me.''

His strong voice echoed hers.

''Sky above; land below; I call upon the fairies glow; send your magic dust our way; and forever bless our wedding day.''

''Now what?'' he asked, bringing his arm down to wrap around her waist and hug her tightly to him. ''Did I call fairy dust to rain down upon us?''

''A special blessing from the fairies is what you asked for, and only if they choose to send it will it come.''

"The blessing will come," he said with such confidence it brought tears to Ali's eyes.

And as Sebastian wiped her tears away, gold fairy dust sprinkled gently down over them in a loving blessing.

"Now, my love," he said and kissed her softly, "we make magic."

Turn the page for a preview of
JILL MARIE LANDIS'S
latest novel,

Blue Moon

Coming in July from Jove Books

Prologue

SOUTHERN ILLINOIS, LATE APRIL, 1819

She would be nineteen tomorrow. If she lived.

In the center of a faint deer trail on a ribbon of dry land running through a dense swamp, a young woman crouched like a cornered animal. The weak, gray light from a dull, overcast sky barely penetrated the bald-cypress forest as she wrapped her arms around herself and shivered, trying to catch her breath. She wore nothing to protect her from the elements but a tattered rough, homespun dress and an ill-fitting pair of leather shoes that had worn blisters on her heels.

The primeval path was nearly obliterated by lichen and fern that grew over deep drifts of dried twigs and leaves. Here and there the ground was littered with the larger rotting fallen limbs of trees. The fecund scent of decay clung to the air, pressed down on her, stoked her fear, and gave it life.

Breathe. Breathe.

The young woman's breath came fast and hard. She squinted through her tangled black hair, shoved it back, her fingers streaked with mud. Her hands shook. Terror born of being lost was heightened by the knowledge that night was going to fall before she found her way out of the swamp.

Not only did the encroaching darkness frighten her, but so did the murky silent water along both sides of the trail. She realized she would soon be surrounded by both night and water. Behind her, from somewhere deep amid the cypress trees wrapped in rust colored bark, came the sound of a splash as some unseen creature dropped into the watery ooze.

She rose, spun around, and scanned the surface of the swamp. Frogs and fish, venomous copperheads and turtles, big as frying pans, thrived beneath the lacy emerald carpet of duckweed that floated upon the water. As she knelt there wondering whether she should continue on in the same direction or turn back, she watched a small knot of fur float toward her on the surface of the water.

A soaking wet muskrat lost its grace as soon as it made land and lumbered up the bank in her direction. Amused, yet wary, she scrambled back a few inches. The creature froze and stared with dark beady eyes before it turned tail, hit the water, and disappeared.

Getting to her feet, the girl kept her eyes trained on the narrow footpath, gingerly stepping through piles of damp, decayed leaves. Again she paused, lifted her head, listened for the sound of a human voice and the pounding footsteps that meant someone was in pursuit of her along the trail.

When all she heard was the distant knock of a woodpecker, she let out a sigh of relief. Determined to keep moving, she trudged on, ever vigilant, hoping that the edge of the swamp lay just ahead.

Suddenly, the sharp, shrill scream of a bobcat set her heart pounding. A strangled cry escaped from her lips. With a fist pressed against her mouth, she squeezed her eyes closed and froze, afraid to move, afraid to even breathe. The cat screamed again and the cry echoed across the haunting silence of the swamp until it seemed to stir the very air around her.

She glanced up at dishwater-gray patches of weak afternoon light nearly obliterated by the cypress trees that grew so close together in some places that not even a small child could pass between them. The thought that a wildcat might be looming somewhere above her in the tangled limbs, crouched and ready to pounce, sent her running down the narrow, winding trail.

She had not gone a hundred steps when the toe of her shoe caught beneath an exposed tree root. Thrown forward, she began to fall and cried out.

As the forest floor rushed up to meet her, she put out her hands to break the fall. A shock of pain shot through her wrist an instant before her head hit a log.

And then her world went black.

One

HERON POND, ILLINOIS

Noah LeCroix walked to the edge of the wide wooden porch surrounding the one-room cabin he had built high in the sheltering arms of an ancient bald cypress tree and looked out over the swamp. Twilight gathered, thickening the shadows that shrouded the trees. The moon had already risen, a bright silver crescent riding atop a faded blue sphere. He loved the magic of the night, loved watching the moon and stars appear in the sky almost as much as he loved the swamp. The wetlands pulsed with life all night long. The darkness coupled with the still, watery landscape settled a protective blanket of solitude around him. In the dense, liquid world beneath him and the forest around his home, all manner of life coexisted in a delicate balance. He likened the swamp's dance of life and death to the way good and evil existed together in the world of men beyond its boundaries.

This shadowy place was his universe, his sanctuary. He savored its peace, was used to it after having grown up in almost complete isolation with his mother, a reclusive Cherokee woman who had left her people behind when she chose to settle in far-off Kentucky with his father, a French Canadian fur trapper named Gerard LeCroix.

Living alone served Noah's purpose now more than ever. He had no desire to dwell among "civilized men," especially now that so many white settlers were moving in droves across the Ohio into the new state of Illinois.

Noah turned away from the smooth log railing that bordered the wide, covered porch cantilevered out over the swamp. He was about to step into the cabin where a single oil lamp cast its circle of light when he heard a bobcat scream. He would not have given the sound a second thought if not for the fact that a few seconds later the sound was followed by a high-pitched shriek, one that sounded human enough to stop him in his tracks. He paused on the threshold and listened intently. A chill ran down his spine.

It had been so long since he had heard the sound of another human voice that he could not really be certain, but he thought he had just heard a woman's cry.

Noah shook off the ridiculous, unsettling notion and walked into the cabin. The walls were covered with the tanned hides of mink, bobcat, otter, beaver, fox, white-tailed deer, and bear. His few other possessions—a bone-handled hunting knife with a distinctive wolf's head carved on it, various traps, some odd pieces of clothing, a few pots and a skillet, four wooden trenchers and mugs, and a rifle—were all neatly stored inside. They were all he owned and needed in the world, save the dugout canoe secured outside near the base of the tree.

Sparse but comfortable, even the sight of the familiar surroundings could not help him shake the feeling that something unsettling was about to happen, that all was not right in his world.

Pulling a crock off a high shelf, Noah poured a splash of whiskey in a cup and drank it down, his concentration intent on the deepening gloaming and the sounds of the swamp. An unnatural stillness lingered in the air after the puzzling scream, almost as if, like him, the wild inhabitants of Heron Pond were collectively waiting for something to happen. Unable to deny his curiosity any longer, Noah sighed in resignation and walked back to the door.

He lingered there for a moment, staring out at the growing shadows. Something was wrong. *Someone* was out there. He reached for the primed and loaded Hawken rifle that stood just inside the door and stepped out into the gathering dusk.

He climbed down the crude ladder of wooden strips nailed to the trunk of one of the four prehistoric cypress that supported his home, stepped into the dugout *pirogue* tied to a cypress knee that poked out of the water. Noah paddled the shallow wooden craft toward a spot where the land met the deep dark water with its camouflage net of duckweed, a natural boundary all but invisible to anyone unfamiliar with the swamp.

He reached a rise of land that supported a trail, carefully stepped out of the *pirogue* and secured it to a low-hanging tree branch. Walking through thickening shadows, Noah breathed in his surroundings, aware of every subtle nuance of change, every depression on the path that might really be a footprint on the trail, every tree and stand of switch-cane.

The sound he thought he'd heard had come from the southeast. Noah headed in that direction, head down, staring at the trail although it was almost too dark to pick up any sign. A few hundred yards from where he left the *pirogue,* he paused, raised his head, sniffed the air, and listened to the silence.

Instinctively, he swung his gaze in the direction of a thicket of slender cane stalks and found himself staring across ten yards of low undergrowth into the eyes of a female bobcat on the prowl. Slowly he raised his rifle to his shoulder and waited to see what the big cat would do. The animal stared back at him, its eyes intense in the gathering gloaming. Finally, she blinked and with muscles bunching beneath her fine, shiny coat, the cat turned and padded away.

Noah lowered the rifle and shook his head. He decided the sound he heard earlier must have been the bobcat's cry and nothing more. But just as he stepped back in the direction of the *pirogue*, he caught a glimpse of ivory on the trail ahead that stood out against the dark tableau. His leather moccasins did not make even a whisper of sound on the soft earth. He closed the distance and quickly realized what he was seeing was a body lying across the path.

His heart was pounding as hard as Chickasaw drums when he knelt beside the young woman stretched out upon the ground. Laying his rifle aside he stared at the unconscious female, then looked up and glanced around in every direction. The nearest white settlement was beyond the swamp to the northeast. There was no sign of a companion or fellow traveler nearby, something he found more than curious.

Noah took a deep breath, let go a ragged sigh and looked at the girl again. She lay on her side, as peacefully as if she were napping. She was so very still that the only evidence that she was alive was the slow, steady rise and fall of her breasts. Although there was no visible sign of injury, she lay on the forest floor with her head beside a fallen log. One of her arms was outstretched, the other tucked beneath her. What he could see of her face was filthy. So were her hands; they were beautifully shaped, her fingers long and tapered. Her dress, nothing but a rag with sleeves, was hiked up to her thighs. Her shapely legs showed stark ivory against the decayed leaves and brush beneath her.

He tentatively reached out to touch her, noticed his hand shook, and balled it into a fist. He clenched it tight, then opened his hand and gently touched the tangled, black hair that hid the side of her face. She did not stir when he moved the silken skein, nor when he brushed it back and looped it over her ear.

Her face was streaked with mud. Her lashes were long and dark, her full lips tinged pink. The sight of her beauty took his breath away. Noah leaned forward and gently reached beneath her. Rolling her onto her back, he straightened her arms and noted her injuries. Her wrist appeared to be swollen. She had an angry lump on her forehead near her hairline. She moaned as he lightly probed her injured wrist; he realized he was holding his breath. Noah expected her eyelids to flutter open, but they did not.

He scanned the forest once again. With night fast closing in, he saw no alternative except to take her home with him. If he was going to get her back to the tree house before dark, he would have to hurry. He cradled her gently in his arms, reached for his rifle, and then straightened. Even then the girl did not awaken, although she did whimper and turn her face against his buckskin jacket, burrowing against him. It felt strange carrying a woman in his arms, but he had no time to dwell on that as he quickly carried her back to the *pirogue*, set her inside, and untied the craft. He climbed in behind her, holding her upright, then gently drew her back until she leaned against his chest.

As the paddle cut silently through water black as pitch, he tried to concentrate on guiding the dugout canoe home, but was distracted by the way the girl felt pressed against him, the way she warmed him. As his body responded to a need he had long tried to deny, he felt ashamed at his lack of control. What kind of a man was he, to become aroused by a helpless, unconscious female?

Overhead, the sky was tinted deep violet, an early canvas for the night's first stars. During the last few yards of the journey, the swamp grew so dark that he had only the yellow glow of lamplight shining from his home high above the water to guide him.

Run. Keep running.

The dream was so real that Olivia Bond could feel the leaf-littered ground beneath her feet and the faded chill of winter that lingered on the damp April air. She suffered, haunted by memories of the past year, some still so vivid they turned her dreams into nightmares. Even now, as she lay tossing in her sleep, she could feel the faint sway of the flatboat as it moved down river long ago. In her sleep the fear welled up inside her.

Her dreaming mind began to taunt her with palpable memories of new sights and scents and dangers.

Run. Run. Run, Olivia. You're almost home.

Her legs thrashed, startling her awake. She sat straight up, felt a searing pain in her right wrist and a pounding in her head that forced her to quickly lie back down. She kept her eyes closed until the stars stopped dancing behind them, then she slowly opened them and looked around.

The red glow of embers burning in a fireplace illuminated the ceiling above her. She lay staring up at even log beams that ran across a wide planked ceiling, trying to ignore the pounding in her head, fighting to stay calm and let her memory come rushing back. Slowly she realized she was no longer lost on the forest trail. She had not become a bobcat's dinner, but was indoors, in a cabin, on a bed.

She spread her fingers and pressed her hands palms down against a rough, woven sheet drawn over her. The mattress was filled with something soft that gave off a tangy scent. A pillow cradled her head.

Slowly Olivia turned her aching head, afraid of who or what she might find beside her, but when she discovered she was in bed alone, she thanked God for small favors.

Refusing to panic, she thought back to her last lucid memory: a wildcat's scream. She recalled tearing through the cypress swamp, trying to make out the trail in the dim light before she tripped. She lifted her hand to her forehead and felt swelling. After testing it gingerly, she was thankful that she had not gashed her head open and bled to death.

She tried to lift her head again but intense pain forced her to lie still. Olivia closed her eyes and sighed. A moment later, an unsettling feeling came over her. She knew by the way her skin tingled, the way her nerve ends danced, that someone was nearby. Someone was watching her. An instinctive, intuitive sensation warned her that the *someone* was a man.

At first she peered through her lashes, but all she could make out was a tall, shadowy figure standing in the open doorway across the room. Her heart began to pound so hard she was certain the sound would give her consciousness away.

The man walked into the room and she bit her lips together to hold back a cry. She watched him move about purposefully. Instead of coming directly to the bed, he walked over to a small square table. She heard him strike a piece of flint, smelled lamp oil as it flared to life.

His back was to her as he stood at the table; Olivia opened her eyes wider and watched. He was tall, taller than most men, strongly built, dressed in buckskin pants topped by a buff shirt with billowing sleeves. Despite the coolness of the evening, he wore no coat, no jacket. Indian moccasins, not shoes, covered his feet. His hair was a deep black, cut straight and worn long enough to hang just over his collar. She watched his bronzed, well-tapered hands turn up the lamp wick and set the glass chimney in place.

Olivia sensed he was about to turn and look at her. She wanted to close her eyes and pretend to be unconscious, thinking that might be safer than letting him catch her staring at him, but as he slowly turned toward the bed, she knew she had to see him. She had to know what she was up against.

Her gaze swept his body, taking in his great height, the length of his arms, the width and breadth of his shoulders before she dared even look at his face.

When she did, she gasped.

Noah stood frozen beside the table, shame and anger welling up from deep inside. He was unable to move, unable to breathe as the telling sound of the girl's shock upon seeing his face died on the air. He watched her flinch and scoot back into the corner, press close to the wall. He knew her head pained her, but obviously not enough to keep her from showing her revulsion or from trying to scramble as far away as she could.

He had the urge to walk out, to turn around and leave. Instead, he stared back and let her look all she wanted. It had been three years since he had lost an eye to a flatboat accident on the Mississippi. Three years since another woman had laughed in his face. Three years since he moved to southern Illinois to put the past behind him.

When her breathing slowed and she calmed, he held his

hands up to show her that they were empty, hoping to put her a little more at ease.

"I'm sorry," he said as gently as he could. "I don't mean you any harm."

She stared up at him as if she did not understand a blessed word.

Louder this time, he spoke slowly. "Do-you-speak-English?"

The girl clutched the sheet against the filthy bodice of her dress and nodded. She licked her lips, cleared her throat. Her mouth opened and closed like a fish out of water, but no sound came out.

"Yes," she finally croaked. "Yes, I do." And then, "Who are you?"

"My name is Noah. Noah LeCroix. This is my home. Who are you?"

The lamplight gilded her skin. She looked to be all eyes, soft green eyes, long black hair, and fear. She favored her injured wrist, held it cradled against her midriff. From the way she carefully moved her head, he knew she was fighting one hell of a headache, too.

Ignoring his question, she asked one of her own. "How did I get here?" Her tone was wary. Her gaze kept flitting over to the door and then back to him.

"I heard a scream. Went out and found you in the swamp. Brought you here—"

"The wildcat?"

"Wasn't very hungry." Noah tried to put her at ease, then he shrugged, stared down at his moccasins. Could she tell how nervous he was? Could she see his awkwardness, know how strange it was for him to be alone with a woman? He had no idea what to say or do. When he looked over at her again, she was staring at the ruined side of his face.

"How long have I been asleep?" Her voice was so low that he had to strain to hear her. She looked like she expected him to leap on her and attack her any moment, as if he might be coveting her scalp.

"Around two hours. You must have hit your head really hard."

She reached up, felt the bump on her head. "I guess I did."

He decided not to get any closer, not with her acting like she was going to jump out of her skin. He backed up, pulled a stool out from under the table, and sat down.

"You going to tell me your name?" he asked.

The girl hesitated, glanced toward the door, then looked back at him. "Where am I?"

"Heron Pond."

Her attention shifted to the door once again; recollection dawned. She whispered, "The swamp." Her eyes widened as if she expected a bobcat or a cottonmouth to come slithering in.

"You're fairly safe here. I built this cabin over the water."

"Fairly?" She looked as if she was going to try to stand up again. "Did you say--"

"Built on cypress trunks. About fifteen feet above the water."

"How do I get down?"

"There are wooden planks nailed to a trunk."

"Am I anywhere near Illinois?"

"You're in it."

She appeared a bit relieved. Obviously she wasn't going to tell him her name until she was good and ready, so he did not bother to ask again. Instead he tried, "Are you hungry? I figure anybody with as little meat on her bones as you ought to be hungry."

What happened next surprised the hell out of him. It was a little thing, one that another man might not have even noticed, but he had lived alone so long he was used to concentrating on the very smallest of details: the way an iridescent dragonfly looked with its wings backlit by the sun, the sound of cypress needles whispering on the wind.

Someone else might have missed the smile that hovered at the corners of her lips when he had said she had little meat on her bones, but he did not. How could he, when that slight, almost-smile had him holding his breath?

"I got some jerked venison and some potatoes around here someplace." He started to smile back until he felt the pull of the scar at the left corner of his mouth and stopped. He stood up, turned his back on the girl, and headed for the long wide plank tacked to the far wall where he stored his larder.

He kept his back to her while he found what he was looking for, dug some strips of dried meat from a hide bag, unwrapped a checkered rag with four potatoes inside, and set one on the plank where he did all his stand-up work. Then he took a trencher and a wooden mug off a smaller shelf high on the wall, and turned it over to knock any unwanted creatures out. He was headed for the door, intent on filling the cook pot with water from a small barrel he kept out on the porch when the sound of her voice stopped him cold.

"Perhaps an eye patch," she whispered.

"What?"

"I'm sorry. I was thinking out loud."

She looked so terrified he wanted to put her at ease.

"It's all right. What were you thinking?"

Instead of looking at him when she spoke, she looked down at her hands. "I was just thinking . . ."

Noah had to strain to hear her.

"With some kind of an eye patch, you wouldn't look half bad."

His feet rooted themselves to the threshold. He stared at her for a heartbeat before he closed his good eye and shook his head. He had no idea what in the hell he looked like anymore. He had had no reason to care.

He turned his back on her and stepped out onto the porch, welcoming the darkness.